A Shot in the Dark

"An outstanding urban fantasy . . . [a] super paranormal."
—*Midwest Book Review*

"Jesse James Dawson is my kind of hero . . . [Stewart] has created an urban fantasy with the same touch of darkness I found in Butcher's Dresden series. . . . [She] also has a wicked sense of humor, which I find irresistible."
—*Fresh Fiction*

"I love Jesse's adventures, that of a modern-day samurai mixed with the paranormal and a bit of mystery. I can't wait to see what's in store for Jesse next!"
—*News and Sentinel* (Parkersburg, WV)

"Stewart provides nonstop action . . . well-developed characters and taut pacing."
—*Publishers Weekly*

A Devil in the Details

"A clever conceit, with a surprisingly moral center. Lots of fun, deftly witty, and one of the most appealing central characters of recent years."
—*New York Times* bestselling author Simon R. Green

"If you want your life saved, you call the cops. If you want your *soul* saved, you call Jesse James Dawson. Humor, action, and a one-way trip straight to Hell, this book delivers it all."
—*New York Time* bestselling author Rob Thurman

continued . . .

Jesse James Dawson Novels
by K. A. Stewart

A Devil in the Details
A Shot in the Dark
A Wolf at the Door

A WOLF AT THE DOOR

A JESSE JAMES DAWSON NOVEL

K. A. STEWART

A ROC BOOK

ROC
Published by New American Library, a division of
Penguin Group (USA) Inc., 375 Hudson Street,
New York, New York 10014, USA
Penguin Group (Canada), 90 Eglinton Avenue East, Suite 700, Toronto,
Ontario M4P 2Y3, Canada (a division of Pearson Penguin Canada Inc.)
Penguin Books Ltd., 80 Strand, London WC2R 0RL, England
Penguin Ireland, 25 St. Stephen's Green, Dublin 2,
Ireland (a division of Penguin Books Ltd.)
Penguin Group (Australia), 250 Camberwell Road, Camberwell, Victoria 3124,
Australia (a division of Pearson Australia Group Pty. Ltd.)
Penguin Books India Pvt. Ltd., 11 Community Centre, Panchsheel Park,
New Delhi—110 017, India
Penguin Group (NZ), 67 Apollo Drive, Rosedale, Auckland 0632,
New Zealand (a division of Pearson New Zealand Ltd.)
Penguin Books (South Africa) (Pty.) Ltd., 24 Sturdee Avenue,
Rosebank, Johannesburg 2196, South Africa

Penguin Books Ltd., Registered Offices:
80 Strand, London WC2R 0RL, England

First published by Roc, an imprint of New American Library,
a division of Penguin Group (USA) Inc.

First Printing, August 2012
10 9 8 7 6 5 4 3 2 1

 REGISTERED TRADEMARK—MARCA REGISTRADA

Printed in the United States of America

PUBLISHER'S NOTE
This is a work of fiction. Names, characters, places, and incidents either are the product of the author's imagination or are used fictitiously, and any resemblance to actual persons, living or dead, business establishments, events, or locales is entirely coincidental.
    The publisher does not have any control over and does not assume any responsibility for author or third-party Web sites or their content.

ALWAYS LEARNING   PEARSON

To you, for all that you do
But more for all that you are.

ACKNOWLEDGMENTS

It's getting harder and harder to thank everyone who deserves it. So many people help me with these books in ways they never even realize. As always, for Scott and Aislynn. For my beta-slaves, without whom this book would never exist in the form that you see it. For the crew at Badger Blades, and Badger himself for creating The Way. For the Purgatorians, who all know why. Also, for those people who make me laugh when I didn't even know I needed it. For the authors who make jokes only another author understands. For the agents and the editors who ride the highs and lows with us. And last but most definitely not least, for the readers. You are why I get to do what I love every day.

1

Four years ago . . .

Once upon a time, this guy stumbled into something big, something way bigger than he could handle, and though he won, he got his ass handed to him in multiple pieces. And while he was recovering from that, this huge white-haired dude with a foreign accent and a black trench coat showed up and said, "Follow the yellow brick road!"

And that's how I wound up here. Wherever the hell "here" was. It sure as hell wasn't Kansas anymore, Toto.

Okay, I knew I was somewhere in Eastern Europe, one of those countries that changes its name every other week. Somewhere that seemed uniformly gritty, until I was sure I could feel tiny granules grinding between my teeth, strained out of the air I breathed. Given that my guide was Ukrainian, we'll say I was in Ukraine. 'Cause I honestly had no idea. You would think for my first trip out of the United States, I would have chosen some-where less . . . frozen.

I hitched the collar of my coat up higher around my chin, but despite the occasional brutality of Midwestern winters, the leather bomber jacket just wasn't living up to the Ukrainian temperatures. I jammed my hands in my pockets and did my best to keep up with the long strides of the man in front of me.

His name was Ivan Zelenko. I got that much a few days ago when he showed up on my front porch. Dude had to be at least six four, and his shoulders were broad enough to be two of me. His white hair was cropped in a short military buzz cut, and the lines of many years made his eyes crinkle at the corners.

Most of the time, I'd have told him to stuff whatever he was selling and get off my lawn, but when I opened the door, he was thoughtfully examining the doorjambs, running a finger down the wood like he was testing for dust.

Finally, with an approving nod, he said, "This is to being good work. Excellent wardings. You are to being Jesse James Dawson?"

That one statement brought me up short. Not the knowing my name part, even as creepy as that was. No, it was the recognizing the wards part. Up until that moment, I'd known only one person besides myself capable of sensing the protection spells on my doors, and that was the woman who'd put them there. My wife, Mira. And to tell the truth, up until that point I wasn't sure she and I weren't both some level of insane. I mean really. Magic? Demons? If I'd have told anyone else, they'd have put me in a nice white coat with extra-long sleeves and given me a padded room to take my rest in. No sane person believes in demons.

Except that I'd seen two of them now, and the second one was nearly the end of me. The muscles down my left side were still knitting, the scars that marred me from armpit to hip angry red and throbbing when I overexerted. I'd gone from wiry to emaciated in the ICU, and even a month after my liberation from the hospital, I was struggling to put the weight back on. The huge man on my front step served only to make me feel as wasted and frail as I was afraid I looked.

So, this Ivan Zelenko knew magic. After proving that he could walk through my doorway unimpeded, I invited him to sit on my couch. He met my wife. He met my daughter. Despite the fact that he nearly filled the room with his sheer size, and booming gravelly voice, he managed to put both the women in my life at ease almost immediately. And then he did a lot of talking in badly fractured English.

Most of it boiled down to the fact that he knew all about demons, and contracts, and fighting. A champion, he called me. He was one too, or had been in his youth. Unabashedly, he unbuttoned his shirt to show me the scars, some of which looked like the ones I was now carrying, and some of which looked like an alien creature had tried to gnaw out a few vital organs. Nothing natural made marks like that.

"I watch for men like you. To be letting them know that they are not alone in this fighting. The more we are to be knowing, the better chance we are to be having."

"That's great, man, really, but I don't intend to be doing this again. This isn't a lifestyle choice." The white-haired man smirked before I could even finish my sentence.

"If you could to be stopping, you would have said no already." He nodded sagely. "When next someone is to be asking you, you will fight again. I am seeing it in your eyes. A champion."

While he may have liked what he saw in my eyes, he was not as impressed with the rest of the examination.

He asked to see my weapon, and I produced my katana, which seemed satisfactory. He asked to see my armor. I didn't have any. That got a deep furrow of his white brows. He asked to see my magic and I laughed in his face.

"I don't have any magic."

The big man looked perplexed. "Apologies, I am not to being so good at the language. The spells on your door . . . ?"

"That wasn't me. That was my wife. She's tried to show me how, but it just doesn't click. No juice." It took me a few more minutes of translation difficulties to get the man to understand that I just wasn't a magic-user. "What's the big deal? It can't be that common or everyone would do it. Don't you have any of these champions without any magic?"

The answer was a resounding no. Not only was it unheard of, it was also unacceptable, and somehow I found myself on a plane to Ukraine, where Ivan believed I would learn something that would correct all I'd done wrong up to this point.

I was still alive. Personally, I thought I'd done pretty damn good so far.

Though we'd started on the outskirts of a small town, our little walk was rapidly leading us across a sparsely wooded area, mostly really old-growth trees. No brush, no saplings, oddly barren compared to the woods I was used to back in Missouri. It had to be almost midnight, local time, but my internal clock was so fried from crossing time zones, I didn't know if it was Tuesday or raining out. Without the slight dusting of snow on the ground to reflect the distant moonlight, I'd have been walking into trees left and right.

Ivan's long strides were outdistancing me, given my still-weakened state.

"Mr. Zelenko? Excuse me?" On he marched, and my chest burned as my newly healed ribs struggled to flex with my breath. "Hey!" Then he stopped, turning to look at me. "You're gonna have to slow down. I'm not fully functional back here, remember?"

That earned me a soft snort, and he set off again, not slowing one damn bit. Well . . . screw him. I'd take my sweet time. I ducked my head down into my coat, and concentrated on keeping Ivan's tracks in my view, listening for the soft crunch of his footsteps on the light snow.

I obviously wasn't listening well enough, because I nearly walked into his broad back when he came to an abrupt stop. I leaned on a tree—oak maybe?—and tried to catch my breath.

"Here. You will to be needing these." He passed me a pair of binoculars so heavy I almost dropped them. He pointed with one gloved hand. "There."

Before us, the tree line ended abruptly, the stumps of recently hewn trees dotting a hillside. Under the snow, I could even see the drag marks where the logs had been moved, loaded into some waiting vehicle, I assumed. A logging site. "Really nice stumps you got here." What the hell was I supposed to be looking for, exactly?

"To be looking farther up the hill. To be watching." He raised his own binoculars to his eyes, illustrating.

With a sigh, I did the same.

My view of the night suddenly flared in bright greens, outlining everything on that empty hillside in sharp detail. "Oh, cool . . . night vision!" The teenage boy inside me was thrilled to bits with my new toy.

"Near the top of the ridge. What are you to be seeing?"

Obediently, I looked. "There . . . Is that a woman up there?" Dialing in a bit on the binoculars, I could see that it was indeed a woman, standing alone near the top of the naked hill.

"Her name is Svetlana."

Young. That was my first thought. If she was my age, I'd eat one of my gloves. Y'know, when I got somewhere warmer. Her hair color was impossible to determine, with the greenish night vision, but I could settle on "dark." It was pulled back into a severe tail. She was dressed in what looked to be white ski gear: a parka, boots, her hood hanging down her back. Her gloves were slim, not bulky like most snow garb, but still white. And was that . . . "A sword?"

"A shashka. A saber once used by the Cossacks."

It was impossible to see details on the weapon at this distance, but I could tell it had a slight curve, like my katana. It lacked a guard, though, and it was hard to tell where the hilt ended and the scabbard began. If it hadn't been belted on like it was, I might have assumed it was simply a walking stick.

If the woman knew we were there, watching her, she never once looked down the hill at us. Instead, she stood on one of the wider tree stumps, doing what looked like warm-up stretches. Still being as stiff and sore as I was after my injuries, I kind of envied her flexibility. Her stretching done, she bounced on her toes a little, rolling her head on her shoulders. Obviously, she was waiting for something, and it wasn't us.

"What exactly are we looking for, here?"

"Quiet. It is to be starting now."

Okay, I don't like being shushed like a hyper kid, but before I could object, something stirred on that hillside. I squinted through the binoculars, trying to make out just what was going on.

For a moment, I thought that some small animals had come scampering out of the decimated tree stumps, capering across the ground around the woman's feet. But it must not have been cute little bunny rabbits and squirrels, because she stepped back up on the tree stump, keeping her boots clear of the darting shadows. They weren't very big, maybe the size of a football at the most, but she definitely didn't want them touching her.

In no time at all, there were dozens of them, probably more, just little balls of shadow flitting and flickering over the ground. I lost sight for just a moment when a full body shudder caught me out of nowhere, and I realized how really freakin' cold I'd become. Beneath the warmest clothes I had, my skin was crawling with goose bumps, and my stomach cramped painfully.

Putting the glasses back up to my eyes, I saw that the little shadows had gained some purpose, clambering over each other, stacking like interlocking blocks. Taller and taller it built, until it loomed over the woman like a thin, teetering tower. Each little segment had a pair of legs now, jointed insectile legs, and they waved and flexed, looking for purchase.

"A centipede . . ." Crap, that's what it looked like. A humongous centipede, scuttling over the ground as it came together piece by piece. And it wasn't finished by any means. The darting shadows kept appearing, kept adding on, and the bug-thing kept getting longer, stretching out along the ground to support the length it had raised up in the air. We still hadn't got to the head yet, and I was suddenly very certain that I didn't want to see what that would look like. "We have to help her."

"No." Ivan's voice was quiet, calm. "To aid her will to be forfeiting the contract. She must do this alone."

"What *is* that thing?"

"A demon. Lesser in strength than some, greater than others. She should to be having no problems."

It didn't look like either of the demons I'd fought. The most recent, the one that nearly made my entrails into my ex-trails, had been a monstrous white-furred beast, with ram horns and gleaming silver claws. That one I called the Yeti. The other one, my first one, had been furry too, sort of, but much smaller, lower to the ground. Something between a cheetah and a Komodo dragon, maybe. It had died much easier than the Yeti.

"She's one of your champions, then?" Of course she was. Ivan was trying to convince me that this was my life's calling, right? Of course he'd bring me to see one of his best and brightest at work. Standard recruiting tactic.

He made one of those generic man-noises, and I got the idea that my question-and-answer period was over. I focused through the binoculars again, dreading what I'd see, but afraid not to watch.

The centipede-demon was almost fully formed, a few stray segments scuttling their way to latch on to what I assumed was the hind end. It had to be nearly twenty feet long, and the half that was raised into the air was nearly twice as tall as the woman it was menacing.

I had to give her credit. If she was scared, I couldn't tell it from where I was standing. Her stance was loose, relaxed, and her hand rested on the hilt of her sword lightly. I think she was speaking to the thing, and I saw two sets of mandibles in its . . . well, we'll call it a face for ease of reference . . . face waggle about with sharp snaps. The terms must have been agreeable, because she drew her weapon—a shashka, Ivan had called it—and sketched a very faint bow.

The demon wasn't one to stand on formality. It struck almost faster than I could see, and my entire body jerked with the impulse to go tearing up that hill. I didn't need to worry. The woman, Svetlana, had been ready.

Almost casually, she rolled out of the path of the striking head, coming to her feet and slashing in one fluid movement. I could tell even then that she was good. Damn good.

The sword connected with the demon's—we'll call it his back—back, and there was a bright flash of light, dazzling in the night vision lenses. I almost dropped the binoculars, blinking spots from my eyes. "What the hell was that?"

"Hm." Ivan frowned thoughtfully behind his own binoculars. "Blessed silver in the blade."

With purple and black dots still dancing in my vision, I turned to watch again. At first, I thought she'd won already. The centipede thing had been cut in half by that flashy strike, the rear end flailing about wildly. The head piece snapped at the woman, and retreated until it could touch its severed half ... and then they just reattached. One segment shorter, but whole again. Damn. That thing had to be a hundred chunks long, if it was one. Taking it apart one piece at a time was going to take forever.

It didn't matter how hard you practiced, how good you were with a sword, long fights took a toll. I knew how tired her arms would get, wielding that long blade. She'd get slower, even just by a split second. She'd hesitate a hair too long, or duck a smidgen too short. Then it would have her. It was just a matter of time.

"We gotta go up there and help her."

"No." He lowered the glasses long enough to give me an amused smile. "Svetlana is never to be losing, Jesse Dawson. She will be fine."

Svetlana seemed intent on proving him right. Twice more, her sword flashed brilliantly in the darkness—I learned to avert my eyes at the last second—and the centipede would flop aimlessly for a few heartbeats before reassembling itself again. Was it just me, or were the flashes getting dimmer?

It wasn't just me. Somewhere around the fifth or sixth clash, there was a sickly flicker and the clang of metal on carapace carried all the way to where I was standing. Whatever she'd had on her sword, it had worn off.

Then the fight began in earnest. Whatever the bug was made of, it was no simple cockroach to be squished.

The sword rang like a bell in the snowy night as she parried and struck, retreated and feinted. She wasn't even pretending to save her strength. Every move was done explosively, with fury. She leaped from stump to stump, throwing in some impressive acrobatics as she avoided her opponent. I'd cut my own leg off if I tried that with a blade in my hand. I caught myself breathing hard, like I was battling right alongside her, and forced myself to stop. God, it was like watching someone try to run a marathon at a dead sprint.

For the demon's part, it seemed a bit frustrated. It seemed no matter where it bit or clawed, the sword was there. And while the bug wasn't hurt, it still couldn't get to her. It wasn't, however, out of tricks yet.

It reared up again, striking like a cobra, only about a foot before it would have made contact, it just . . . vanished. Well, half of it did. The demon poured itself through some invisible rip in thin air, disappearing segment by segment. Svetlana dropped into a defensive position without hesitation, proving that this was something she'd anticipated.

The night vision lenses caught a faint shimmer in the air behind her, and only sheer astonishment kept me from calling out in warning. She didn't need it, though. As the front half of the centipede burst out of whatever realm it had retreated to, the woman's sword was there, meeting the gnashing mandibles with a clang of steel. The back half of the worm writhed through its little portal, spitting the entire length out at its new location, and they kept on.

Christ . . . how do you fight something that can disappear and reappear at will? That had always been my greatest fear during the two fights that I'd had. Fighting something that just wouldn't stand still and get thumped. I'd negotiated magic out of my fights. Since I wasn't using any myself, it was a small loss to swear it off. But this woman . . . she was facing the demon's full arsenal.

The next time it tried to pull the portal trick, the return opened up right under Svetlana's booted feet. In a spectacular display of acrobatics, she left the ground as the thing came up beneath her, snapping and clacking. She twisted in midair, her landing bringing her sword down full force on the back end of the creature, pinning it to the ground, caught between the two portals. The front half whipped about, the back half struggling to get free, and in the middle, there was just nothing. Dead space. It thrashed there, apparently not having the brainpower to figure out how to find reverse.

A faint buzzing sound reached my ears, and I adjusted the binoculars, trying to get a better look. The night vision made clear details hard to see, but there was a ripple that passed up the back of the centipede, travelling from segment to segment toward the head. The demon-bug's head suddenly focused on her and spat something thick and steaming through the frigid night air.

She rolled out of the way, taking her sword with her, but the tree stump that took the shot for her started to smoke forlornly, parts of it dissolving as I watched. "Holy shit . . ." Freed, the centipede finished its travel through the portal, coming out whole on the other side again. The portal had become its downfall, though, and it didn't try that trick again.

The pair came together in a flurry of slashes and snapping fangs, moving so fast, and it was hard to follow what exactly happened. Pretty sure no human should be able to move that fast without some sort of help. I could tell the moment Svetlana started to tire, though. The bug tail-swiped her, knocking her sprawling, and then the buzzing started again, the little waves moving through the thing's carapace. It loomed up and spewed that toxic gunk at her, and she only had time to pull her hood up over her head, taking the hit square in the back.

The white of her coat vanished as the smoke rolled, and she stripped out of the parka quickly, leaving it to melt into the snow. That left her in what looked like a Kevlar vest, with mail sleeves attached, covering her from shoulder to wrist. A twist and yank produced another blade from somewhere, and she faced the thing with her shashka in one hand and a reversed dagger in the other. When it came at her again, she met it head-on, the sword defending her upper body as she lunged in to bury the dagger between the first and second segments.

The worm-demon whipped itself away from her, writhing as it tried to scrape the dagger free. Everywhere it touched, it left a blackness behind, and that smudge on the white snow started to move, oozing together like blobs of black mercury.

I recognized that. It was how demons bled, a wispy black fog that would eventually form another type of portal, a big one, ushering the creature back to Hell. The wounded bug was leaving a lot behind. Whatever she'd done with that dagger had hurt it, badly.

When it was unable to remove the blade, the demon

came back, raising itself in the air and slamming its entire body down in an attempt to crush her. She leaped to the side, avoiding the smash, but the tail snapped around and took her feet out from under her again. Her head cracked against a tree stump loud enough that I could hear it, and inside I cringed. This was not going to end well.

She didn't get up. Christ, she wasn't getting up! I didn't even realized I'd taken two steps toward the hill until Ivan's big hand landed on my shoulder, freezing me in place. "*Ni.* Watch carefully."

Despite the fact that every instinct was demanding I dash up that hill and . . . well, probably get my ass kicked again, I raised the lenses to my eyes, spinning the dial until I could focus in on Svetlana's still form as closely as I could. "Come on . . ."

That close, I could see her chest rising and falling. I could see her hand lying across her waist. I could catch the moment her fingers twitched with purpose, easing something small off a clip on her belt. It was small enough to conceal in her hand and though I couldn't see what it was, I recognized the distinctive flick of her thumb. A pin. She'd pulled a pin on something.

Oh, shit. Unable to scrape the dagger loose, the demon finally remembered its fallen opponent, and whipped around to face her again. It approached warily, advancing one rattling segment at a time, its mandibles nibbling at the toe of her boot, examining the texture of her pants, feeling its way up her body as she lay there in the snow.

Wait for it . . . I couldn't risk yelling, couldn't distract her, but I willed her to hold her ground, to wait for the proper moment.

Reaching her head, the centipede picked at strands of her hair, tasting it. Finally, satisfied that Svetlana was no longer a threat, it raised up a bit to get a decent strike, its mandibles gaping wide. That's when she struck.

Her eyes snapped open and she thrust her hand into the creature's mouth, clear up to her elbow. Whatever she had, she was jamming it clear down the bug's gullet. She was moving so fast, the thing didn't even have time to bite her arm off before she'd yanked it out and scrambled away, taking shelter behind the biggest stump she could find.

The demon didn't bother to follow, hacking and choking, trying to dislodge whatever she'd stuffed into its mouth. Its head whipped violently, the venomous rattle starting again as it tried to launch the foreign object out in a burst of toxic goo. For a moment, I thought it was going to succeed. Then it exploded.

The blast echoed forever, and took half the centipede demon with it. Bits of it rained down, drifting like falling white-hot stars in the night vision goggles, burning in the snow until the entire hillside looked like it was covered in fireflies. The parts that weren't left burning promptly dispersed, wafting and swirling into a shining disk in midair. I lowered the glasses in favor of putting my hands over my ears, but I could still hear the high-pitched whine, a wail I could feel only in the back of my head. It seemed to go with the portal, like for just a moment we could hear the souls in Hell screaming.

And then it was gone.

Ivan put his binoculars away, and nodded. "Holy hand grenade."

I couldn't help it. I busted up laughing, choking it off only when I realized that he had no idea why it was funny. The big man gave me an odd look, and I just shook my head. "Never mind." Not a Monty Python fan, obviously.

The sounds of feet scuffing through the snow made me look up in time to see Svetlana come staggering down the hillside. Her hair was a deep brown, I realized, matted to her head with sweat, but her eyes were a striking pale blue, lighter even than my own. A trickle of blood gleamed wetly down the side of her neck, oozing from the back of her head, if I had to guess, where she'd smacked it on the stump. Still, she was moving damn good. Better than I had after my last fight.

She drew up short to find us in the trees, her glance dismissing me immediately, and fixating on the big Ukrainian.

"Svetlana." Ivan dipped his head to her in acknowledgment.

Okay, I have no idea what she said, because it was in whatever language Ivan spoke, but trust me, I know the sound of a pissed-off woman, and that was it. She was *not* happy to see us there. There was more venom in her voice than the demon had spewed all over that hillside. She waved her hands as she talked, and I had to duck a couple of times to keep her sword from taking off an ear.

Ivan never got riled, never got ruffled, just calmly responded to her. Finally, she kicked a pile of pine needles at him and stalked off, muttering to herself as she stumbled her way through the trees.

I raised a brow at Ivan. "That went well?"

He shrugged his massive shoulders. "As well as to be going, with her. She is . . . strongheaded."

Yeah, I could see that.

"So, what are you to be learning, Jesse Dawson?" He turned and walked off, I guess assuming that I was going to follow him. I did, of course. I mean, what else was I going to do, stay out here and become a lumberjack?

"What did you want me to learn?" That seemed the safest question.

"I wanted you to see what is to being possible, with the proper tools and resources. With her magic, Svetlana is faster, is stronger. Her weapon does more damage, her armor protects longer."

"Is that why she didn't break her skull open on that tree?"

"*Tak.* Yes. Special reinforcements on her person. Coatings on her sword, her dagger. Blessed phosphorous grenade."

I blinked. "Maybe over here, you can get phosphorous grenades at the local gas station, but where I come from, they're a bit harder to get ahold of."

"*Tak.* But resources will to being at your disposal. Is amazing what we can to be doing when we harness our potential, is it not?"

Resources? What resources? What the hell was I getting myself into? Though he was right, it was amazing. The last demon fight I'd had nearly killed me. Maybe if

I'd have had some armor, like Svetlana's. Maybe if Mira could work a little voodoo on it. Maybe next time would be better.

We were nearly back to the village before I realized that I was thinking in terms of "next time." *Dammit.*

2

Now . . .

There are a few things every guy dreads seeing in a
trash can. His favorite boxers, for example. His comic
books, or baseball cards. But first and foremost, at the tip
top of the list, is the empty box to a pregnancy test.

I stood there and pondered the little blue and white
box, sitting so innocuously in the trash can, my tooth-
brush hanging out of the corner of my mouth forgotten.
It could have been old, I suppose. My wife cleaning out
the bathroom cabinets from days gone by, maybe. There
were no tests in evidence, just the box, lying there in the
used-up tissues, empty.

Toothpaste dripped down my bare chest, and I wiped
the sticky blob away absently. "Um . . . Mira?"

Of course, she was clear out in the kitchen, so she
didn't hear me.

I caught a glimpse of myself in the mirror, and the
man in the glass had this wide-eyed stare, like a deer in
headlights. And a huge smear of blue toothpaste across
his chest. I managed to clean myself up, still eyeing the
very scary box in the trash can like it might bite me, then
went in search.

"Mira?" I followed the sounds of bacon frying toward
the kitchen, and only a quick sidestep kept me from get-

ting mowed down as my daughter rounded the corner on her new bicycle, still trailing the Christmas bows from yesterday. Her gangly English mastiff puppy thundered around the corner a split second later, and nearly knocked me flat a second time. "Anna! No biking in the house!"

"Okay, Daddy!" She disappeared down the hall, pedaling her little legs as fast as they could go, and the puppy Chunk galumphing along after.

In the kitchen, my protégé Estéban was flipping pancakes while my wife stood beside him, frying the bacon. Even with her back turned, she was stunningly beautiful. There was just something about the set of her shoulders, the curve of her hips, the spill of dark curly hair down her back ... I could watch her all day, if it wouldn't have made me creepy.

She laughed at something Estéban said, and elbowed him in the ribs. He just grinned back at her. His black hair was getting shaggy again. I figured he had about a week before Mira started hounding him about a haircut. Tall, lanky, still growing into himself. So far from the angry kid he'd been a few months ago, he was actually starting to become a pseudo-grown-up. Don't tell him I said that.

"Kid." He looked at me and I jerked my head toward the hall. "Go make sure Anna's hair gets brushed, 'kay?" He had little sisters, he could brush hair. And he didn't need to hear this conversation.

Estéban gave me a puzzled look, flipped his pancake once more, then handed the spatula to me as he passed. *"Todo está bien?"*

"Sí."

"Y'know, speaking Spanish to hide what you're saying from me is a poor choice," Mira reminded us. "It *is* one of the languages I'm rather good at."

"Off with you." I shooed the kid out the door—and I use the term "kid" loosely, 'cause he was taller than me now—and went to tend the pancakes before something burned. For a few moments, Mira and I cooked breakfast in silence. "So . . . there was this box in the trash in the bathroom . . ."

She didn't look up at me, just kept turning the sizzling bacon. "Mhmm."

"So . . . were you gonna say something about that?"

"Nothing to say, yet." She fished the last of the bacon out of the pan and set it aside, bracing her hands on the counter with a sigh. "It was negative, so . . . nothing to say."

"Oh." The pancakes were fascinating. I kept my eyes on them. "But . . . you had a reason . . . ?"

"I'm late, Jess. I . . ." In the corner of my vision, I could see her rake her fingers through her thick hair. "I thought it couldn't hurt to be sure."

"Oh." In the back of the house, Chunk started barking, a precursor to the deep bellow he'd have when he was full grown. I tried to tune him out.

Annabelle was six years old now. She was destined to be an only child. After three miscarriages, Mira and I had accepted that. Mira's magic took such a toll on her body . . . well, the pregnancies had always been over before we even knew it was happening. We'd never really talked about not trying anymore, it had just . . . happened.

The pancake was burning, and I dumped it out of the pan. "So . . ."

Mira sighed at me again, turning to lean against the counter, hugging her arms around her. "So, yes, it is still a possibility. I . . . if the test is negative again, I'll have Bridge do a blood test. We need to know as soon as possible, right?"

"Right." Okay, I gave up on pretending to cook. I was sucking at it anyway. Reaching over, I caught her around the waist and pulled her into my arms. She tucked her head under my chin, fitting perfectly. "Do you want the test to be positive?"

"I don't know." We stood there for a long time in silence. Well, as silent as it could be with a dog yowling in the background.

How different this was from when she told me we were having Anna. We'd been younger then. Married just a couple of years. So excited about this whole new "baby" part of our lives.

That was before. Before my brother Cole sold his soul to a demon. Before I'd gathered up an impressive collection of scars. Before I knew magic was real, before the forces of Hell had put a hit out on me. Before.

Mira's thoughts were the same as mine. I knew her well enough to know that. The part of her that desperately wanted another child warring against the side that knew it would be difficult, if not impossible, and majorly unwise on top of all that. I held her closer, silently telling her that those thoughts were okay. I was having them too, after all.

I had to ask myself, if Mira *was* pregnant ... what the hell kind of world was I bringing a baby into?

And the dog was *still* barking.

"Estéban, would you shut the dog up," I yelled. It came out harsher than I'd intended, and I winced, adding "please" belatedly.

Chunk didn't shut up, and his clamor almost drowned out my daughter's tiny voice. "Daddy?" She peeked around the corner at me from the hallway, her hair in haphazard pigtails. Well, at least Estéban had tried.

"What is it, button?"

"The funny man is knocking on the door, Daddy." One little hand pointed at the sliding glass door behind me. "I put Chunk in my room, because Chunk doesn't like him."

I turned to look, and firmly pushed Mira behind me. Funny man, indeed.

He looked human, I'll give him that. My height, almost as skinny as me, blond hair cut into a Mohawk. More piercings than I could shake a stick at. But he was also standing on my patio dressed in just a T-shirt and jeans, despite the fact that there were four inches of snow on the ground. He wasn't even pretending to be cold. Mindful of the magical wards my wife had placed on our doors, he tapped at the glass with a stick. *Tink, tink, tink.*

When I was in a good mood, I called him Axel. When I was in a bad mood, I had more ... interesting names for him.

I murmured quietly to Mira, "Take Anna in the back.

See if you can get Chunk to quiet down." I knew now why the dog was going apeshit. There was no dog in the world that would tolerate Axel's presence. Hazard of being a demon, I guess. *Gee, everybody's got their burden to bear.*

"Jesse . . ." Mira hesitated, her fingers knotting in the back of my shirt.

"Do it." I glanced at her over my shoulder and gave her a small smile. "Please. It'll be okay."

In the hallway, Estéban appeared, his worn machete in one hand. I shook my head at him, holding up a hand to stop him before he stepped into Axel's view. "Kid, take the girls. Stay with them."

He wasn't happy with that, but he gave me a short, tense nod. Mira wasn't happy with it either. I could tell by the way her green eyes went dark and the muscles in her jaw got all tight. But she nodded. "Yell if you need me." She scooped Anna up as she vanished into the hallway. "Come on, button, let's go get ready to play in the snow!" Obediently, Estéban followed them back down the hall, even if he did keep casting uncertain glances over his shoulder at me.

I waited until they were out of sight before I looked back to the man-demon still tapping on my door. "You know I can see you, right? You can stop knocking."

He grinned at me through the glass. "Gotta get my annoyance quota in early." Even through the door, he sounded like me. I mean, exactly like me. I was getting a little tired of the demon borrowing my voice whenever he felt like it. That was like . . . borrowing my underwear. You just don't do that.

I wasn't even sure if Axel and I were friends or not. I mean, we weren't, 'cause he was a demon and that would be bad, but ... I guess what I meant to say was, I wasn't sure if we were enemies. The events of the last year had started to muddle my very clear view of what exactly "good" meant.

I grabbed my bomber jacket and slipped on my sneakers before I stepped out the door. Axel may be impervious to winter, but I wasn't. Even bundled up, the snow-cooled air snuck past the leather, and I shivered as I shut the sliding door behind me.

The man-demon stepped back, probably glad to be away from my wife's anti-demon magic, and I couldn't help but notice that his footprints began and ended in a two-foot space, like he'd teleported there. Which he probably had. "That's subtle. It's broad daylight, Axel, what if someone saw you just blink in like that?"

He looked around, squinting in the morning sun. "They didn't."

"But they could have."

"But they didn't."

I deliberately took a deep breath, in through my nose, out through my mouth, concentrating on why I was *not* going to reach out and punch him in the face. Because I knew I could now. Despite the fact that we shouldn't have been able to cause harm to each other without a formal contract in place, one little experiment last fall had proven that those restrictions were no longer as firm as they'd once been. That made dealing with Axel a lot more unpredictable. It also meant the temptation to reach out and tag him was harder to resist.

"Here, put a coat on. You look conspicuous." I reached back in the door long enough to grab my snow-shoveling coat, some ratty denim thing, and tossed it to him. And yes, the puppy was still having a cow in the back of the house.

He eyed it for a moment, then shrugged it on. "If you say so."

We stood and stared at each other for a minute, while I shifted my weight as the snow trickled into the tops of my sneakers. "Listen, if you have something to say, can you do it sooner rather than later? I like my toes, they're one of the few parts of me I haven't broken. I'd hate to see them freeze off."

He stuffed his hands in his—my—coat pockets, rocking on his heels a bit. "I came to ask a favor."

"*A* favor, or *the* favor?" Because I owed him a favor, you see. A few months ago, I'd been desperate, alone, and to save the lives of my best friends, I'd offered him an unnamed favor. And in the grand tradition of negotiating with demons, if I didn't pin down just what kind of favor this was, I'd owe him forever.

"*The* favor. It's a big one." He scuffed his boots in the snow, drawing a little design with his toe. "I need you to do something for me."

I eyed him suspiciously. "You're going to ask me to do something awful, aren't you?"

Axel snorted. "No. At least, I don't think it's awful."

"Then you do it." Ha, had him there.

He shook his head, the sunlight sparkling off all the metal in his face. "No can do. My ice is thin enough as it is, I can't get involved in this one."

"Y'know, I'm getting damn sick of fighting your battles for you. At no point did I agree to be your pet champion."

Axel's eyes flared red for a heartbeat. "No, but you did ask for my help. So now I'm asking for yours. Tit for tat, Jesse. You know how this works."

Boy, did I. The fact that I'd come out of this so far without a nasty black demon brand down my arm and my soul in Hell's pawnshop was a constant amazement to me. My own ice was dangerously thin, to be brutally honest. "Fine. What's the favor?"

"I need you to go to Los Angeles. There's a girl there, and she's in danger. I need you to protect her."

I admit, I stood there and blinked at him for a few moments. Of all the things I expected him to say, that was ... well, pretty far down the list. Maybe in the footnotes, or something. "Is this girl ... a special friend of yours?"

He gave me a puzzled look until he realized what I was asking, then made a face. "Ew! No! What do you take me for?"

"You really don't wanna know." I frowned a bit, thinking it over. "You realize that it's the holidays, right? If I take off, Mira's gonna be pissed."

The man-demon snorted. I realized that his breath didn't fog in the air. What the hell did that mean? "Your holiday was yesterday. I waited."

"And your thoughtfulness touches my heart, really." With a sigh, I brushed some snow off the patio table so I could lean up against it as we talked. "Are you going to give me any more information, or do I have to bargain it all out of you?"

"I can tell you most of it. The pertinent bits, anyway."

I guess that was as good as I was going to get. "Okay. Tell me about this girl. What's so important about her?"

"She's soulless. I'll tell you that right off. But this isn't a champion request. I don't need you to get her soul back."

"Good to know. I guess."

"She sold her soul years ago, and she sold it so that she could be beautiful and famous for her entire life." Axel shuffled his feet in the snow, making a nice packed-down space that was going to be a bitch to shovel later. "Only, as part of her contract, she also agreed to collect souls herself, to store them until the time of her death."

"You can do that?" I'd never heard of that before. Didn't mean it couldn't happen, just . . . taking other people down with you? That was kinda dick.

Axel nodded. "It was more common in the old days, but . . . yeah." The old days. Which could be anywhere from the 1960s to biblical times. "Currently, she is holding within herself two hundred and seventy-six additional souls, mostly from men she's seduced."

I had to whistle lowly at that. That's a helluva lot of seduction. "Damn, who *is* this girl?"

"Gretchen Keene. I don't know if you've heard of her—"

"Gretchen Keene, the movie star? Seriously?" Heard of her? Hell, you couldn't flip on the TV without some news or entertainment show dribbling her name all over themselves. I think she had four movies come out last year, and another couple due for the summer blockbuster season coming up. "Blond" and "bombshell" were the words most frequently associated with her.

"Oh good, you know her!" Axel seemed delighted.

"Well, not personally." The whole seduction thing made a bit more sense now. I mean I'm sure there were easily two hundred and seventy-six men who would sell their souls to spend the night with Gretchen Keene. I was honestly surprised it wasn't more. And a demon contract did explain her meteoric rise to fame, starting about five years ago. It explained a lot. Dammit, didn't anybody get by on their own merit anymore? "That makes her like a succubus or something, right? Using sex to get souls?"

"More or less. As you know the word." Axel nodded agreement. "For one of us . . . one like me . . . that many souls equates to a tremendous amount of power."

"When she dies, what happens to those souls then?"

"Well . . . that's the kicker." Axel rocked on his heels, pursing his lips thoughtfully. "See, the demon who made her contract was fairly inexperienced. He left an amazingly large loophole, and really those souls are going to go to whoever can be there to claim them when she dies." For a moment, he shook his head with a faint expression of awe in his eyes. "That kind of power . . . that power wins wars, Jesse. Or loses them."

Axel never did anything for purely charitable reasons, and I'd been confused about his motives up until this point. Now things were starting to become clear.

There was a war brewing in Hell. At least, that's what I'd managed to piece together from stray Axel comments and a bit of research. Axel was on one side of the conflict, I'd gleaned that much. I had no idea who was on the other, or even which side was the "good" one. I mean really, when they're all demons, *is* there a good side?

"You basically have a loose nuclear weapon, and you don't want the other side to get their hands on it first."

"Roughly, yes." Axel mulled that over for a moment, then nodded. "A rather apt analogy."

"So why send me to play bodyguard? Why don't you just go yourself and collect the extra souls?"

He drew a breath through his teeth, making a soft hissing sound. "It's . . . complicated. If I were to go myself, it could tip some things, and I have no way of knowing if it would be in my favor. Thankfully, the other side is in the same position. They can't send one of their own, so they'll send someone else. Some*thing* else."

Leaning on the table like I was, the snow was melting and soaking through my jeans. I shifted position uncomfortably. "Do you think their man's in place already?"

"I have no way of knowing. Assume someone is already there, and then you won't be surprised if they are."

There was a lot to mull over in Axel's simple little request. I sat quietly for a few moments, and he just watched. "What exactly is it that you want me to do, Axel?"

"Just keep her alive."

"For how long? I mean, how long do you expect me to play babysitter? I have a life here, Axel. I can't just pick up and move to L.A. for the foreseeable future."

"No! No no, it wouldn't be like that," he hurried to assure me. "I only need you until New Year's Eve. Either

I'll have something else arranged, or it'll all be decided by then."

"What happens at New Year's, Axel?"

"Honestly?"

"If you can."

"I have no idea. I just know that it'll all be done by then." I think he could still see my reluctance. "If it helps, I'll cover your expenses."

That made me blink at him again. "Where do you get money?"

"Investments. Like anybody. Where do you get yours?" He grinned at me then, and I still have no idea if he was kidding or not.

I rolled my eyes at him. "I need to talk to Mira about it."

He shook his head. "This isn't really a 'choice' kind of thing, Jesse. You owe me, and this is what I am asking for."

Fuck. I couldn't even argue with him on it. I had agreed. "When do you need me to go?"

"Your flight leaves tomorrow morning." Reaching inside his coat—my coat!—he produced an envelope, handing it over with a snap.

"How did . . . ?" I changed my mind. How he yanked a large envelope out of a coat that wasn't even his was his business. I wasn't going to ask. Examining the contents, I found a plane ticket to L.A., hotel information, and a credit card with my name on it. A company card, I noted. I was apparently an employee of "Axel Rhodes, LLC."

"Axel Rhodes? Really?"

"Hey, you named me. I just ran with it." He gave me a small smirk. "You should go start packing."

I sighed, knowing he was right. I did, however, have one last question. "So why me? Why not someone more sympathetic to your cause?"

"Honestly?"

Y'know, it probably says a lot about him that he had to keep asking if I wanted the truth or not. "If you can without choking, sure."

He smirked at that, chuckled even. "Because you're the only one I can trust not to steal those souls for himself. You're the only honest man I know."

And how do you argue with that, really? "I've never been to L.A."

"Don't worry, I'll have someone meet you at the airport. Everything's arranged, you just have to get on that plane."

And explain to my possibly pregnant—*Holy crap, possibly pregnant!*—wife why I was running out to guard the body of a really hot movie star instead of staying home with the family for Christmas break. There was no way this was going to end well for me. No way out of it, either.

"Will I be seeing you out there?"

"No. I need to be as far away from that city as possible. Establish an alibi, that sort of thing. I can't be connected."

I snorted. "If you didn't want to be connected, you shouldn't have sent me." Somewhere, in some big demon library in Hell, my name was down, with Axel's right next to it. He'd marked me as his soul to claim, if he could. We were definitely connected.

"Desperate times." He shrugged. "I'll see you when you get back." And with a gust of sulfur-tainted air, he was gone.

The bastard took my coat.

3

I hollered "All clear!" as I came back in the door, stomping the snow off my sneakers, but they already knew. Chunk had fallen silent, and in fact the puppy came galloping out on his dinner plate paws to jump up on me, tail wagging happily. "Good boy, Chunk. Very good boy."

The fawn mastiff rolled his eyes in ecstasy as I scratched his favorite place under his chin. I didn't care if he raised hell every time Axel showed up. That's why we had him, after all. He'd protect my daughter, no matter what. Y'know. Once he got bigger.

Annabelle wasn't very far behind the pup, waddling her way into the kitchen all decked out in her snowsuit. "Ready to go play in the snow, Daddy?"

"I . . . uh . . . button, I gotta run out and do some stuff." Her face fell and my heart broke. I crouched down to look her in the eyes. "I'll try to get back as soon as I can, okay? We'll have hot chocolate and go out again this afternoon."

It obviously wasn't enough, but she nodded a little. "Okay, Daddy."

I stood to find Mira in the doorway, one brow raised. "What stuff?"

Before I could answer, Estéban barreled through the room, scooping Anna up and bolting out the door with her, leaving only shrieks of little girl laughter behind. Chunk followed with a surprised "growf!" leaving Mira and me alone. I slid the door shut behind them to keep the cold air out.

Mira was still looking at me expectantly, so I handed over the plane ticket. "Los Angeles? What for?"

"Some bodyguard work. I'll only be gone a week, he said."

"*He* said. That thing." She slapped the ticket down on the table and planted both hands on her hips. I was in so much trouble. "You're going out there for that thing."

"I owe him, baby—"

"Don't you 'baby' me!" Her green eyes flashed. "Dammit, Jess! You promised to spend this week with Anna and Estéban. I need to be at the shop, remember? You promised Anna you were going to do all kinds of things this week!"

"Estéban can watch her . . ."

"That's not the *point*, Jesse! Explain to me just why your promises to him mean more than your promises to us."

That hurt. That hurt a lot. "Mir, he saved Cole. He saved Marty and Will. I *owe* him."

"Never make a deal, Jess. Isn't that what you always said? What Ivan taught you? One small deal, one harmless little arrangement . . ."

"Should I have let them die? I'd be without three of the most important people in my life, but gee whiz, my soul would be lily-white spotless!" Instantly, I regretted snapping. She didn't deserve that from me.

Mira just glared at me, grinding her teeth together for a few moments. Finally, she shook her head. "Go. Just . . . go run your errands or whatever. I'm too angry to talk to you right now."

I started down the hallway, then came back to try to kiss her. She turned her head and it landed on her cheek instead. "I love you."

"Mmf."

Ouch.

She was right, though. We weren't going to get anywhere in this discussion if we were both pissed off. One of those things you learn as you try to get through married life.

See, I was the hotheaded one, quick to anger, quick to forget. Mira was the calm pool, the steady force. Once she got angry, though, we were gonna be there for a while. Truthfully, as I got dressed, I had to wonder if the emotional response was maybe an indicator of something off-kilter with her. Y'know, something like pregnancy hormones. Guys, even if it's true, *never* suggest that to a woman's face. You *will* end up dead.

Mira had gone outside with the kids by the time I got back out front, and I poked my head out the door. "Kid! Saddle up!"

Estéban obediently abandoned the snowball fight, though he took one in the back of the head as he trotted to the door. He turned long enough to stick his tongue out at my daughter, then darted inside when he was answered with a barrage of snow from my two lovely ladies.

Mira just looked at me through the sliding door and didn't say a word. Later. We'd discuss this later. At much length, no doubt.

The kid waited until we'd pulled out of the driveway at least before he offered his two cents. "You should apologize to her."

I shifted gears roughly, and my truck gave a little jerk. "For what?"

"For whatever you did. Just say you're sorry." Wise words, but somehow I didn't think that was gonna cut it this time. When I didn't answer him, he dropped it. "So where are we going?"

"Marty's. I need to pick up my new sword."

About four months ago, I'd broken my katana in a bad fall that nearly broke my neck, too. I'd also nearly broken the friendship with the man who had made the sword for me. Marty hadn't signed on to get chased by zombie demon minions. He didn't volunteer to risk his life. I'd done that. I'd forced that on him.

He'd promised me a new sword, but I wasn't sure if I rated a new friendship, too. I guess we were about to find out. To be perfectly frank, I'd asked Estéban to come, 'cause I wasn't sure I wanted to have this showdown alone.

For his part, the kid pulled out his new cell—a gift from Mira and me for Christmas—and started texting.

"So...how's old what's-her-name?" Instantly, he flushed red, and I grinned to myself. I had no idea what Estéban's girlfriend's name was, or if he even had one. But mentioning "old what's-her-name" was guaranteed to get a blush out of him, so I did it whenever possible.

Marty's Suburban was in the driveway when we pulled in, so at least he was home. His wife was due to go into labor any second now, and I'd half imagined missing them as they left for the hospital or something. But no, he was there, and he stepped out his front door as we pulled up in front of the house.

"Stay in the truck, kid." He grunted acknowledgment and never looked up from his phone. Yeah, I didn't want to be here alone, but I also wasn't sure the kid needed to hear all the gritty details. He'd missed out on last fall's debacle.

I stepped out into the snow, nodding to the man on the porch. "Marty."

"Jesse." He looked good, at least. Way less beat up than the last time I saw him. Built like a damn fireplug, shaved head, bristly black beard for winter, his heavily tattooed arms crossed over his chest.

The two of us kinda stood there in the snow, the silence uncomfortably taut between us. It felt like two gunslingers, waiting to see who was gonna twitch first. Turns out, it was Marty.

"You come for your sword?"

"Yeah, if you've got it done."

"It's done." He jerked his head toward his workshop behind the house. "Go on back, I'll meet you back there."

Yeah, I noticed that he didn't invite me into the house. So that's how it was gonna be. I trudged through the yard to the back, and Marty met me at the workshop, unlocking the door.

"Wait here." Shit. He wasn't even gonna let me into his man-cave?

I stuffed my hands into my coat pockets and waited and pretended that it didn't feel like a rock in my guts. I knew this could happen. Pretty much counted on it, really.

I mean, I nearly got the guy killed. It's a little hard to be best buds after that no matter what the cop movies say. What Marty had been through last fall ... no one should have to do that. I couldn't blame the man if he wasn't all puppies and sunshine with me anymore. Couldn't blame him at all.

A few minutes later, Marty reappeared, a cloth-wrapped bundle in his arms. "Here. Check it out, make sure it's okay."

He balanced the bundle across his arms, and I un-wrapped it slowly. I think I stood there gaping like a landed fish for a good long while, but if you could see this sword, you might too.

It was a katana still, that didn't surprise me. It was the weapon I was most comfortable with, the fighting style I knew. The polished steel blade swept out in a graceful curve, and just looking at it I could tell it was silk-slicing sharp.

He'd done the circular guard in brass, big enough to just cover my fist as I held it. The pommel was brass too, and came to a subtle point. A skull-breaker. The hilt though ... oh the hilt. My old sword had been plain, the hilt just wrapped in blue cord. For the new one, Marty had chosen some kind of bone, smooth and white, and etched into each side was a line of kanji.

"The way that is spoken here is not the eternal way," I murmured quietly. "The name that is spoken here is not the eternal name." I knew those lines. They were tat-tooed down each of my biceps. The first two lines of the *Tao Te Ching*. Marty had carved them into the sword, specifically for me.

"I named it The Way." Apparently deciding I'd looked long enough, Marty shook the wrappings back over the sword and thrust it at me. "The pommel makes it a bit heavier on the back end than you're used to, but the hilt is lighter, helps balance it out. The bone is lion bone."

I didn't even bother to ask him where he'd found lion bone. If he said it was, it was. I couldn't even think of anything adequate to say. The man had just handed me a goddamn work of art. Finally, I settled for, "Thank you, Marty."

He grunted a little. "This is the last one, Jess. I'm not gonna do this anymore. I got Mel, and the baby, and . . . I just can't."

"I know. It's all good, man. I understand." A small part of me even envied him. What would it be like to have the luxury of just . . . walking away? The rest of me, well frankly it hurt. Marty had been my best friend for years now. And now he just . . . wasn't anymore. "You uh . . . take care of Mel, okay? Call Mira when the baby comes, she'll want to know."

He grunted again, and retraced his tracks in the snow, disappearing into his house. The door slammed with ominous finality.

I stared at the bundle in my arms for long moments, until my truck's horn beeped at me impatiently. "Yeah yeah, I'm coming." With a shake of my head, I started back to the truck.

What's done was done. No changing that now, no use dwelling on mighta-coulds or maybe-shouldas. Marty and his family would be safer for it. I had to believe that.

I handed the sword to let Estéban as I climbed into the truck, and he unwrapped it immediately. "Oh wow . . . I don't think I could use it. It's too pretty."

Though I was inclined to agree with him, I knew I'd use it. I'd had my chance to give up this glamorous life, and I'd passed it by a long time ago. Just one of those sacrifices a hero makes, or some shit.

"Hey, kid. How's your spell casting going?" Like most champions, Estéban had magical ability. His mother—a powerful *bruja* in her own right—had been teaching him a little, and Mira had picked up there when he came to live with us. He wasn't up to either woman's skill level yet, I knew that, but every smidgen of power he had was a smidgen more than I possessed. Me, the great magic-less wonder.

The kid looked at the weapon in his lap, and quickly shook his head. "No way. I'm not good enough to do this. You have Miss Mira do it."

I ran the truck through its gears as we bounced down the road, pondering that notion. There was no way I was having Miss Mira do *any* magic in the foreseeable future. Not until we knew for sure. If there was even the slightest chance she was pregnant, I couldn't ask her to risk that. Not again.

When I missed the turn that would have taken us home, Estéban gave me a look. "Where are we going?"

"We're gonna go find Cameron." I knew one other powerful magic-user, and I had absolutely no qualms about asking him to drain himself for my benefit. He was still on my shit list anyway.

Cameron—*Brother* Cameron if you wanted to be formal—had moved out of his little hole of an apartment shortly before Thanksgiving, saying something about black mold or whatever. Personally, I think he needed to suck it up and suffer.

Of course, the woman he was dating, my wife's best friend Dr. Bridget, had taken him in. She didn't know he was really a priest, sent to spy on me, and whatever discussions they'd had about him sleeping in the spare bedroom were none of my business. Seriously, how could she *not* question why the man wouldn't sleep with her?

Bridget looked surprised when she answered her door to find us standing there. "Jesse . . . Estéban . . ."

"Heya, Bridge. Cam here?" I gave her my best charming no-nefarious-deeds-to-see-here grin. Pay no attention to the teenager standing to my right with a sword behind his back. Bridget was still in the dark concerning magic and all things demonic. I wasn't going to be the one to burst that bubble.

"Yeah . . . come on in." She gave us both a wary look as she stepped back from the door. "Cam . . . ! Jesse's here!"

Cam appeared from the direction of the kitchen, drying his hands on a towel, and his look of faint curiosity faded almost instantly, seeing me standing in the entryway. "Jesse . . ."

"Cam. Got a second?" My words were friendly, but my tone of voice said "*yes*, you have as many seconds as I require."

"Uh yeah, sure." He passed the towel to Bridget and kissed her on the cheek. "The biscuits are ready to go in the oven, hon."

I waited until the good doctor had vanished into the recesses of the house before turning a flat look on Cameron.

"I'd say Merry Christmas, but I'm guessing you're

not here delivering gifts." The priest raised a brow. "What's up?"

"I need that voodoo you do so well." Estéban brought the sword forward when I nodded, unwrapping it.

Cam's eyes went wide. "Wow . . . that's . . . did Marty make that?" He reached out, but stopped just short of touching the blade. No matter what he called himself, in the end, Cam was just a champion like myself. He knew good weaponry when he saw it, and he knew that you didn't just reach out and grab another guy's sword. It's rude.

"Yeah. And now I need it magicked."

The priest frowned in puzzlement. "Why don't you have Mira do it?"

"She just can't right now. And this has to be done before tonight. My armor's in the truck, and I need those spells refreshed too." If I was going to be fighting a soul challenge, bargaining for a demon to retrieve someone's lost soul, I wouldn't have bothered with blessing my gear. I usually negotiated those protections out anyway. But this job wasn't normal, and I had no idea what I was going to need in the next week.

Cam frowned thoughtfully. "All right . . . um . . . I can't do it here, for obvious reasons. Do you know where Redemptorist is?"

Of course I did. Everyone in Kansas City knew that church. "Down on Broadway. Sure."

"I need to get some stuff first. Meet me there."

As we stepped out the door, I could hear Cam inside explaining to Bridget that he had to run out for a little bit. It sounded oddly like the conversation I'd just had with Mira, only with a lot less "angry" in it. I think it just made me dislike him a little more.

Cameron was a part of the Ordo Sancti Silvii—the Order of St. Silvius. You ask any Catholic about that saint, and they'll look at you like you're crazy. It's a saint that doesn't, as far as most of the world knows, exist. The men in the order were champions, like me, who operated under the direction of the Catholic church. They tended to look down on the more secular champions, like me, and in return, I usually referred to them as the Knights Stuck-up-idus.

A few months ago, Cam's superiors sent him to KC to keep an eye on me. Too bad none of them bothered to tell *me* that the demons were gunning for me. I had to admit, without Cam we'd have all been zombie chow, but I still didn't appreciate the deception. Especially when it involved him lying to a woman I greatly respected.

If the jerk hadn't seemed to genuinely care for Dr. Bridget, I'd have probably kicked his ass months ago. As it was . . . I couldn't bring myself to break her heart like that. Maybe I'm a big ole softie on the inside.

Our Lady of Perpetual Help, better known around Kansas City as Redemptorist Church, was one of the most amazing churches I'd ever seen. What I know about architecture you could fit on the head of a pin, so I couldn't tell you if it was Gothic or Baroque or whatever. I could tell you that it looked like a medieval castle with spires and turrets sweeping to the high heavens. The stained glass windows were amazing, and the sun cast multicolor images across the parishioners as they sat in their quiet prayers. It seemed like there might just be angels lurking in the shadows of the vaulted ceilings, listening to those prayers.

Yeah, I know. I don't really believe in god-with-the-big-G, but if I did, this was what church should feel like. Like there was something so much bigger than me out there, looking out for us.

Luckily, we'd just missed the midmorning service, and I slipped in the door feeling like a long-tailed cat in a room full of rocking chairs. Estéban paused to dip his fingers in the font, making the sign of the cross like the good Catholic boy he was, then we walked up the center aisle toward the altar.

Damn, were my boots always this loud? I shifted my equipment bag on my shoulder and I swear it sounded like I had a herd of Santa's reindeer in my bag, jingling away. Even the slightest footstep seemed to echo off the cavernous ceiling. There were only a couple of people still in the church, their heads bowed as they tended to whatever spiritual needs they had. They never looked up at me, so maybe it was my imagination.

I glanced at the kid, but he was gazing around with wide eyes, entranced by the ornate beauty. "I wish *mi madre* could see this. She would love it so much." Even his quiet awe seemed to reverberate in hushed whispers from up above.

"Is there something I can help you gentlemen with?" Both Estéban and I flinched at the soft question, and the priest who'd snuck up behind us smiled his apologies. "Sorry, I didn't mean to startle you. I am Father John." He was seventy if he was a day, bristles of white hair sticking out above his ears, but leaving the rest of his head shiny and bald. Smile lines were etched deep around his pale blue eyes, and his face was simple and kind. I can think of no other way to describe it.

"It's okay, no harm done." Though it was a good thing the sword was in Estéban's arms, or things coulda got nasty there, real quick. Don't startle the paranoid guy, 'kay? "We're just waiting for someone to meet us here."

The priest's eyes swept over my duffel bag, and the bundle clutched to Estéban's chest, but he didn't ask. "Well, our next service isn't until tomorrow morning at seven, and we take confessions a half hour before all of our weekday masses."

"Thank you." Geez, the things I could confess would probably turn the man's hair white. Y'know, if it hadn't been already.

Deciding that perhaps we weren't potential parishioners, Father John excused himself, leaving the kid and me standing before the altar.

"Um, Jesse? Would it be all right if I sat here for a while?" I raised both brows at the kid, and he studied his toes intently. "I have not been to church since Miguel died. I think perhaps I should spend some time."

"Yeah, kid. You do what you gotta." I thumped him on the shoulder once and he gave me a very small, grateful smile, handing me the bundle containing my new sword. I mean, what was I gonna say? The kid really hadn't had a chance to deal with his brother's murder, almost a year ago now. If he wanted to sit and commune with God or whatever, who was I to question?

Estéban found a seat in the front pew and clasped his

hands, murmuring quietly to himself. I turned away. It seemed too private to watch, this whole religion thing. Thankfully, I spotted Cameron coming in the big double doors, which saved me from trying to figure out what to do with myself in the interim.

The incognito priest also stopped to dip his fingers in the holy water, making the sign of the cross, then strode down the center aisle toward me. "Where's E— Oh." He spotted the kid, I guess.

"He's dealing with some stuff. I'll grab him on the way out. So where do we do this?"

"I need to let them know I'm here; they'll have a place available, I think." Cam hefted a black duffel bag on his own shoulder, eerily similar to mine, and I followed him toward the recesses of the big church.

Behind the scenes, the church looked just like any other generic building. There were several doors that opened into what appeared to be classrooms. A janitor's closet. And several doors that simply had nameplates on them. We stopped at one labeled REV. RICHARD STRONG and Cam rapped lightly with one knuckle.

The man who opened the door wasn't as old as I was expecting. I'd been picturing another elderly fellow, like Father John, but this guy was young. Ish. Forties, maybe, athletic build, sandy hair. In a blue polo shirt and khaki pants, I never would have guessed he was clergy.

Reverend Richard's eyes lit up, landing on Cameron. "Cameron! Damn, it's good to see you!" They traded rough, backslapping hugs, while I was pondering the concept of cussing in a church. "I was beginning to think you weren't going to come see us."

Cam chuckled and shrugged. "The life of a busy man, you know how it is. Um, Jesse, this is Ricky. Ricky, Jesse."

"Pleased to meet you." I had to juggle stuff so that we could shake hands, but once managed, I found the reverend's grip nice and firm. I also noticed the calluses, the sign of a man who worked with his hands. And I mean worked hard. Either this man was only pretending to be some administrative lackey, or he had some really interesting hobbies.

"So what brings you in?" Reverend Ricky asked, eyeing the bundle in my arms curiously.

"I need a place to work." Cam nodded toward his own bag of supplies. "Thought I'd ask if we could borrower your Sanctum?" Reverend Ricky gave Cam a curious look, and a dart of his eyes toward me. Yeah, that was subtle. "Jesse's fine. He's one of Zelenko's."

"Ah. I was wondering. It's back here."

Ricky led the way and I brought up the rear of our odd little train, trying to decide if I was offended to just be known as "one of Zelenko's" or not. Especially since I wasn't technically speaking to Ivan, right now. See, that's what happens when people lie to me. I get all pissy.

Ivan had been lying to me from the moment he'd turned up on my doorstep almost five years ago. I'd seen proof of it last fall as picture after picture scrolled across Viljo's computer screen. Images of more champions than I'd ever been told about, people who weren't supposed to exist. It might seem like a small deception, but my life depended on being able to trust Ivan's information. If he'd lied about that, what else was he less than truthful on?

No, we're not going to talk about me lying to other people. I'll struggle with my hypocrisy on my own time, thank you very much.

There were more hallways in the back of the church than I really realized, and then we even found a staircase leading down beneath the building. The air temperature dropped about twenty degrees, and what might have been dampness during the summer felt like pinpricks of frost on my bare face. Yay for being underground in a brisk Missouri winter.

Despite the aged feeling of the natural stone walls, the lighting was thoroughly modern, and pointed our way to a room at the farthest end of the hall. I glanced up, estimating that we were under the nave. Part of me wanted to bang on the ceiling, see if I could scare the people sitting above us.

"Everything should be ready, we refresh the supplies every morning." Reverend Ricky gave Cam a polite nod, and included me in it at the last second. "Let me know if you need anything else."

He left us down there in the dungeon (yes, I know it wasn't, but the image was stuck in my head) and the door above boomed shut. Cameron gave me a small shrug and pushed open the plain wooden door, revealing nothing but a dark featureless room in front of us. "Ready?"

"Guess so." I had to wonder, ready for what?

4

While I had visions dancing through my mind of medieval torture implements and manacles hanging off the walls, when Cameron flipped on the light, it was just another room. Two rooms, actually, and the first one had a row of old porcelain sinks against one wall, a shelf above it holding a row of clay pitchers. The doorway to the second room was low—I'd have to duck to get through it without knocking myself out—and I couldn't see much except the same stones as the walls, set in concentric circles to make up the floor.

Cameron dropped his duffel bag on the floor and went to select a pitcher. "You should scrub up too, I may need your help."

"What is this, surgery?" I set my gear down with a bit more care and moved to the sinks.

Cameron ditched his coat, then poured water from the pitcher into the basin in front of him. He dunked his hands in it up to the elbows, so I quickly followed suit with another pitcher from the shelf.

"Jesus freakin' Christ!" I snatched my hands back just as quickly, splattering freezing-cold water every which way.

"Language, please?"

I glared at the priest as he performed his ablutions in the ice-cold water. "You could have warned me."

"It's winter. It's cold down here." He glanced at me once. "It's holy water. You may feel a tingle."

"After my fingers go numb and fall off, I may never feel anything again," I muttered to myself, but plunged my hands back into the ice bath. Keee-RIST that was cold!

He was right, though. Once I got used to the frigid liquid, I could feel more than just the cold lancing through my bones. Under that was the telltale prickle, the only trace of magical power that I was able to sense. I brought a handful of water to my face to sniff at it, and caught the faintest hint of cloves. It was distant, but discernible if you knew what to look for. I may not be able to use it, but I could usually tell when it was present.

My scrubbing didn't take nearly as long as Cameron's, and I shucked back into my coat so I could pretend I wasn't shivering. "You guys just leave holy water sitting down here in case someone happens by?"

"Yes." Apparently, he was clean to his own satisfaction, because he pulled the stopper on the sink and moved to his duffel bag again. "The function of a Sanctum is to be prepared whenever someone needs it."

"That's a lot of wasted juice," I observed, watching the blessed water draining out into the local sewer system.

"Not really. Most novices have enough latent ability to bless the water, even if they don't know their results have actual power. Faith is an amazing phenomenon."

"Mmhmm." Cam and I had discussed this whole magic vs. religion thing before. What it boiled down to, for me, was that my pagan wife's magic smelled and felt just the same as Cam's prayers. You can call it an elephant if you want, but for me it all still quacks like a duck.

Cameron was unloading his duffel bag right there on the floor, setting out vials and bells and small containers of unidentifiable powders. "Only take what you need inside the next room. Leave your bag out here, the wrappings on the sword, that kind of stuff."

Hey, I don't ask. I leave the whys and the how-comes to the magic folk. I unpacked my gear, like he said, managing somehow to carry all my armor and padding with one arm, leaving my other hand free to carry the precious new sword. It was heavy as hell—the armor, not the sword—and it took only a few minutes for my arm to start complaining.

Cam appeared to be taking his sweet time, mulling over the other ingredients of his all-purpose bag of magic paraphernalia. "What exactly do you think you'll be needing?"

That was a damn good question. This wasn't one of my usual soul challenges, and I really had no idea what I'd be going up against, if anything at all. Axel had said they'd send someone, or some*thing*. One of those zombie things, like what we'd faced last fall? No, that didn't make any sense. Even in L.A., those things would start a raging panic.

A person, maybe? Somebody like me, but demon-sworn? I'd never turned my sword on another human being in my life. I honestly don't know if I could. Let's all just hope I'm never faced with making that decision.

"General protective spells on the gear. Bionic me up." I didn't think I could run down a Los Angeles street, waving a katana, so I'd need more than just my weapon in case things went bad. "A way to set up wards would be good, something portable. I've got mace already, but you could snazzy it up a bit." Demon mace was only cayenne and cumin mixed together, but a little magic oomph couldn't hurt. "Anything else you think might be useful. General anti-demon stuff?" Yeah, a font of information. That's me.

"The wards are easy." He pulled a spool of thick string out of his pack and laid it with the rest of his supplies. "And maybe . . ." He plucked a few more things out, then folded all the bottles and jars and knickknacks up in a cloth I hadn't even seen him produce. Standing, he looked at me very seriously. "Once we're inside the room, we don't leave until we're done. If you gotta piss, you should do it now."

"Are you allowed to say that in a church?" He just rolled his eyes at me and disappeared through the low door. What could I do but follow?

Ducking to get through the doorway, I saw that there were also a few steps down, an awkward maneuver with an armload of armor and weaponry. The room itself was perfectly circular, as I'd guessed, with a raised altarlike surface in the dead center. A plain wooden cross hung from the ceiling above it, the end centered over the stone table where Cameron gently laid his supplies.

Though there were electric lights in this room as well, the priest then went around to wall sconces and lit torches—*actual torches!*—narrating as he did so. "Once we start, we'll probably lose the lights. Trust me when I say that being down here in the pitch black isn't fun."

"I thought you'd never been here before." Finding no place to set down my heavy burden, I was forced to just stand there and wait.

"The Sanctum is the same in any church that has one. Most of them on this continent were even built by the same man, back in the early 1900s. Until that point, the Order was solely based in Europe." With quick, precise movements, he started setting things around the altar, a place for each one and everything in its place. I couldn't help but smirk a little, watching him. "They're scattered all over the country, available for whoever might need them."

"So, everybody knows that demon-hunting knights might come strolling in at any time?"

"No. Only a few in each parish. Most think this is just a room for meditation and prayer." He flicked his lighter one more time, lighting a tiny candle in his array of random objects. "They know it as the Sanctum. The rest of us know it as the Sanctum Arcanum."

Finally, I leaned against the wall, careful not to get my long hair anywhere near the flickering torches. "Why is the Order a secret, even within the church?"

Cameron finally looked up from his fiddling. "Why doesn't Marty want to talk to you anymore?" I frowned, and he nodded. "Because some people, even those in the church, just can't handle that reality." He turned his gaze back down to his work, examining everything on a microscopic level, it seemed. "Those who can handle it . . . they get recruited, either as knights or as support staff."

"Like Reverend Ricky."

"Yeah, like Ricky." Cam smiled a little. "We went to seminary together, actually. He's a good man."

"So why's he not a knight?"

"He was." With a few minor adjustments, Cam seemed satisfied with his toys. "You can't tell, but he's blind in his left eye now. They pulled him out of circulation." He stood up straight, stretching a little, then motioned to me. "Bring me the sword first, we'll start with that."

Pulled him out of circulation. A retirement plan. I had to wonder how many of Ivan's champions had ever retired. Ivan no longer fought, that I knew of, but the rest of us . . . our life expectancy wasn't good. Retirement meant just one thing, and it had nothing to do with long afternoons spent fishing.

I laid the new sword on the altar where Cam directed, and stepped back. The priest took another moment to just look over the wonder that was my blade. "This is the kind of sword that ought to have a name."

"He called it The Way."

"The etchings . . . that's the same as your tattoos, right?"

"Yeah." I was still touched that Marty had gone to such amazing effort, all for me. For a guy he didn't even really like anymore. "Get this moving, it's freezing down here."

"Step back a little more." I did, and Cameron closed his eyes, placing one palm on the hilt, the other on the tip of the blade.

His lips moved silently for a few moments. That was one thing I'd noticed, Cameron's magic required words. Mira's didn't. I found the differences fascinating. Mira would have cast a circle, a barrier of her own will. Cam scrubbed down like a brain surgeon. My wife's implements usually involved a scrying bowl and various herbs.

I spotted salt on Cam's altar, alongside saltpeter, wine, and a tiny bottle of magnetized iron shavings. A cross, of course, in addition to the one already hanging overhead.

The priest mouthed something, in Latin I think, and the thick scent of cloves wafted out of nowhere. My skin tingled again, like pins and needles, and I couldn't help but rub my fingertips together, like I could almost grab it if I just knew how.

To my left, one of the lightbulbs shattered with a pop and a fizzle. I flinched just in time to avoid being peppered with glass fragments, and brushed the sparks off my shoulder before it could catch my hair on fire. Two more bulbs across the room followed suit, eliminating three of the four electric lights. The torches kept flickering merrily, but the place looked even more like a dungeon than it had before.

In the dimmer lighting, I could make out the faintest of glows around Cameron's hands as he prayed, and it spread slowly from his fingers to the metal of my sword, oozing along the blade like syrup. It met in the middle, gained in intensity for just a moment, then sank into the weapon and vanished. His hand trembling, the priest dipped his fingers into a small bowl of water and spattered it across my sword. The water sizzled when it touched the metal, apparently to his satisfaction. Cameron took a shaky breath and leaned hard on the altar.

"You all right?" Magic—*all* magic, no matter what Cam wanted to believe—was fed from the life force of the user. The bigger the effect, the greater the price. It was entirely possible to cast yourself to death, just pouring out your own life until there was nothing left.

Luckily, things like wards and protections were fairly minor on the magical spectrum. Defensive spells had minor costs. Not like the big flashy stuff. That's why even those champions who had magic didn't use it in combat. No great wand duels or fireballs. That'd kill a champion faster than any demon.

"I'm fine. Just gotta catch my breath between, you know?" Cam gave me a small grin that faded when he remembered we weren't quite friends. "Let's get the armor next."

I traded out my newly blessed sword for my pile of tarnished mail armor and padding, Cam clearing more space on his altar for the heap of metal. As he reset some of his supplies, he casually asked, "So, why is Mira not doing this for you?"

"She just isn't." It was none of his damn business.

He gave me a flat look. "I heard Bridget talking to her on the phone." *Crap.* "If she is pregnant, you're right to keep her from casting any spells."

"I know that." I'm not stupid, I swear.

"Are you excited?"

That was a damn good question. I mean, I love my daughter. She's one of the most amazing things in my life. And I'm sure I would love any other kids that came along just the same. But was that being a responsible parent, bringing another kid into this mess? Poor Annabelle, she was here before I got involved in the lunacy. But another kid? It was a daunting prospect.

"Can we just save our male bonding for another time when I'm not freezing my balls off?" When I'm uncomfortable, I snap. Sorry.

Cam went to work without answering me, spreading his fingers to touch as much of my armor as he could. Again, the faint blue glow started at his palms, trickling through his fingers and into the gear in front of him. Topping the pile of armor were my leather bracers, and I could see the sigils on the inside surface flare brightly when Cameron's magic passed over and through them. Mira's runes, carved by Marty's hand. In the pile of chain, tiny sparks danced in the links, adding a metallic hint to the clove-scented air. I didn't remember seeing that happen when Mira worked her stuff. Interesting.

Watching the priest work over my armor, it occurred to me what else Marty's absence in my life would mean. Damn, where was I going to get my armor worked on when it was damaged now? The stocky blacksmith had crafted every link with his own two hands, fitting and designing it by trial and error over the course of the last four years. It wasn't like I could just drop it at the dry-cleaners and pick it up a couple of days later. I could ask Cam, sure, but I'd rather choke. Maybe I could call Avery, out in San Fran. Surely he'd know someone . . .

The spells on the armor went much the same as the blessing over the sword, except there was just more to cover and thus it took longer. It cost us the last lightbulb, leaving us with the torches and the increasingly smoky air, and despite the icy temperatures, Cameron was soaked with sweat when he finished. As he recovered from the second round of hoodoo, chugging a can of energy drink that I didn't see him bring in, I grumbled about the lack of ventilation. "It's actually a safety mechanism."

"How's that?" I eyed the shadowy ceiling and the murky layer of smoke that was accumulating up there.

"Eventually, we'll pass out from lack of oxygen."

"And that's *safer*?" That's it, they were all nuts, every one of them.

"If you're unconscious, you can't pray anymore. Better to wake up with a raging headache than not wake up at all."

He was right. Even magic use had its addicts, and apparently the church wasn't immune. There were those who would simply cast and cast until they fell over dead, and they would do it willingly. Power of all kinds corrupts.

Armor and sword sufficiently tingly to my senses, Cam went about arranging a few other things for me. Lengths of the thick string became portable wards—or so he said. He blessed my demon-mace canister on my key chain, and gave me a charmed disk to add to my collection that was supposed to change color in the presence of danger. I didn't bother to tell him about my own ingrained danger sense. Mira insists it's the one vestige of magic I possess. I don't care what we call it, so long as it works.

All the while, the air got thicker with smoke and clove-scent. My eyes burned, and I wasn't sure if it was the torches, or the magic. And with every spell he cast— wait, sorry, prayer he said—Cameron's face got paler, and the shadows under his eyes got darker. When his hands were visibly shaking, I stopped him.

"That's enough. I don't need anything else." For just a moment, I thought he was going to argue with me.

Like I said, power is tempting, even for a priest. I guess maybe I don't really envy them after all. Finally, he nodded and I started helping him pack up his gear. "You can't drive home like this."

Cameron shook his head. "I'll stay here for a bit, have some coffee with Ricky or something. I'll be fine."

"What are you gonna tell Bridget?"

He snorted. "I'm gonna tell her you took me out back and kicked my ass. What do you think I'm gonna tell her?"

Okay, I had to smile at that. I left him down there, making sure I propped the outer door open so there would be a little fresh air.

Estéban was right where I'd left him, but he was leaning back in the seat instead of being all hunched over his clasped hands. There was a sense of peace in his face that hadn't been there before, and for a moment, I wished I could have that too.

He hopped up when he saw me coming, and I hit him in the chest with my duffel bag of armor. He threw it over one lanky shoulder, looking like a demented Santa. "C'mon, kid. We gotta go home so Mira can rip my head off."

"What exactly did you do, by the way?"

I waited until we were outside before I answered him. "I'm heading out to L.A. tomorrow."

"For what?"

"It's . . . complicated." But if anyone was going to understand my reasoning, it would be Estéban. He was from a family of demon slayers. He'd lost a father and two brothers to it already.

As we drove home, I tried to lay it all out, as I knew it. The actress, the botched deal, the extra souls. The promise I'd made to Axel. His dark brows drew closer together, the more I talked, his frown deepening with each passing mile.

"Can't you just . . . tell him no? You are not tattooed, it isn't a contract."

Yeah, I probably could have. I hadn't promised Axel my soul. I'd just promised him a favor. What could really happen, if I said no? I'd cease to be the kind of man I wanted to be, that's what would happen. I was already straining the limits of what the *bushido* might call acceptable. I couldn't ditch my honor too. "No, kid. I owe him a legitimate debt. Cole would be dead without him. You'd have done the same for Miguel."

Estéban shook his head slowly. "You are either braver than I realized, or crazy as fuck."

"Language." I'd had a bad influence on his English since he'd been living with us.

He only snorted at my admonition. "I don't think there is anything in the world that would compel me to anger Miss Mira. The only thing worse would be angering *mi madre*."

He was right. Either woman was likely to take a skillet to my head. "Well, you work on her while I'm gone then, okay? See if you can get her to soften up."

The teenager snorted again. "Oh, hell no. You are on your own with this one."

"Thanks. Thanks a lot."

5

The discussion with Mira got put off for a few more hours, even after we got home. There was the Christmas wrapping mess to clean up still, and dinner to get on. There was the promised outing in the snow with my daughter, which somehow turned into an impromptu lesson in hand-to-hand combat for Estéban. I put him down twice, but the third time he managed to sweep my legs out from under me, and I landed in a giant heap of snow. I was so proud.

Anna was in bed and Estéban had retreated to his room before Mira and I found time to actually converse.

I was carrying the trash out through the garage when I caught her standing near my truck, examining my duffel bag of armor. "Hey!" I moved quickly and snatched her hand away from the bag. "Don't even think about it."

She looked a bit shamefaced, proving that she *had* been thinking about it. "I wasn't going to do anything. I was just checking it. Cam's work?"

"Yeah. Figured he may as well be useful, right?" Taking a chance, I slipped my arm around her waist. She leaned into me, which was way better than the elbow in the ribs I was expecting. I rested my chin on top of her head. "You doing okay?"

She was quiet for a while, before taking a deep breath. "I'm pissed off, Jesse. I'm scared, and worried, and I desperately do not want you to go to Los Angeles. I think this is a horrible idea, and I wish you'd never asked for that thing's help."

"If I'd have had another way, baby . . ." Standing in the middle of a dark road in Colorado, so many months ago, it had seemed like the only course of action. I hadn't had time to think of something better.

"I know." She patted my chest lightly. "I do know, I just . . . I'm not happy about it. It seems like this whole thing suddenly got way more complicated than we bargained for."

Boy howdy, did it. "What do you want me to do, baby?"

I wasn't sure if the sound she made was a laugh or a sob. "Run far, far away? Go hide in a cave somewhere? Just . . . quit?"

A simple request, one she'd been very careful not to make before. But you know . . . I could. After this little errand for Axel, all I had to do was never take another contract again. That simple. My own retirement plan. Let it all be someone else's problem. Hell, as of last fall, I knew there were way more champions under Ivan's watchful eye than I had ever realized. Surely one of them could take up my slack? "Can we revisit this again when I get back?"

"Yeah." She straightened herself, squaring her shoulders. "Come on, we need to get you packed up. You'd head out there with a pair of underwear and one clean sock if I let you."

"Mir?" I caught her hand as she turned to head back inside, and when she stopped, I rested my other hand on her flat stomach. "You call me the second you know something, okay? No matter what time it is."

She nodded, but her smile was faint at best. "I will. You'll be the second to know."

The night passed uneventfully. I even managed about seven hours of actual sleep. My dreams, when they came now, seemed to be ordinary, boring things. Showing up at work in my underwear, running late to take a test I hadn't studied for, and once this really weird thing involving a penguin and an escalator made of Gummi bears. (I blamed the buffalo chicken pizza for that one.) The Yeti no longer visited me in my sleep, tearing out my heart night after night after night. Guess once you kick a guy's ass twice, he's just not as scary.

When dawn came, I kissed Mira and Anna good-bye, patted Chunk on the head, and crawled into the truck to let Estéban drive me to the airport.

We stopped briefly on the way to mail off my sword and armor. They don't like it when you try to take stuff like that on an airplane, and it was easier to just ship it ahead. I charged it to Axel's credit card. S'what he gave it to me for, right? Now I just had to hope that nothing requiring weaponry happened until tomorrow morning.

Hitting the highway toward the airport, Estéban shifted gears smoothly in my old clunker, and I nodded a little. Teaching him to drive this past summer had actually been way easier than I'd expected. I almost felt okay, leaving my baby with him.

"You put a single scratch on this truck while I'm gone, and we're gonna have problems."

He gave me a sidelong smirk. "How would you even find a new scratch in all the old ones?"

"Trust me, I know every mark on this truck. A new one will shine like a beacon." Still, I grinned to myself. I wasn't worried, not really. Not about the truck at least. About another mile down the road, I asked him, "You can take care of Mira and Anna, right?"

He took his eyes off the road just long enough to give me a quizzical look. "I think Miss Mira can take care of herself."

"She can't use magic right now, kid."

"Why not?"

"Because it's possible that she's pregnant." I cringed when the truck gave a little swerve, Estéban glancing with his whole body instead of just his head.

"Really? That's great!"

"Simmer down. We don't know for sure yet. But until we do, she absolutely can*not* cast any spells, okay? If something happens, you do it yourself, or call Cameron. Got it?"

"Yessir." The kid was grinning ear to ear, and it was a little contagious. I found myself smiling right along with him. "Congratulations."

"Thanks, kid." You know, it did feel kinda good to be congratulated. Maybe this wasn't going to be such a terrible thing after all. Maybe I could walk away after this. Just be a dad. Get a real job. Join the PTA. Hell, I dunno. Something.

After a few minutes of silence, the kid glanced at me again. "Jesse, are you sure this is a good idea? This trip, I mean. Demons . . . they lie."

Yeah, I knew that. Except Axel never had. Not that I could remember. "Pretty sure this is one of the worst ideas I've ever had, kid. But I gotta go. I gave my word."

He frowned, keeping his eyes on the road. "I know that you say honor is the most important thing, but . . . does it count if the person you gave your word to isn't honorable themselves?"

"That's when it matters the most. You can't control what other people do. All you can do is, at the end of the day, make sure you can still hold your own head up and think 'Hey, I did right.' "

"Have you ever had to do something bad, because it was right?"

"Not yet. That's one of those dilemmas you gotta hope you never run up against."

He mulled that over in silence for the rest of the drive. I think, at the end of *my* day, I just wanted to be able to think "Hey, I taught the kid well." I owed his family that much.

I just had the kid dump me out at the airport, checking the suitcase Mira had insisted I pack, and taking my backpack in as a carry-on. ('Cause really, that's where my important stuff was.) In order to make my trip more cheerful, Annabelle had decorated the pack with a bunch of fluorescent stickers, all of which had a garish logo that read SOLDYOURSOUL.COM! Thanks, Viljo.

Our pet computer geek had started the Web site as a joke, I think, an exercise in Web design. Self-help for the demon-sworn among us. But despite the fact that most of the world viewed it as only amusement, it had found an audience, and was going like gangbusters last I heard, getting however many hits a day they considered a lot. If any of those hits had resulted in an actual soul challenge, no one had told me, mostly because I think Viljo thought I was pissed at him.

He was right. I wasn't as mad at him as I was at Ivan, because Viljo had just been following the old man's orders, but still. He'd lied to me too.

And because even on my best days I have a petty streak, I was leaving town without registering with Viljo's champion database, Grapevine. Yeah, that's right, I'm a rebel through and through. Wasn't any of Ivan's business where the hell I was, anyway.

Getting through security at the airport was its own kind of special hell. My backpack, my steel-toed boots and my collection of anti-demon key chains got dumped in the tub to be scrutinized by overworked and underpaid TSA folks. One of them poked and prodded at my tangle of gizmos with a pen. I had a blessed mirror for seeing invisible creepies, a carnival token that could turn any vessel of water into holy water, Cam's mood-ring danger device (which stayed neutral, thankfully), a pentacle of my wife's for extra protection, and a small photo of my girls, which had no magical properties, but made me smile every time I looked at it. The security lady finally decided I couldn't take over a plane with that stuff, and passed me with a grumpy snort. Damn good thing I'd thought to take off my demon mace canister. It was currently stuffed in my checked suitcase, and I could only hope the damn thing didn't leak cayenne all over my clothes.

I got a window seat in the plane and set my backpack

by my feet. Hopefully, I could put on some headphones and ignore the world while we zoomed along overhead. Give me time to do some thinking, some meditating. Get my head on straight about this whole baby thing.

For a few brief, joyful minutes, I thought I was going to have the row all to myself, but right as the attendants were getting ready to button us up, a man came scrambling on board, out of breath and flushed. "Woo! Almost missed it, didn't I?" And of course, he was directed right toward me.

The guy plopped down in the seat beside me, jostling my elbow without even saying excuse me. I tried to ignore him. It didn't work. "Hey, how's it going? I'm Spencer, Spencer Law." He stuck his hand in front of me with every expectation of me shaking it. I did so with the barest modicum of enthusiasm.

"Hey."

"Man, had to run for my connection! Just knew I was gonna miss it and be stuck in this hick town forever." I suppose it never occurred to him that I was very fond of this "hick town," but my frown was wasted as he busied himself stowing his bag.

He was preppy, in a fresh-out-of-college kind of way. Looked a lot like Cameron, with short dark hair in stylishly gelled spikes. His khaki pants were already wrinkled from whatever flight he'd just dashed off of, and his polo shirt was salmon pink. Seriously? Pink? He flopped down, jostling me once again. "Can't wait to hit L.A. Babes in bikinis beats waist-deep snow any day."

I snorted to myself. The snow was barely ankle deep. A dusting, really. Wuss.

"So, what're you headed out to La La Land for?" Before I could answer him (even if I'd had any intention of doing so) he held up his hand. "Wait, don't tell me, let me guess. I'm pretty good at reading people."

While he looked me over good, I contemplated what his face would look like if I had him in a choke hold. He took in my blond ponytail, still at shoulder-length, the fading scar high on my cheek. His eyes narrowed as he observed my steel-toed combat boots, my worn jeans and my T-shirt that said I HATE YOUR FAVORITE BAND.

Finally, he nodded as if he'd discovered the answer to life, the universe and everything. "I'm thinking . . . stunt man."

Seriously? "No, not really."

"Really? Damn, I'm usually so good at this stuff." Chatty-Spencer made himself comfortable as the plane started to taxi, and I fished in my backpack for my headphones. I was going to need them. "Sold your soul dot com? What's that?"

Inwardly, I sighed. Damn Viljo and his freakin' stickers! I could tell already that this was one of those airplane buddies who was just *not* going to shut up, even if the plane went down in a fiery heap. We'd plummet to our deaths with this guy narrating all the way down. "It's a Web site a buddy of mine runs."

"Yeah, what's it about? One of those Christian things?"

"No." I have never wished for teleportation technology so hard as I did just then. "It's just a thing." I put my headphones on, even though I had no music playing, and pretended to be fascinated with the takeoff process.

The ruse seemed to work, at first, Chatty-Spencer settling in for the flight and directing his incessant babbling to the flight attendant and the lucky passenger across the aisle. But the moment we got up in the air, he whipped out a laptop and pulled up Viljo's Web site. "Oh wow . . . is this guy serious?"

"Mmf." Maybe if I didn't look at him, he'd go away?

"He really believes that people sell their souls to the devil, hunh?" He snorted. "Geez, if somebody can point me at one of those demons, I'll do it in a heartbeat. There's stuff I need to do!"

I had to turn and look then, checking out every inch of bare skin I could see on the man. No demon brands. No twisting, writhing tattoo to scramble my senses and add to the ache I was already getting behind my eyes. Hey, it was worth a look. You never know. "And just what do you deem important enough to sell your soul for?" I swear, if he said something stupid, I was going to punch him.

"Well, see . . . like, I'm heading out to L.A. 'cause I have this movie idea. I'm a writer! A screenwriter, anyway, and a buddy of mine knows a guy who knows a guy . . . you know how Hollywood is." He rolled his eyes and chuckled, deciding that, with no evidence to support his assumption, I must know all about Hollywood.

"And you think a movie deal is more important than your soul?"

Chatty-Spencer laughed. "Hell, what are you gonna do with a soul? I figure in Hollywood, you're a nobody if you still *have* one. Amirite?" He elbowed me jovially, and I imagined myself crushing his skull. It was a sweet thought. I also set my mental clock for six months, a year at the outside. Viljo'd be getting an e-mail from this idiot, I just knew it, wanting one of us to come save his ass.

"But I won't have to sell my soul or anything. This thing I've got, it's gonna be huge. Nobody's got anything like it." He patted his laptop like a cherished puppy, and I had to wonder what would happen if I "accidentally" spilled my complimentary paper cup of water all over it later.

"Well, good luck to you."

To me, that sounded like a conversation ender, but the man just kept talking! Four hours of unrelenting drivel, and I couldn't even say for sure that the guy stopped to take a breath.

I found out all about his super-secret movie idea, because he could tell I was a trustworthy sort. (And I've seen the same plot done at least four other times; trust me when I say it was not as groundbreaking as the guy wanted to think.) I learned where he went to college, about the crazy ex-girlfriend he'd left behind in Chicago, all about the online video game he played fanatically. He told me about his friend-of-a-friend-of-a-friend inside studio connections, which basically boiled down to a janitor for Someone Important's intern. He confessed that he only had a hundred bucks in his pocket and no idea where he was going to stay once the plane touched down, but he had a cousin who promised to get him a job somewhere with lots of celebrity interaction.

Part of me had to wonder just how many people every year headed out to California with just the change in their pockets and dreams the size of Canada. How many of them had those same dreams crushed and went crawling home, broken? How many of them stayed past the point when they *could* go home, unwilling to admit to anyone else that they'd failed in an industry where success was the rarity, not the norm?

See, that's the problem with having a philosophy degree. I have a crappy job, and my brain works way too much.

I almost cried from happiness the moment the wheels touched down. At that point, I was dangerously close to selling *my* soul for a moment of peace and quiet.

"Aw, man, here already? And we were just getting to know each other." Spencer gathered up his stuff, carefully putting his laptop back in its bag. "We should totally keep in touch, man. You on Twitter?"

I wasn't even sure what the hell a Twitter was. But something told me this guy was gonna need help in the near future, and even if I planned on retiring, I could still direct him to the right people. "Here." I handed over one of my self-printed business cards. It was plain white card stock and said simply JESSE DAWSON, CHAMPION. My cell phone number was printed beneath it.

I squeezed past him and down the aisle, ignoring the puzzled "Champion?" behind me.

I'd never been to Los Angeles before. Typically, the entire west coast fell into Avery Malcolm's territory, the champion based out of San Francisco. I mean, I'd seen pictures on TV, like anybody, but we all know how true-to-life those can be.

People rushed around me, greeting loved ones with squeals and kisses, or just hustling off to the next stop on the journey of their life. Christmas travelers, I decided, just coming home after the festivities. Things looked off for some reason I couldn't put my finger on, until I realized that no one was wearing a winter coat. Light jackets, yeah, but nothing like the parkas we'd been bundled up in at home. Winter in California, I guess.

Standing in the midst of the human flood was a man in a dark suit jacket over a white T-shirt and blue jeans. The crowd parted around him, I think because running into him may have caused bodily harm. Dude wasn't tall really—no taller than my six foot one—but he was solid muscle and the nice coat did nothing to disguise the breadth of his shoulders. In fact, if he flexed, I bet he'd shred that nice jacket right in two. Black hair, the kind with natural blue undertones, caramel-colored skin, and most notably a stark black tattoo down the right side of his face. Oh, and he was carrying a sign that said J. DAWSON. Since my name happened to be J. Dawson, I walked over and introduced myself. "I am J. Dawson."

"Taiaho Otimi. You can call me Tai." He offered me a handshake and the foreboding expression morphed into a genuine smile. I mentally took about five more years off his age. Mid-twenties, if I had to guess. His friendly grin was only slightly marred by the tribal markings from his forehead to his chin. I stared at those black marks, waiting to see if they would move under my gaze, until the guy gave me an odd look.

"Sorry. Jet-lagged, I guess. Call me Jesse." The second his hand touched mine, I felt a jolt all the way through my arm into my neck. Like whizzing on the electric fence. I jerked, breath hissing between my teeth, and he looked at me strangely. "Old carpal tunnel injury. It flares up when I fly." When he glanced away, I shook the numbness out of my fingers.

Cheezus Christ on a piece of freakin' toast! That jolt had been pure unadulterated magic, and if my hair were shorter it might have been standing straight on end. *He's Maori.* I'd heard about it, sure. It was one of those subjects Ivan covered in Demonology 101, but I'd never seen it in practice before.

The Maori were one of those few remaining peoples of the world who, through some quirk of genetics or culture, had innate magic coursing through their veins just as a matter of common birth. And despite the influence of the outside world, they'd managed to hold on to most of their old legends and stories. Magic was not as unbelievable to them as it was to pretty much the rest of the world.

This Tai, though . . . he didn't know. He had no idea he'd just zapped the living shit out of me. "Do you have luggage?"

"Um . . . yeah. One." I fell in behind him as we headed for the baggage pickup, letting him clear a path through the crowd. "So you're Maori, right?"

He gave me a surprised glance. "That's right. Most people guess Samoan, 'cause I played football. Like only Samoa has big, dark-skinned dudes that play football, right?"

That small fact clicked in my head, and I realized why he looked vaguely familiar. "You used to play for USC, right?"

"Yeah, 'til I blew out my knee. That's the breaks, I guess."

We found a place surrounded by everyone else waiting for their luggage, Tai clasping his hands in front of him casually. His shoulders strained the cloth of his suit jacket, but the fact that it didn't just rip right in two proved that it had been tailored expressly for him. Tailored so well, in fact, that it almost hid the outline of a shoulder holster rig across his back. Damn. I was starting to wonder if maybe limo drivers in L.A. had New York taxi drivers beat.

"So you're a limo driver now?"

"Sometimes. Mostly, I'm a bodyguard who also drives." Okay, then the shoulder rig made a bit more sense, I guess. Though I now had Whitney Houston stuck in my head.

"You often find use for a gun in your limo driving-slash-bodyguarding?" Maybe I really am from some kind of backwater hick town. Aside from the president, I'd never met anyone who warranted a bodyguard, let alone an armed one. Even my wealthier clients hadn't been that far up the fame scale.

"Not yet. But the world is full of crazies. Stalkers and stuff, y'know?" He shrugged his broad shoulders.

"I assume you're working for Miss Keene?" He grunted an affirmative. "So who's watching her while you're here?"

"Other guard. His name's Bobby. You'll meet him when we get to the hotel."

We stood in semiawkward silence for a bit. But I couldn't help but notice that there were three teenage girls standing off to one side, giggling and pointing at me. Great, did I have toilet paper on my shoe or what? Finally, I sighed and looked at them. "Is there something I can help you with?"

They whispered among each other, finally poking the bravest one until she stepped forward. She kept glancing back at them for support, giggling like a lunatic. "You're him, right? That guy?"

"What guy?" I mean, I know I'm a legend in my own mind, but this was ridiculous.

"From that show. With the island and the polar bear."

"Um . . . no. Sorry. You must have me mistaken for someone else." You'd have thought I popped their balloons or kicked their puppy or something. Instantly they deflated with a chorus of "aaawwwws" and wandered off.

I glanced at Tai, who gave me a thoughtful look. "You do kinda look like him."

"Like who?"

"That guy. But I've seen him in person. You're taller."

"Well, I'm not him. Whoever the hell he is." I don't watch a lot of TV. I had no idea who they were talking about. An island and a polar bear? Sounded lame. I spotted my suitcase forlornly circling the baggage carousel and moved to grab it. "Are we far from the hotel?"

"You've never been to L.A.?" I shook my head to the negative. "Well, you'll get to do a bit of sightseeing on the way there, then."

I grinned a little. "I get the dollar guided tour?"

Tai smiled again. The small gesture seemed bigger on his tattooed face. "Yeah, I guess I can do that. Come on, let's get outta here."

6

Tai led me to a silver Lincoln Town Car in the parking lot, and after some internal debate, I tossed my luggage in the backseat and climbed into the front. I don't do well with a chauffeur, okay? It's just not natural.

"Excuse me." Tai leaned over to reach for a black box under my seat. Fishing a silver key out, tiny in his large hands, he unlocked it to reveal a handgun, which he quickly slid into the holster under his arm. "Can't take it into the airport, obviously."

"Yeah, I get it." Okay, coming from the land of deer hunters and gun racks, maybe I shouldn't have been so concerned by the sight of the weapon, but really, I didn't know anyone who openly carried a sidearm. Except my brother, the cop. He doesn't count. "You all go armed like that?"

"No, most don't. Bobby and I do because . . . well, Gretchen had some nasty stalker stuff a few years go, so now we just don't take chances."

I vaguely remembered hearing about that in the news. The dude went to jail, maybe? Celebrity gossip wasn't something I kept up on really. "You been with her long?"

Tai nodded as we drove through a tunnel leading out of the airport. "Couple of years. Bobby's been with her a little longer. We're kinda the rarity. She goes through staff pretty quick." He darted a glance at me. "To be honest, I'm not sure why you're here, other than Reggie said you were coming."

"Reggie?"

"Her agent." Oh great. Another agent. I didn't have a good history with agents. "So, you don't know Reggie?"

"Guess my people talked to her people." If this Reggie knew I was coming, that meant he knew Axel. I had to wonder if that made him another demon, or one of Axel's demon-sworn, or maybe just Axel himself, in disguise. Should be interesting to find out.

"So . . . why *are* you here?"

"I'm a specialist."

"In what?"

"In the kind of problem that Miss Keene may or may not have." Yeah, that sounded suitably vague. I was actually kind of proud of my evasion techniques. "Somebody asked me to come check on things, so I am."

The bodyguard eyed me up and down. "No offense, but you don't look like much."

Couldn't argue with the guy there. I mean, I was six one, yeah, but the Maori masher sitting next to me outweighed me by a good seventy-five pounds. Probably more. A heavy hitter I was not. "I'm wiry."

Tai snorted his laugh, and shook his head in amusement. "'Kay, man, if you say so."

The drive into L.A. wasn't nearly as interesting as I'd hoped it would be. The sun was shining brightly, which was nice after the overcast Missouri winter. But whatever highway we were on, it seemed to be just another gray stretch of pavement looming over the streets below, like every other gray stretch of pavement I'd ever seen.

What local color I could see involved a few scraggly palm trees (not nearly as many as TV would have you believe), some other spindly trees I couldn't name, and nondescript buildings that occasionally sprouted tall enough to be seen over the sides of the guardrails. Really, it looked remarkably like Johnson County, back home, only with more lanes and fewer cows.

The only point of curiosity was the elevated train running down the middle. When I expressed interest, Tai identified it as "The green line. Rapid transit."

Once the loops and turns of the highway got us headed in the right general direction, Tai also pointed out a gray smudge in the distance. "That's downtown, where we're headed."

I squinted a little. "Is that the smog?"

"Yeah. It's lighter in the winter. In the summer, you can't even see the mountains." That was light? Ugh. "Not as much traffic, this close to the holiday." I eyed the lanes and lanes of cars streaking along beside us and decided I never wanted to see actual traffic. There seemed to be more of the iconic palm trees, but when I remarked on how pretty they were ('cause isn't that what you're supposed to say?), the big man next to me just wrinkled his nose.

"Giant rats live in those trees."

"Seriously?"

"Dead serious. I saw one the size of a cat once."

Well, isn't that . . . special. I made a mental note to be on the lookout for any giant rodents, especially any of them with glowing red eyes. I didn't trust Axel not to check up on me, and that'd be the perfect hiding spot, given his predilection for small vermin disguises. "So . . . any local points of interest I shouldn't miss while I'm in town?"

Tai chuckled again. "Aside from the usual touristy stuff? Not really. I imagine we'll get dragged to a few parties in the next week or so, hitting up the New Year's celebrations. Might see some interesting places then."

Mentally, I started planning how to actually guard someone's body in a room full of Hollywood's elite. It would be easier if I had the foggiest idea what I might be up against. And why couldn't this be Halloween instead, when I might get away with carrying my sword in public? "She go to those kind of things a lot?"

"When she's not on set somewhere, yeah. Usually, security's pretty high at the big-name shindigs, so we mostly just stand against the wall and talk among ourselves. Not a lot to do, and the food is pretty good. Hot girls there too, sometimes, if you're interested."

"Nope. Married." I waggled my fingers to show off my very plain wedding band.

"Oh yeah? Got any kids?"

"One. Little girl. She's six." One so far, anyway. I added calling Mira to my mental to-do list, once we got to the hotel.

Forty minutes of idle chitchat, several harrowing turns down side streets to avoid traffic, and a few cuss words I'd never even heard before, we arrived in front of the Masurao Grand Hotel.

As I stepped out of the Town Car I had to chuckle, looking up at the elegantly designed sign. Tai gave me a curious look, so I pointed up at the name. "Masurao. It means warrior." The guy gave me one of his "oooookay" looks and grabbed my suitcase out of the backseat. Guess I was the only one interested in Japanese trivia.

More precisely, *masurao* meant warrior with the connotations of a gentleman, a hero. I chose to consider it a good omen. Tai tossed the keys to the valet, and I was about to follow him inside when a strange figure accosted me.

"And he shall come forth from the land of bread and honey!" It was impossible to tell if the man was old or young, but if I had to guess, I'd say he was more than sixty. Steel-gray hair hung from his head in long dreadlocks, interwoven with bits of brightly colored yarn and string. His clothes were thrown on with no rhyme or reason, in equally garish hues, in more layers than the mild California weather warranted. His skin was dark in a way I'd come to associate with Haiti and Jamaica, though he had no accent that I could discern.

The old man caught my hand before I could react, just holding it between his palms, patting gently. His skin was leathery and dry, but not in an unpleasant way. "He shall walk the earth, and he shall know no rest, so long as steel is in his heart."

"Um . . . yeah, thanks for the tip." I carefully extracted myself from his grasp, and just then the doorman noticed my predicament.

"Felix! Go on, get out of here. I told you yesterday you can't bother the guests!" The man gave me an apologetic smile. "Sorry about that. He's one of the local eccentrics, always spouting mixed-up proverbs and stuff. He's harmless, really."

I watched the strange fellow shuffle off down the sidewalk, muttering to himself. Mixed-up proverbs, indeed. Sounded like he'd confused the Bible with the old *Kung Fu* series. Walking the earth . . . *Felix, hm?*

Tai came back to see what was keeping me and frowned when the doorman explained. "Crazy old man. They need to put him in a home somewhere. Come on, we're late and she'll be pitching a fit."

The interior of the hotel was stunning, every bit worthy of the moniker "grand." The lobby had been done with a nod to Asian flavor, bamboo and paper screens abounding, but it was done subtly, fitted in between modern lighting and furniture.

We passed through a circle of flickering light on the elegant tile floor, and I looked up to find myself beneath a skylight, many floors above. The light danced and moved, and it took me a moment to realize that there must be water on the glass, breaking the sunlight into tiny rainbow bits.

"It's a reflecting pool," Tai offered, seeing my interest. "There's a big garden on the roof, with waterfalls and everything."

"Wow." What else could I say? I was impressed. Hell, even my luggage felt shabby, compared to this place. "Oh hey, I shipped myself a package here. I need to make sure the desk is expecting it."

"Yeah sure, this way. We gotta get you on the approved list anyway."

All the pertinent details arranged—and the concierge gave me an up-and-down look like he thought I was single-handedly bringing back the plague—Tai and I headed up to the penthouse suite on the uppermost floor. The bodyguard showed me how to swipe my key to allow me access to the restricted floor, much to the ill-concealed amusement of the bellhop, following along with my one lonely suitcase.

"This'll be your room." Tai opened a door with his own keycard, which made me frown a little. I didn't like the idea of someone else having a key to my room, but apparently everything on this floor responded to one. "Sometimes, some of Gretchen's friends stay in the others, but there's nobody in them right now. She got ticked and tossed a bunch of them out a couple of weeks ago."

"Lovely." I dumped my backpack off for the time being and even tipped the bellhop. See, I can be civilized! "Let's go meet her then."

As we stepped into the hallway, the double doors at the end flung open, and a harried-looking attendant pushed a cart out, the plates on it full of barely touched food.

Tai shook his head a little. "Let me guess, her rare steak was too rare and her three-minute egg was in thirty seconds too long?"

"And later, her porridge will be too cold and her bed will be too hard." The waiter just rolled his eyes, and the two men exchanged fist bumps before he wheeled the rejected food back toward the elevators.

The bodyguard caught the door when it would have closed, and gestured me inside. "Welcome to the penthouse, Jesse Dawson."

The penthouse was everything you would expect of a room tagged with that designation. Spacious, sumptuous, elegant, extravagant. It seemed to be a central sitting room, with several doors leading off. I mentally mapped them as the master bedroom, a second bedroom, a second bath, and off to the side there was a kitchenette and a full dining room with a twelve-seat table. The living room—which looked nothing like *my* living room, I might add—was crowned by a TV the size of my bed at home, and a couple of plush couches in dark brown leather.

I might have noticed more, had there not been a topless woman standing in the middle of the room. Okay, she wasn't *totally* topless, but she stood there in only her bra and panties with her hands on her hips like she owned the world. In the split second before I averted my eyes, I recognized her as Gretchen Keene, movie star extraordinaire. Hell, maybe she *did* own a good chunk of it.

"Is it Take a Homeless Guy to Work day, Tai?" A small smattering of chuckles sounded from around the room. I mentally marked the positions of two other people, both male, but refused to look toward the crazy half-naked chick.

"This is Jesse James Dawson. Reggie told you he was coming, remember?" If Tai was uncomfortable with her nudity, it wasn't evident in his voice. Maybe this was normal? Naked Tuesdays or something? Geez.

"Oh yeah. The demon slayer." That made me look up in surprise. Very few people knew what I did. It wasn't like demons ran PR campaigns or took out television ads. For her to speak so openly, in front of witnesses and everything . . . I wasn't expecting that.

Dear God, where was I supposed to put my eyes? I

mean, the girl was smokin' hot and the next best thing to buck naked. I think her legs went all the way up to her eyebrows, and even without makeup on, she was stunning. Her hair was piled up on top of her head, gold like only comes out of a bottle and all artfully messy-like, but it only made her even more gorgeous. Was this what demon magic could do? I could feel warmth in my face and fought the urge to look away again. Instead, I focused on her eyes. They were blue—darker than mine, I could tell from a distance—but there was that slight shadow behind them that I recognized instantly. She was soulless.

That forced my eyes to her left forearm, looking for the telltale black tattoo. It was there. I could see one dark curlicue snaking toward her elbow, but it was mostly obscured by her stance. Still, if it stretched that far, it was a helluva tat. A helluva contract.

Gretchen raised a brow when I finally raised my eyes to meet her gaze. "Well, are you any good?"

"The ones who aren't good don't live to get better." Every eye in the room was on me, which struck me as odd when they could have been staring at her. I could feel Tai standing behind me, and off to my right at the bar was another big man with a crew cut who had to be the other bodyguard. The third man was hanging over the back of the sofa, watching me, his short dreads dyed an unnatural shade of fire-engine red. I couldn't see much of him except his head, but somehow I didn't think he was a fighter.

"Well, show me something." Gretchen waved her hand and plopped onto the leather couch, curling her bare feet beneath her. "Do a spell or something."

This day was just getting weirder and weirder. "I don't perform on command, Miss Keene." Never mind that I couldn't "do a spell" if my life depended on it. "I will, however, check the room over if you don't mind." What I couldn't do, my friends could do for me.

My mirror was still in the bundle of anti-demon stuff hanging off my belt loop. I picked it up and turned it toward Tai first. It was hard as hell, trying to get a look at the big man in such a tiny glass, but I managed it while walking a few slow circles around him. He was clean.

"What are you looking for?" He watched me curiously when I headed next toward the man at the bar.

"Fleas." More precisely, I was looking for huge demonic fleas, things I called Scrap demons. As long as Gretchen had been demon-sworn, I'd be amazed if there weren't at least a couple of the little beasties lurking around. They tended to latch on to the soulless, sucking their life force like greasy little parasites.

"Seriously?" I ignored Tai's incredulous question in favor of examining Bodyguard #2. Crew Cut eyed me with a raised brow, but held still as I passed the mirror over him. I mentally put him at a couple of years older than me, and though it was hard to say for sure with him seated, but I thought he was a bit taller than me, too. The requisite muscles filled out his plain white T-shirt, just like Tai's, but he wasn't some grotesquely built weight lifter. Those were usable muscles. Fighter's muscles. Seriously, if these guys were already familiar with the concept of demons, what the hell was I doing out here? They looked like they could handle themselves.

"And what's your name?"

"Bobby McGee."

That made me pause, and I looked up from checking out the guy's boots to see if he was screwing with me. "Really?"

He scowled, a scar at the corner of his mouth puckering the skin along his jaw. "Hey, your name is Jesse James."

"Good point."

Bobby McGee was likewise clean, and I went next to check out the guy on the couch. He raised a brow at me too, but where Bobby's had been calculating—no doubt measuring me up as I had him—this one was decidedly lecherous. "Oh, I love your hair! Can I braid it?"

"No." No one braided my hair. Except my wife. And me. You know what I meant.

"I'm Dante, by the way." He offered his hand, but I left it hanging there until I'd looked him over thoroughly in my tiny little mirror. Mentally, I labeled him "groupie." He didn't seem to serve any purpose that I could see, yet. "You find what you were looking for?"

"No." Thankfully, we seemed to have a distinct lack of Scrap demons so far. When I was done checking the groupie over, I shook his hand (that he'd left hovering there in midair, waiting). His grip was firm, but his touch was cold. Scraps or no Scraps, I let go quickly.

And that just left Miss Gretchen Keene. She stood up as I turned toward her, holding her arms out to the sides. "Take a good look. Most men would kill for this."

Already, her attitude was starting to grate on my nerves. I didn't think we were destined to be friends.

The first thing I examined was the black tattoo

scrawled down the inside of her left arm. Some small part of me expected to recognize it, expected to hear the Yeti's low chuckle from some dark corner of the room. But the Yeti was gone for now, dispatched by my own hand a few months ago, and her demon brand wasn't from a demon I'd seen before. The black coils curled and writhed under my gaze and I forced myself to look at it longer than I should have, just to be sure. My head ached when I finally looked away.

"Turn please." She did. It was easier to examine her when I didn't have her lovely . . . assets sticking in my face. Her back, though . . . I wasn't expecting that either.

At first, I thought my eyes were just protesting the hard work I'd had them doing, staring at Gretchen's demon brand. But when I'd blinked them a few times, I realized that what I was seeing was real.

Her skin was pale, as most true blondes will be, but just beneath the skin was something even lighter, shining faintly when the light hit in a certain way. It reminded me of butterfly scales, a shimmer seen for only a split second when the sun shone just right.

Her back was covered. The iridescently white tattoos spread from the tops of her shoulders to the small of her back, ending right where a married man should stop looking anyway. Once I really tried to see them, I could see the intricate loops and whorls, the whole complicated design almost swaying under my gaze. I caught myself swaying in time to it and looked away.

So that's what a trapped soul looked like. Many trapped souls, actually.

It was fascinating and sickening all at once, and I

wasn't sure if I wanted to reach out and touch those faintly seen shimmers or turn and walk right out the damn door.

"Are you done?" Her tone of voice told me I was, whether I liked it or not. I stepped back, tucking my key chains and such away.

"Yeah. You're all clean." When I really thought about it, I guess it wasn't surprising. I mean, Gretchen was some demon's pride and joy. They wouldn't want some skuzzy little parasite sucking on all those glorious souls she was carting around.

"Good. Now let me make a few things perfectly clear to you." Again, the hands on the hips. "I don't like you. I don't want you here. The only reason I'm allowing this is because Reggie thinks it's a good idea. So you will sit down, you will shut up, and you will stay out of my way, are we perfectly clear?"

Oh, that was it. "Then let me make *my*self perfectly clear. I don't like you either. I think what you've done to other people puts you one rung below slime on the evolutionary ladder. I am here because I owed someone else a huge favor. At no time did I say I'd take orders from a spoiled little rich bitch, so what you do or do not allow really means diddly-squat to me."

I don't know what I expected from her, but it wasn't a very satisfied smirk. She nodded once. "So long as we know where we stand." Turning on her heel, she snatched a satin robe up off the couch—proving she could have dressed any time she wanted, she'd just chosen not to— and marched back into her bedroom.

I don't know what I expected from the other men in

the room either, but when Tai and Dante laughed, I felt some tension ease across my shoulders.

Even taciturn Bobby nodded his approval. "You'll do just fine here."

I had my doubts.

7

I escaped to the safety of my own room after that. "Freakin' California." I'd just tossed my suitcase on the bed earlier, so I made some vague motions toward unpacking it. "The problem with California is that it's full of Californians," I told the empty room.

It was a nice room. Not the sprawling paradise down the hall, but nice. I'd never had a king-sized bed, and most definitely hadn't had one all to myself. The comforter was black satin, and looked like you could sink into it forever, and the bed was piled high with eleventy-billion pillows. I had a small bar to one side, and a fully stocked office area to the other. The closet was bigger than my den at home. Cripes.

I threw the curtains on the windows open wide, staring out at L.A. for a few long moments. Buildings stretched as far as the eye could see, all different and yet oddly the same as what I'd see in Kansas City. Somewhere out there was the ocean, and I wondered briefly if I'd be subjected to it during my stay. Sunlight and me, we don't exactly get along. I'd wind up looking like a samurai lobster if I was out there for more than an hour or so. Still, a city was a city apparently, especially from this height. Stone and concrete, brick and asphalt. I had to wonder if all the seductive tinsel and bright lights only glimmered at night.

But enough of that foolishness. Top priority was getting Cam's portable wards put down. When I opened up my suitcase, the first thing to catch my eye was a tiny piece of quartz, resting on top of my neatly folded T-shirts. I picked it up, rolling it between my fingers.

Ivan had given the crystal to me, years and years ago. I was supposed to do some meditation exercises with it or something, try to awaken the magic Ivan was just sure I had buried deep inside me. I think the crystal was supposed to react in some way if I ever got it right. Needless to say, it had always remained still and quiet, perfectly clear except for the one milky white flaw deep inside it.

Mira must have packed it for me, but I couldn't for the life of me fathom why. I tucked it into the pocket of my suitcase, and kept digging through my clothes. I found the Ziploc bag containing my magical goodies stuffed under my socks. The canister of demon repellent had survived intact, and I hooked it on to my belt loop with the rest of my doohickeys. I uncoiled the lengths of blessed string from the bag, examining the tiny tingles that spread across my skin like a band of ice-skating fleas. The trip had no ill effect on Cam's spells, then.

I eyed the expansive windows first. That was a lot of glass, a lot of entry point. With the coin on my key chain, I could make some holy water, paint protections on the windows. I finally opted not to. This high up, I didn't think a window entry was likely, and I hated to waste spells when I didn't have an easy way to replenish them.

So that just meant warding the doors. I briefly thought of doing the elevator too, but I wasn't sure how the constant motion would affect the spell, and I wasn't sure I had enough string, either. Only the occupied rooms would get the warding treatment.

It took me a few minutes to figure out just *how* to go about applying said string, but it finally came down to a liberal application of tape and staples, which I just happened to have on the nicely equipped desk. The string was long enough to make the entire loop around the inside of the doorjamb, and once in place, I verified that I could feel the boundary as I passed in and out of my door. It glided over me like a soap bubble, making the short hairs on my arms stand on end.

I had to wonder just how powerful it would be, though. Cam's wards had failed us in the past. Granted, he'd also been close to "spelling" himself to death at that point, so I wasn't sure I could hold that against him. I just ... wasn't sure I could trust him, yet. If it had been Mira's work, I wouldn't have questioned it at all. I had more faith in her than I did in myself, most days.

Speaking of . . .

With my room at least nominally secure, I flopped on the monstrous bed, listening to the phone chirp in my ear, and smiled when she answered on the third ring. "Hey, baby."

"Jess! You made it there okay?"

"Yup, just got to my room. You should see this place, Mir, it's a freakin' palace. We totally have to come here on vacation sometime."

She chuckled a little. "Because your last vacation went so well."

"Point." I sighed, putting one arm behind my head to get comfy for a bit. "So how are you doing?"

"I'm fine." She answered too quickly, which meant she knew it was a loaded question. "Did you tell Estéban that I'm pregnant?"

"Um ... no?" Technically, I hadn't. I told him she *might* be pregnant. "Why, what's he said?"

"He hasn't said anything, but I'm apparently not allowed to reach for things on high shelves or pick up anything that weighs more than five ounces without him right there, doing it for me." I could hear the annoyance in her voice. Nothing pisses my wife off faster than being told she can't do something.

"He means well, hon. Cut the kid some slack."

"So you did tell him."

Oops. "Was it supposed to be a secret?"

She sighed, and I could picture her raking her fingers through her long curly hair. Her green eyes would be dark, a small crease between her brows. "I just don't want a lot of people to know, if it's a false alarm. Or if ... if it doesn't last."

Yeah. Three miscarriages in, we knew very well that sometimes things just didn't last. "Just ... take it easy, okay? Let the Boy Wonder do some of the heavy lifting around the house for a change. It's good for him, builds character. And do *not* cast any spells. Not even little ones. You need something done, let Estéban do it. Or Cam." That last part was bitter to say. I wasn't sold on Cameron, not yet, but if it was a choice between using his skills or losing a baby ... well, I knew which I'd pick.

"I know." She fell silent, then. Sometimes, those silences say more than the words. I could hear the uncertainty in it, the desire to be hopeful, and yet dread at the same time. The fear of the what-ifs and the joy of the maybe-coulds. Everything I was feeling, too.

"Whatever happens, baby, I love you. You know that, right?"

"Yeah, I know that." There was a small smile in her voice. "I love you too."

"Listen, I gotta go put some wards up around the diva's door. You call me as soon as you know something, 'kay? No matter what time it is."

"I will, Jess. And I'm sure if I don't, Estéban will send up smoke signals or something."

I lay there for a few minutes more after we hung up, just rolling things over in my head. Another baby ... Christ, I didn't even know which outcome to hope for. I wondered if that made me a bad person.

Tape and stapler in hand, I went to go ward Miss Gretchen Keene's door next. I was almost done, crawling on my hands and knees across the carpet, when the door opened and Tai looked down at me with a raised brow. "Do I want to know what you're doing?"

"I'm willing to say no." One last staple held the blessed thread in place, and I nudged Tai back so I could pass through the door several times. As expected, a subtle shock passed over my skin, marking the location of the protective barrier. "What do you feel, Tai? When you wave your hand through here?" I admit, the entire concept of Maori magic made me curious.

Eyeing me like I was bonkers, Tai waved his hand through the door negligently, then hesitated and did it again, slower. "It's some kind of ... electrostatic barrier? What's it for, jamming listening devices?"

"Not quite." He could feel it! First, this meant it was really working. Second, it meant that he could pass through it without harm. That worked in his favor.

I hadn't forgotten Axel's warning that an enemy could already be here, and the presence of such strong magic was . . . very convenient. It was possible that Tai didn't know what he held. It was also possible that he was just hoping I hadn't noticed. "Hold this a second." I passed Tai my key chain, pressing Cameron's danger-sensing doodad into the big man's palm. I wasn't sure what color it was supposed to turn if things were bad, but the little disk remained a flat black slate. We stood for long moments while nothing happened, and I finally took it back.

"What was that about?"

"Oh, nothing. Just something I had to see." If Tai was demon-sworn for the other side, surely I'd have known by now. For one thing, he didn't have the eyes of someone who had sold their soul. It's always in the eyes. Gretchen even had the eyes, under her perfectly practiced smile, proof that part of her was missing.

The bodyguard frowned in puzzlement. "What are you, like the James Bond of demons or something?"

"Nah. I hate martinis." Glancing around the suite, I saw a distinct lack of Dante-the-groupie or Miss Keene. Bobby was sprawled on the leather sofa, idly surfing the channels. "Things chill out in here?"

"Oh, yeah. Dante bailed, and Gretchen is in her room setting up some stuff for some party thing she's dragging us to later." Tai closed the door behind me as I stepped inside. "You'll have to dress, if you're going."

Dress? I looked down at my snarky T-shirt and worn-but-comfy jeans. I wasn't exactly naked at the moment. I'd leave those kinds of displays to the starlet. "What's wrong with what I have on?"

The big man chuckled. "She'd never be seen with you in that. If you have some black jeans and a plain black T-shirt, it should be good."

Well, I did, and I could easily go change, but the obstinate part of me balked at having my wardrobe dictated. "Nothing like pinning a big sign on your back saying 'Hey, I'm a bodyguard!'"

"The appearance of force often does more good than the application of force." Tai shrugged his broad shoulders and had a seat on the other couch while I blinked in surprise. I liked him already. Man, I hoped he didn't turn out to be the bad guy.

The next hour was rather pleasant. I put Bobby through the disk test too, with the same unimpressive results, then sat and watched some TV with the bodyguards and got to know them a bit. They seemed like decent guys, really, and serious about their duties. They weren't just arm candy for some celebrity princess.

Tai, of course, had played college football until he blew out his knee. He'd gone on to finish his degree after his injury, and had been drafted into some light bodyguard work due to his impressive size and tattoos.

"Most people don't care if their guards can actually do the job, they just want the scariest-looking mother they can find." He shrugged. "I decided, if I was gonna call myself a bodyguard, I should at least know how to do the job. Got into some training classes, some certifications, found out I had a knack for it. Bounced around a little, mostly working big events instead of any specific celebrity. Then Gretchen had that stalker thing going on, and she put the word out she was looking for some help. Hired me after the first interview."

"And you?" I looked at Bobby.

"I was a marine for twelve years, did two tours in Afghanistan. When I came back, a buddy suggested this kind of work. Like Tai, I bounced around a bit before Gretchen hired me. People hire for appearance and reputation. I don't look scary like the animal man over here." He nudged Tai with his boot and a grimace that I was starting to understand passed for his smile. "So I had to get some cred behind me to get the good gigs."

The military background didn't surprise me. It was more than his buzzed haircut. It was something in the way he stood and sat, something in his posture. I can't really describe it, but I'm pretty good at spotting it. Ivan stood the same way, and I'd always suspected he was military at some point, too.

"Do you like it?"

Bobby thought for a moment before answering. "It's not like being in combat or anything, and the money's decent. So that's good. But it can be pretty damn stressful at times anyway. Gretchen can be pretty demanding."

Inwardly, I cringed. Yeah, I'd noticed that. "She get like that a lot?"

The two men traded looks, trying to decide how much to reveal to a total stranger. I could respect that. I imagine bodyguards didn't stay employed long if they started blabbing secrets all around Hollywood.

Finally, it appeared that Tai relented, but I caught a

subtle nod from Bobby. Well, that settled which one of them was in charge. "Gretchen can be a bit . . . high maintenance. I mean, everybody knows that. But she's not some dumb bimbo either. She's wicked smart, and really good at what she does. She has Reggie managing her stuff, sure, but she keeps super-close track of every penny, every investment. And if she's really into getting her own way, it's because she knows her shit and how it all needs to be done."

"And she's good to us," Bobby added. "We always get a Christmas bonus, and she's real good about vacation time if we want it, or sick days or stuff. I've had way worse jobs."

It occurred to me that I'd constructed some kind of preconceived notion of what I'd find in Miss Gretchen Keene. A spoiled, self-entitled princess, walking all over everyone around her and making unreasonable demands just for giggles. The imperious orders from on high earlier had kind of borne that out. But I hadn't expected this kind of genuine loyalty from her people. I thought I had a pretty good handle on what kind of men Bobby and Tai were, and if they were willing to back her up, there had to be more there than I was seeing.

Still, there was that whole "collecting souls" thing. Selling your own was one thing. Screwing other people over was another. Wasn't sure I could get past that part.

But, wasn't my job to decide what kind of person she was. It was my job to watch her back. "So, what do you make of all . . . this?" Neither of them had even blinked when Gretchen called me a demon slayer, and their reaction—or lack thereof—intrigued me.

"What, like this whole demon-slaying thing?" Bobby

shrugged his shoulders. "This is Hollywood, man. Anything goes. Doesn't surprise me that there's people running around selling their souls."

Tai nodded his agreement. "Just one more crazy thing in the long line of crazy things we see every day."

"So you've seen one? A demon?"

They exchanged looks, then shook their heads again. "Nothing like that. Just . . . seen stuff sometimes, y'know? Weirdness. Figure it's all part and parcel."

"Have you guys noticed anything weird going on lately?"

"You're gonna have to be more specific than that. Weird like how?" Tai leaned forward, his elbows on his knees.

"I don't know. Unexplained oddities? Noises, or the feeling of being watched. Or even just someone new lurking around more often than you'd expect?" Would have helped if Axel could have given me a clue what to be watching for.

Bobby chuckled. At least, I think it was a chuckle. It was a sharp, staccato noise, reminiscent of a machine gun rattling. "We work for Gretchen Keene. We're *always* being watched." Again, they traded looks, silently talking over just how much to tell me.

Finally, Bobby said, "We always gotta be careful, with Gretchen. Her fans . . . well, they're not always the sanest bunch."

"Tai mentioned a stalker, earlier. That was a couple of years ago, right? What happened?"

Tai nodded toward Bobby. "He was there, for the last of it. Happened before my time."

Bobby nodded a little. "Several years ago, Gretchen had a guy stalking her. To the point where he got into her house a couple different times. Killed her dog, once, left it for her." I couldn't help but grimace. Don't care how bitchy you are, no one deserves that. "About the third time he got in, the cops were waiting. They shot him. He lived, of course, went to jail, but he's due for release in the next few months. That's why we're staying here instead of a private house. Figured security is better, here."

"But nothing recent? Nothing even weirder than usual?"

"Nah. Just the paparazzi, like always."

Hm. Hadn't factored in cameras. Probably should have. "They follow her pretty close?"

Bobby grunted. "Gretchen's made a kind of deal with them. She allows so much without protest, if they go away when she says. Works out well for them, and gives her a little privacy. But they'll be at the club tonight."

"The only rule is, don't lay hands on them." Tai made a face. "No matter how up in your face they get, decking one of them is really bad. If they create too much of a problem, we just call the cops." Geez, this was sounding better and better.

"So, only this room and mine have people in them? Where do you guys stay?"

Tai pointed toward the extra bedroom. "Neither of us have families or anything, so we crash there. We're out at all bizarre hours of the night, so most of the time we take turns sleeping during the day, just in case she needs us for something. Everything else on this floor is empty, since Gretchen tossed all the freeloaders out a couple weeks ago."

"And good riddance," Bobby muttered.

So far, my suspected bad guy list consisted of a big fat lot of nothing, sad to say. But disgruntled moochers sounded like motivation. "Who were they? The people she tossed?"

"Just . . . people. Hollywood people. Gretchen had a party . . . oh, about a month ago? Opened up the other rooms so folks could crash here if they wanted. Only some of them didn't leave. Apparently had no intention of leaving, sponging off the room, charging up room service." The older man made a face that indicated what he thought of such freeloaders. "Then last week, Gretchen got fed up with it and booted them all out. Didn't break my heart any, they were making security a nightmare."

Tai chuckled, shaking his head. "You thought earlier was bad, you shoulda seen her then. I swear, lightning was gonna come down and smite them dead, the way she was going on."

"What about Dante? He's still here." The groupie had vanished while I was unpacking, so I still didn't have a good feel for him yet.

"Dante? Hell, they've been friends since they were in diapers, you hear them tell it. He's kinda permanent. Good guy. Little loud. He'll flirt with just about anything that moves, including you, but he doesn't mean anything by it. It's just his way. Most of the time, when she's on the warpath, he can get her to chill out. She yelled at him for tracking mud across the carpet last week, but I think that's the only time I've ever seen her mad at him."

The doorbell rang, and Bobby tossed the remote to Tai as he got up to answer it. I turned to watch, curious as to what kind of visitors Miss Keene got on a daily basis. What exactly did a movie star *do* when they weren't being in movies?

"Hey, Reggie. 'Sup, man?"

Reggie was the agent, or so I'd been told, and I was real interested to see who this guy was. More importantly, I was interested to see *what* he was. I half expected to find out he was Axel in disguise, which would make the next few moments very interesting if it turned out to be true.

He looked normal enough, I'll give him that. Older than me, if I had to guess, but out here in the Botox-and-lipo belt, his exact age was impossible to determine. A nice tan, probably fake but well done. Personal trainer kinda body, not overly muscular, but no visible fat. Slacks and a polo shirt with a real polo guy on it. Highlighted, sandy hair. Not at all as stuffy and high-strung as I'd expected. I'd dealt with agents before (it hadn't gone well), and Reggie didn't fit in the little shoebox in my head labeled "agent."

Bobby stepped back to let the newcomer in, affording me a good look at the guy's face when he passed through my newly placed ward. If I hadn't been watching for it, I'd have missed it entirely.

Reggie stepped over the threshold and there was a slight hesitation in his stride. Not a stumble, really, but a hiccup when he should have put his foot down. In fact he tapped the floor twice with his foot, as if feeling for the floor beneath him uncertainly. Once he had his bearings again, he glanced behind him, and when he turned back, his eyes landed on me with a thoughtful look. "And this must be Mr. Dawson."

"Yessir." I stood, offering my hand, but he had to cross the floor to take it. As he reached for my hand, I kept a close eye on his other arm. Nope, no black, wriggling tattoos. If he was demon-sworn, he hid it better than anyone I'd ever seen. "And you're Reggie."

"Yes." His grip was warm and firm, and when he let go, he produced a business card for me. As I examined it, he nodded toward the door. "You come highly recommended by certain parties. I see that you more than live up to your reputation." So he had sensed the ward. And more than that, he knew what it was, and that I'd set it. Our Reggie was turning out to be a rather interesting fellow.

"Well, I try not to make liars out of people. I'm just glad I can help." I might have said more—dunno what, really—but Her Highness chose that moment to make her reappearance.

"Reggie!" A far cry from the cold orders she'd snapped earlier, Gretchen now sounded as joyful as a child, all but bounding from her sanctuary to throw her arms around the agent's neck. And oh look, she had clothes on now. "Oh, I'm so glad you're here. Julianne is being positively *horrid* about tonight. She wants to send a Town Car instead of a limousine!"

The sandy-haired man chuckled and untangled himself from his enthusiastic client. "All right, princess, let's see what I can do with Julianne, hm?" He patted her head like a fond papa.

Gretchen gave him a grateful smile. "Thanks. She likes you better than me anyway."

As Reggie disappeared into Gretchen's room, she

fixed her gaze on her bodyguards. "We're going to Purgatory tonight. Black." Almost as an afterthought, she noticed me standing there too. One elegantly sculpted brow rose in disdain as she looked me up and down. "I suppose you're going too."

"That's what I'm here for."

She sniffed, the wrinkle to her nose letting me know exactly what she thought I was there for. "Dress in all black, if you can find something that isn't too disgusting." With a whirl, she vanished into her tiny little kingdom again.

Tai snorted a laugh. "Hell, she likes you."

I raised a brow at him. "How can you tell?"

"She's letting you come, for one thing," Bobby chimed in. "And she didn't order you to wear a suit she knows damn well you don't have."

"I could have a suit." I didn't, but I also didn't think anyone had had a chance to rifle through my luggage. Yet.

"You might, but not up to her standards, I promise. If she really wanted to make trouble for you, she'd have asked for the impossible."

Tai nodded his agreement, grinning. His tattoos gave it a slightly manic appearance. "See? Told you she liked you."

8

Now, I wouldn't say I'm movie-star-level handsome, but I haven't been kicked out of bed for eating crackers. Yet. I mean, I do clean up okay. A quick shower and shave, and I'm almost presentable in civilized company.

But next to Tai and Bobby, I felt like that little cartoon Chihuahua, bouncing along at the feet of the much bigger dogs.

Decked out in their evening attire—black slacks, black T-shirts, black tailored jackets—both men managed to look suave and businesslike all at the same time. Tai had confined his hair into a short ponytail, not unlike mine, and if you could ignore the facial tattoos, he could have been heading to any boardroom meeting. And with Bobby's stiff military-trained posture, I couldn't see how he could look anything *but* professional.

And then you had me. A pair of black jeans, never worn, a plain black T-shirt and a pair of ratty combat boots. Not to mention that both bodyguards looked like they could bench-press me without breaking a sweat. *One of these things is not like the other . . .* I felt scrawny, extremely conspicuous, and without some pithy slogan emblazoned across my chest, I felt practically naked.

Gretchen emerged from her bedroom as I was checking the wards on her doors one more time, and gave me the old up-and-down. "You'll do, I guess."

Well well, I had the queen's approval. La-de-freakin'-da.

Her Highness was mind-bogglingly gorgeous, of course. It was a nice little bit of nothing she was almost wearing, her silver dress baring more skin than it covered. The height of her spiked heels almost put her eye-to-eye with me, and I had to marvel that she didn't break an ankle in those things. I also made a mental note that if anything nasty went down, there was no way Gretchen would be running away from it. Not in those shoes. Mira doesn't wear stuff like that. She's more practical.

"The limo's waiting downstairs." Bobby held the door for all of us, and we were off.

Whoever named the place Purgatory should have just gone all out and named it Hell. At least, it was pretty close to my idea of it.

First off, I had no freakin' clue where I was. Turns out riding in the back of a limousine is fairly disorienting, especially when in a strange city to begin with. No one else seemed perturbed by it, but I kept peering out the tinted windows to try and get a look at my surroundings. I knew we were close only when there was a sudden increase in bright lights and honking horns.

The limo drove around the block three times for no reason I could see other than making sure as many people as possible were watching when we got out. Bobby and Tai exited first, clearing an opening in the rabid throng by means of their sheer size, and Gretchen slid out behind them, leaving me to cover the rear. Watch her tail? Follow behind? Wow . . . none of these things sound innocent. I walked last. There we go.

And oh dear lord, these people were crazy. There were camera flashes from every direction, screaming women (and some men), a hundred hands reaching out and grabbing at anything and everything they could. Any one of those hands could have held a knife, or a gun, or anything really, and there wasn't a thing any of us could have done about it.

Only a few short yards separated the car from the door, and still I was tight and on edge by the time we got through the gauntlet. I wasn't worried so much about the demons making a try for her in a crowded club, but what about these crazed fans the guys kept talking about? Any of these people could be armed, and I don't know that we would have known. The very thought made me want to crawl out of my skin. How Bobby and Tai did this on a daily basis, I would never know.

Gretchen walked through it like the crowd wasn't even there. She wore her short, slinky dress like it was a royal robe, and she held her head regally high, waving to the crowd at large, but careful never to stop and pay too much attention to one person. I was willing to bet, if I could see her face, that she was meticulously avoiding eye contact with the rabid throng. Wouldn't do to encourage the crazies.

The bouncers at the door didn't look at us twice, just sweeping us through and into relative safety. Tai paused behind us for a moment, having a brief talk with the head bouncer. No doubt the club's security staff was accustomed to things like this, but I could appreciate Tai taking a moment to make sure things were up to snuff.

I couldn't say much for the décor of the place. Metal grates and bare steel beams seemed to dominate, punctuated now and then by a splash of black-light paint, glowing coolly against the brick walls. Oddly, it reminded me a lot of my workplace back home, and as I looked around, I realized I could pick out at least seven outfits that had been purchased from my store. I also realized I was a teeny bit homesick. My teenybopper, punk coworkers would have loved it here. Kristyn, my boss in the loosest sense of the word, would have fit right in with her multicolored hair and flamboyant fashion sense.

There were dancers in hanging cages flanking both sides of the stage, dominated at the moment by a DJ and his rig. The girls had on glittery devil horns, and not a whole lot else, writhing inside their faux-steel prisons. I spotted one of the bartenders across the room passing one of the devil horn hair bands to another girl who had earned his favor somehow. No doubt I'd be seeing her up in one of the cages later.

The music was loud enough to be completely incomprehensible, distinguished only by the low thud I could feel through the thick soles of my boots. Strobe lights and disco balls cast rainbow streamers across the seething, writhing dance floor, and I was more than a little grateful when Gretchen and her boys steered us around that mess and into some private tables toward the back.

Walking in front of me, I could see Gretchen's back, bared almost indecently low, and in the black light, the iridescent tattoos glowed softly. They rippled under my gaze in a way that had nothing to do with how she moved, and part of me squirmed. It was like watching ghosts moving under her skin, the remains of living people glowing like cave worms. It struck me as eerie and sad all at once.

The starlet claimed a large round booth, big enough for at least a dozen people, and slid across the black leather seat to the very center, while Bobby and Tai took seats at each end of the bench, obviously there to deter . . . everyone, really. After a moment, I grabbed a chair from a nearby table and dragged it over so I'd have a seat too. Tai gave me an apologetic smile. "Sorry, man, not used to there being three of us."

"It's all good, don't worry about it." I straddled the frail little chair and rested my arms across the back. It would be easier to get out of this fast, if I had to. Better than being all caught up between the table and the leather booth.

Out of nowhere, a man appeared, oozing charm and champagne. "Gretchen, darling! Oh honey, I wanted to meet you at the door! Sly girl, sneaking in like that!" He too wore one of the devil horn headbands. He looked ridiculous.

I will say that Gretchen's smile never faded, but behind her eyes was something that said this man was barely on her tolerance list. He wasn't a friend. "It's all right, Leo, I know my way in." They did that air kissy thing that makes no sense to me, especially since he had to lean way over the table to do it. "Is there anything in particular you have on the agenda tonight?"

"Not at all, my lovely. You sit right here and have anything your heart desires. I'll send a server over." With that, he was gone again in the blink of an eye. I'm not sure I've ever seen a normal human move so fast.

Gretchen settled against the seat with a terminally bored sigh, examining her nails.

"So . . . what exactly do you do at these places?" I had to ask twice, raising my voice to shouting, before she could hear me.

"Nothing." She shrugged. "They just pay me to show up. It makes the club look good to have celebrities here. Leo's business will triple tonight, just because people hear that I'm hanging out."

Seriously? I am *so* in the wrong line of work. "So we just sit here, and you drink champagne or whatever, and then . . . we go home?"

"That sums it up."

The server showed up and the guys ordered soda, while Gretchen asked for a spring water with lime. Not what I expected, but hey, go with it. I passed, not really wanting anything in my hands.

Gretchen's entrance had been noticed. I could almost watch the word ripple through the crowd, see the wave as faces turned toward our table to take furtive glances. *Look, but don't let her see you looking!* The noise level doubled, drowning out what was left of the music.

I examined the crowd, trying to pick out anything odd, anything that didn't belong, all the while wondering what I was expecting to find. They were kids, mostly. Old enough to drink, I guess, to get in here, but still kids. Most of them wearing way too much makeup and hair gel, and way too little clothing. If Anna ever tried to dress like that, I was gonna lock her in her room until she was forty-five.

I think that means I'm officially old.

The server came back, delivering the drinks with quiet efficiency. I suppose celebrities were nothing new to her, and she even gave Tai a smile like they'd met before. "If you need anything else, just flag me down." She seemed nice, and fairly normal. Maybe not everybody was crazy.

I have to say, whatever I'd thought about the profession of "bodyguard" before this, it was way more boring than I'd expected. Bobby and Tai did their duties seriously enough, one of them walking the room from time to time while the other stayed close to Gretchen. Their eyes constantly scanned and analyzed, though how they were going to pick one single dangerous face out of that hustle and bustle, I wasn't sure.

Bobby also watched Tai, I noticed. Whenever the former soldier was out doing his rounds around the dance floor, his eyes always came back to the table, just long enough to be sure that all was right in the world. It took me a bit to realize that it was the same watchful gaze I often directed toward Estéban. A teacher, keeping an eye on his student. It made me like the grumpy cuss just a bit more.

But mostly we sat there while the music cycled from one identical song to the next. The crowd on the dance floor cycled too, the tired ones bowing out to be replaced by those recently refreshed with their beverage of choice. As the night went on, the dancing got dirtier and the crowd got drunker. Not totally unexpected.

Twice, we were approached by adventurous fans looking to beg an autograph or photo from Gretchen. She allowed it, Tai moving aside after Bobby's almost invisible nod of approval so the girls could slide into the booth with their idol. I got drafted into photographer mode, fumbling with their cell phones until they were satisfied with the results. (Though, I overheard one of them mention to her girlfriend as they scampered off "Oh my God, it was *him*! From that one show!" I don't know if I should feel bad for me, for looking like him, or him, 'cause no one could remember his name.)

"That was nice of you," I pointed out to Gretchen after the second time. "You could have told them to piss off."

Gretchen shrugged her bared shoulders. "Those girls will tell everyone they know how cool I am. It's good press."

"Do you ever do anything that isn't directly beneficial to you?"

"No." And there were no regrets there, that much was obvious.

The hours dragged on slower, the later it got, and my body was adamantly reminding me that it was still on Missouri time. I folded my arms across the back of my chair and rested my chin there, just watching the swirl of colors around the enormous room. It was almost hypnotizing, a big swirling riot of noise and shiny.

A hiccup in the general movement of the place caught my attention, and when I brought my eyes back into focus, I spotted our server across the room, at another table. Now, why did that stand out? Something in the way she stood just didn't flow.

I'd talked to her as the night went on. Her name was Traci-with-an-i, she was a college student, and wanted to be an actress. Her hair was dark and curly, just like Mira's, and she reminded me a lot of my wife in younger years.

Now, I couldn't see her face, but there was something to the set of her shoulders that bespoke tension, and when her serving tray clattered to the floor, I was already on my feet.

"Jesse?" I ignored Tai's question and started working my way around the dance floor.

From the changed angle, I could see the man at the other table, just your typical nondescript douche bag if I had to guess. His dark hair was slicked back against his head, and his suit probably cost more than my mortgage payment. His mustache looked like something had died on his upper lip. One hand was clamped around Traci's wrist, and I was pretty sure the hand I couldn't see was planted firmly on the girl's behind. She was obviously not happy about the situation, trying in vain to free herself without causing a scene.

"Hey, Traci?" Arriving at the table, I butted in like I had any right to. "Gretchen was wanting another drink, do you think you could . . . ?"

The guy let her go when I approached, and she gave me a grateful look, gathering up her tray quickly. "Tell her I'll be right there." She vanished into the crowd.

Then I turned my gaze on Douche Bag, simply staring

until he finally realized I wasn't going anywhere. He raised a challenging brow at me. "What?"

"Do you have children?" I could see him blink, his mind trying to process a question he'd never expected.

"Do I what?"

"Do you have children? Y'know, kids? Offspring?" He was alone, I thought. There didn't seem to be any menacing figures lurking in the background, waiting to jump to his defense. Alone and out trolling for a little piece of tail.

"Yeah, I do actually. And what the hell does that have to do with anything?"

"Did you teach them about the Golden Rule?" I could tell this was getting nowhere fast. Not a rocket scientist, our Douche Bag. "Did you teach them to treat people the way they want to be treated?"

"What the f—" He bit off his words when I leaned down right in his face. I wanted to make sure he heard what I had to say.

"And—following the Golden Rule—since you can't seem to keep your hands to yourself, I assume that you also want some random stranger slapping their hands onto intimate parts of you?"

Ah, now he was following where I was going. His lip curled up in a snarl. "Do you know who I am?"

"Nope. Now ask me if I care." I smiled. It's a smile I practice, sometimes. It says "You're about seven seconds away from learning about the afterlife." "Don't touch her again. Clear?"

I knew it was coming. I'd deliberately provoked it, af-

ter all. A guy like this, he couldn't let some other dude
come slap him down like a bad puppy. It's hard on the
reputation and even harder on the ego.

"Listen, asshole . . ." He raised both hands to shove
me out of his face and I caught one before it could even
touch me. With a small twist, his wrist was facing the
wrong way, his fingertips touching the inside of his forearm, and whatever else he was going to say was lost in
the surprised cry of pain. I held him there like that,
pinned to his chair by a light grip on one hand. A bit
more pressure, and I could snap it. I didn't.

"You're leaving now. I'll cover your tab. Have a good
night." There were bouncers moving in on my flanks. I
could see them from the corners of my vision. When they
didn't immediately jump in to break it up, I decided they
were at least nominally on my side.

Douche Bag's face was pale under his fake tan, sweat
beading on his forehead as he debated his options, but
finally he nodded his acquiescence. I released the hold
on his arm and he rubbed his sore wrist as he fled, glaring at me every step of the way.

"You didn't have to do that." Traci appeared at my
elbow, wiping the table down quickly.

"Somebody did." I passed her Axel's credit card. "Pay
his tab. Add a good tip onto this for yourself, too." Funny
how easy money was to spend when it wasn't mine.

Traci shrugged and swiped the card through the reader
on her belt and handed it back. "Whatever the man
wants."

When the hand landed on my shoulder, only one
thing kept me from ripping it off. Tai's innate magic

jolted me even through my T-shirt as he leaned in to speak. "Gretchen says we need to blow, before they connect you with her."

They? Who the hell is "they"?

Letting the bigger man break us a path through the room, we caught up to Bobby and Gretchen near the door. The starlet gave me an irritated roll of her eyes, but Bobby grinned. At least, I think it was a grin. It could have been a snarl. It showed the same amount of teeth.

"That dude about pissed himself. That was awesome." I bumped the offered knuckles, but now that my righteous indignation was wearing off, I felt a bit sheepish. Starting fights in public really wasn't cool, no matter how right I was.

The rabid crowd was still outside, and the limo was not. "We didn't have time to call for the car," Bobby explained. "Leaving in a bit of a rush."

The look Gretchen slung my way let me know just who she was holding responsible for that inconvenience. "Just clear me a damn path."

The limo was parked about two blocks down, and we set out at a swift march. I had to admit, I was impressed at her ability to not fracture something in those shoes.

Luckily, most of the teeming throng held their positions near the club, waiting for the next celebrity to pass within their line of sight. We were in the clear fairly quickly.

"You wanna tell me what the hell that was back there?" Every syllable was punctuated by the sharp click of her stilettos.

"Which part?"

"The part where you attacked one of the most prominent producers in the *world*?"

"He was a douche." I wasn't going to apologize for that. It was true.

"Yes, he's a douche. Everyone knows that. But he's also powerful. And over a waitress? Really?" Gretchen stopped in her tracks, almost causing a pileup, and whirled on me, her eyes flashing.

"Just because he has money doesn't give him the right to treat people like that. Waitress or no."

She rolled her eyes at me. "Are you really that naïve? This is Hollywood. Money gets you anything you want."

"Not when I'm around. No one puts their hands on a woman if she doesn't want it. I'd have done the same for you, and I don't even like you. Women are to be respected, not manhandled."

Whatever else she had to say on the subject was lost when her eyes flicked to something over my shoulder. I had a split second to see something dark moving up on my left side, and I reacted instinctively.

One perfectly executed hip throw later, a very startled man with a camera stared up at me from the ground. He blinked twice, then the flash went off, blinding all of us.

"Wonderful! Now we've moved on to attacking the paparazzi! Perfect." Belatedly, she glanced at the man on the ground. "Sorry." Maybe someday, if she practiced this "acting" thing she was supposedly so good at, she might even sound like she meant it. "Get his ass in the car before he beats up something else."

The camera kept snapping as we got in the limo, flashes going off around us like strobes. Gretchen took up one whole seat herself, making it very clear that the three of us "animals" weren't to soil her personal space. I found myself sandwiched between Bobby and Tai, who kept exchanging grins behind my back.

Finally, I sighed. "Okay. Out with it."

They both busted up into snickers, and Bobby asked, "Jumpy much?"

I gave him a very serious look. "You have no idea."

9

Someone was pounding a sledgehammer into my skull, and I didn't much appreciate it. After some flopping around in a bed that was way too huge and very much lacking a Mira, then struggling to untangle myself from a comforter that was way too puffy, I finally realized that the pounding was on my door, not my dome.

What the hell time is it? The clock said it was eight a.m., but my body said "Hey, jerk, you're not sixteen anymore." Obviously, my days of partying all night were long over.

"Coming! Coming . . ." I grumbled as I padded across the room. "Keep your pants on."

The peephole revealed a room service cart outside, and the scent of bacon was already wafting under the door. My brain pointed out that I hadn't ordered breakfast, but my stomach pointedly refused to care. I opened the door.

"Where would you like me to put it, sir?" The attendant wheeled the cart past me while I stood there trying to figure out why I knew that voice. When he stood up, looking expectantly at me for his tip, I knew.

"Spencer?" Yes, Chatty Spencer from the plane trip blinked at me in surprise, then broke into a broad smile.

"Oh, hey! Jesse Dawson from the airplane. The champion! I remember you!"

I remembered him too, and I didn't really believe in coincidences. I grabbed him by the collar of his neatly pressed chef's coat and slammed him against the wall hard enough to hear his head thump. "What are you doing here?"

"Dude! Man, leggo!" He pried at my hands futilely.

"How did you find me? Who sent you?" With my forearm firmly across his throat, he didn't really have any choice but to answer my questions. With my free hand, I roughly shoved his coat sleeve up, revealing a forearm bare of any marks. Even though he'd been clear yesterday, it was not what I'd expected to find.

"Dude, I work here! My cousin Leslie is a housekeeper, she got me the job." The fear in his eyes was slowly replaced with something else, something excited and curious. "Who did you think I was? Are you, like, a spy or something?"

I didn't answer him, and after a moment I relaxed my hold, stepping back. He'd passed through my warded door without incident, but . . . "Stand right there. Don't make any sudden moves."

Spencer held his hands up. "Sure, man, anything you say." We watched each other closely as I backed my way to the bedside table where my collection of gadgets lay discarded.

Pressing Cam's danger disk to the man's forehead resulted in nothing remarkable, but he nearly went cross-eyed trying to see what I was doing. "What does that do?"

"Right now, it keeps you from getting your ass kicked." If the thing was working, this guy wasn't any kind of danger to me. Maybe it *was* just a coincidence. I finally let him go, but I refused to put my back to him. "I didn't order breakfast."

Spencer advanced slowly, making sure I could see his hands at all times, and picked up a slip of paper from the cart. "Standing order for this room. You'll have breakfast every morning, unless you cancel it."

"Who requested it?"

"Doesn't say, so probably whoever set up the room reservation?"

Somehow, I wouldn't have expected Axel to order me breakfast. It was more than a little odd. I lifted one of the metal lids to find a heaping pile of bacon and sausage and a couple of eggs over easy, just the way I liked them. I almost sent it back right then, out of sheer spite. Axel didn't deserve to know me that well.

Still, bacon was bacon. I munched on a piece, figuring if it was poisoned, I'd at least die happy. "So . . . giving up on screenwriting already?"

Spencer chuckled. "Nah. Just gotta eat between now and my multimillion-dollar deal. Figure pushing a cart is better than digging ditches, right?"

"If you say so."

"It's weird that you're here, 'cause I was just thinking about you this morning." He picked up a folded newspaper off the cart, flipping to one of the inner sections, and offered it to me. "You made the news."

My heart sank as I found my own picture gracing the front page of the entertainment section. The headline read GRETCHEN KEENE'S MYSTERY DATE, and the picture was obviously one from the club last night. Probably one from the photographer I'd flattened, judging by the background. "Fuck."

Spencer grinned. "I was trying to tell my cousin I knew that guy, and she didn't believe me. Can't wait to tell her you're up here. How long have you been seeing Gretchen Keene?"

"I'm not." Mira was gonna kill me. I prayed to all higher powers that this didn't make it back to Missouri. "Just doing a job." I skimmed the article a little. Most of it was wild speculation, though there was a rather lengthy mention of me attacking the poor guy with the camera. He was magnanimously declining to press charges.

"Like what kind of job?" I could tell that Spencer had dreams of intrigue and scandal running through his head.

"Don't you have other orders to deliver?"

"Oh, yeah. Probably." He stared at me for a few moments.

"What?"

"You gonna tip?"

"Get out." I threw the newspaper at him as he retreated.

This was so not how I wanted to start my day. Even half a pound of bacon and a long hot shower didn't really perk me up any. My shirt for the day said STICK THAT IN YOUR JUICE BOX AND SUCK IT, and that was really how I felt about things so far. Last night had left me grumpy and annoyed and feeling increasingly useless here. As near as I could tell, Gretchen was just fine. Could I go home now please?

When another knock sounded at my door, I just knew

it was Spencer, probably with the entire kitchen staff in tow. *"Hey, I know! Let's go gawk at the sideshow freak!"* I threw the door open, ready to rip his annoying head off, only to find another employee standing there with a two-wheeled dolly bearing my armor and sword case. "You were expecting these, sir?"

"Oh. Yes, I was." Him, I tipped.

It felt good to have my gear again. I unpacked everything, double- and triple-checking it even though I'd just had my hands on it yesterday morning. The metal still tingled under my fingers, evidence of Cam's good work.

The Way had travelled well it seemed. I went through a few slow strikes with the new sword, feeling the differences between it and my original. Heavier on the back end, but it seemed to fit well with my own personal fighting style. As I held it, the bone hilt warmed in my hand.

I know, swords don't really have personalities and all. But ... when it's the one thing between you and dying most of the time, you couldn't help but assign it traits, characteristics. My old sword had been female. Don't know why I always felt that way, but I did. This one wasn't. It was male, rock steady in my grip but with a brightness to it that reminded me of a shooting star. Fire in the night.

Since I hadn't really had a chance to put it through its paces before I left town, I grabbed the first thing I could find—a piece of paper off the desk—and slid it along the sharp edge of the blade. The paper curled off like butter melting. *Verrrrry nice.* I found out the sword would also slice through the apple that came with my breakfast, my plain black T-shirt from the previous night, and the entire newspaper. The confetti-like shreds of paper fluttering all over my floor made me feel a little better.

Gear unpacked and safely stowed out of sight, I salvaged the breakfast coffee and finally went in search of Her Highness.

I could hear the voices down at the end of the hall long before I got to the door. Gretchen I recognized. The other woman was new.

Tai answered the door when I knocked, murmuring under his breath, "Watch it, we're in the blast zone."

His meaning became clear once I got a look at the two females squared off against each other in the middle of the room.

Gretchen may have just rolled out of bed—at least, I assumed that's why she was still wearing a tiny little satin nightgown—but her hair and makeup looked like she'd just stepped out of a salon. Demon magic, or just natural beauty? Hard to say.

The other woman was older. Her blond hair was sprinkled liberally with gray streaks and gathered up into a utilitarian ponytail. Her blue jeans showed no signs of wear, and her blouse was fashionable, but I recognized them as cheap brands. You know, stuff normal people wore. When she turned her head a bit, I could see the high cheekbones and flashing blue eyes, just like Gretchen's. A relative, maybe? *A mother*.

The instant I thought that, I knew I was right. Moms stand a certain way, take a certain tone with their children. Mine could still reduce me to a tiny little ball of shame with one glance, when warranted. That's a mother-son thing. I hear with daughters, it's different. Lotta emotions tied up in those relationships, both good and bad. So this was definitely some kind of mother-daughter ... thing.

The tension in the room was thick enough to cut, and I saw that Bobby and Dante had already taken refuge over near the bar, pretending not to see the uncomfortable face-off.

"If you want to tell her you're not coming, you make that phone call yourself. You explain to her why you can't be bothered to come to your sister's wedding." Mom planted her hands on her hips, and I know if I'd been the recipient of that glare, I'd have caved instantly. I'm a big weenie when it comes to my mom.

"I already told her I'd probably be busy that week." Gretchen waved her hand dismissively. "It's not like they've missed me at any other event."

"Busy, my rear end. You had eight months to *make* time to be with your family. Eight months, Gina."

"Gretchen! Is it so hard to say?" Uh-oh. The starlet's hands were likewise planted on her hips, the two women nearly identical. I knew that stance. That stance said there would be no resolution today. Maybe not ever. "The only reason she even wants me there is so I can buy her some expensive damn wedding present. I'll mail her a fucking gift card and she'll be thrilled."

The sharp crack of a slap echoed through the room before I even realized Mom had moved. "You will not use that foul language in my presence, young lady. I raised you better than that."

Gretchen's hand pressed over her reddening cheek,

the rest of her face pale white. "Get out. Don't you ever come back here again."

"Fine." Mom bit off the word and snatched her purse up off the couch, slinging it up on her shoulder. "Call your sister." The woman stalked past Tai and me without even looking at us, but her dramatic exit was ruined by some kind of stumble at the door. "Oh, excuse me . . ."

Before any of us could say anything, she was gone, and a hotel employee was inside, bearing a giant bouquet of assorted flowers. How the poor man could even see to walk was beyond me. I could barely see a pair of staring eyes through the leaves of something that looked like a fern. "Um . . . where should I set this?"

"Goddamn it, all deliveries are supposed to be halted at the desk!" Bobby nearly knocked the hapless delivery man over, getting out the door, no doubt headed to kick some ass.

Gretchen was apparently not interested in the flowers, and stalked to her room, slamming the door with more force than strictly necessary.

Every eye in the place turned toward Dante, who sighed heavily. "I know, I know. I'm the best friend. But if she bashes my brains in, I'm haunting every one of you." With a major show of reluctance, he went after her, disappearing into the inner sanctum.

When no one else seemed inclined to answer the delivery guy, I pointed over at the bar. "Just set them there, I guess."

"Yessir." He did as instructed, then looked at me expectantly.

"Look, you're apparently not even supposed to bring those up here. You really think you're going to get a tip?" He looked a bit crestfallen, but nodded and departed without further comment.

Tai shook his head. "Bobby's gonna have someone's head on a platter."

"Yeah, sounds like everyone is just puppies and rainbows today."

He snorted. "Just another day in the glamorous life of a movie star."

"Noticed that. The woman was . . . Gretchen's mother?" I took Dante's vacated seat, sipping at my lukewarm coffee. Even halfway cold, it was better than what I usually had at home.

"Mhmm. Her name is Patricia, but everybody calls her Patty." Tai found a cheese Danish somewhere, munching as he talked. "They're what we'll call 'strained.'"

"No kidding. Gretchen's not big on acknowledging her roots, I take it?"

"It's not like that." Tai mumbled around his breakfast. "After that last stalker go-round, Gretchen cut ties with her family to protect them from stuff like that. But her mom doesn't see it that way."

"Can't blame her there. Her mom, I mean." Tai looked at me curiously when I said that. "If someone was threatening my daughter? They'd never find all the pieces when I got done. That's every parent's first instinct, to protect their child."

Tai nodded thoughtfully. "Yeah, I guess I could see that. But I kinda see where Gretchen comes from, too.

It's hard enough to live in the spotlight without dragging folks along with you. She's doing them a favor, whether they realize it or not. If she showed up at that wedding, the paparazzi would make it all about Gretchen, and that's not how she wants her sister's wedding to be. Gretchen loves Chelsea to death. She's just trying to do what's best for her."

Sadly, explained like that, Gretchen's actions made sense. I still didn't like her—that whole soul-stealing thing and all—but I thought maybe I understood her a little more.

Bobby returned from his rampage, face still red and the scar on his jaw standing out in stark white contrast. Tai smirked as his mentor stalked the floor, too wired up to sit down. "Any of them wet their pants?" The former marine just snarled, not ready for humor yet.

About that time, Gretchen's door opened, and Dante emerged unscathed. "Hey, Tai? Could you call down for the car?"

"Yup." Tai pulled his cell out of his pocket. "Where are we going?"

"Spa day, apparently." Dante shrugged. "She called and got an 'emergency' appointment with Rolf, and then maybe some retail therapy after. She's got a meeting at the studio later, too."

There was a short phone conversation, then Tai plucked at my sleeve. "C'mon, come get the car with me. Bobby'll bring her down."

Heading out into the hallway, I paused at the door when the wards felt a bit . . . off. The invisible barrier was still there, but it wasn't nearly as strong as it had been yesterday. *Dammit, Cam.* Were his spells fading already?

A quick examination revealed that the blessed string was still in place, firmly taped and stapled right where I'd left it. Still, there was a distinct difference in how it felt when I passed my arm through it. "Tai? Who's been in or out of this room today?"

"Um . . . Me, Bobby . . . Dante. You. Patty. Room service. The flower guy."

"Was room service a new guy?" *Spencer, maybe?*

"No, one of the regulars. His name is Todd." He came to lean over my shoulder, watching what I was doing. "Why?"

I ran my fingertips along the jamb, but I couldn't find any specific weak point. Just a general drain of power. "Something's not right." Crouching down, I examined the carpet, looking for . . . well, I didn't know what. Something that didn't belong, I guess.

Tai knelt next to me, tilting his head curiously as he wiggled his finger through the barrier. "It's not as strong as yesterday, right?"

"Right."

"Is the circuit broken anywhere?" He was still thinking of it as an electrical device, but he wasn't entirely wrong. If there was an opening in the circle anywhere, it would cease to function. I checked the entire length of string again, and found it all intact. "Maybe your power source is dying? Like, it needs fresh batteries?"

That made something cold settle in my stomach. If Cam's power was flagging this soon, these things were going to be worthless before day's end. And I had no way to renew them. "Maybe . . . I wonder if . . ."

"Dear God, what *is* that stench?" Gretchen's voice startled me out of my thinkings, and we turned to find her planted in the middle of the living room, her pert nose wrinkled in disgust. "Which one of you didn't shower?" There was a general chorus of "not me's" from the menfolk, and Gretchen looked at us like we were crazy. "Seriously? None of you smell that?"

Bobby, standing near the dining table, frowned faintly. "Now that you mention it . . . what is that?" His nose wrinkled as he sniffed the air. "Smells like . . . like stale sweat. Only worse. Like . . . an entire football team of stale sweat."

I tested the air myself, dreading that I would find the telltale scent of sulfur. But no, I caught nothing but the subtle fragrance of Gretchen's perfume. "Where do you smell it?"

"This way." After a few moments of wandering, Bobby found himself facing the flower bouquet. "Here. It's something in here, I think."

Now, what I know about plants could fit on the head of a pin. That's my wife's department. But once I got close enough to the assorted flowers and caught the distinctive aroma, I knew exactly what it was, and why it was there.

"Shit." A little digging into the bouquet revealed a double handful of small leaves, fuzzy-ish, already turning black where the edges had dried. It had been tucked in among the flowers like decorative greenery. "Black horehound."

"Black whore what?" Dante gave me an accusing look.

"Black horehound," I enunciated carefully, holding the leaves up for display. "It's a member of the mint family, but it reeks to high heaven, so no one uses it for much." The only reason I recognized it was because Mira had received some of this instead of the less offensive white horehound in some supplies for her shop a few summers ago. The smell was . . . memorable.

Gretchen came closer to examine the offending foliage. "Why would someone put it in a bouquet?"

"They wouldn't." But I knew exactly why it was there. "Black horehound has some medicinal values. I forget what all right now. But it also has the unique ability to absorb magical energies." Soaked it right up like a sponge, if I remembered Mira's lecture correctly. Which explained a whole lot about the wards on the door. "Someone thinks they're gonna need to get in here. They're trying to disable my wards."

You know, up until this point, I'd been tempted to pack it all in and go home. I'd seen no signs of danger that Tai or Bobby couldn't handle, no overt attacks, no hints of anything nefarious. Until now.

And of course, there was no card. That would have been too easy. Why, just once, couldn't the bad guy just walk up and introduce himself? "Hi, I'm Frank. I'll be your nemesis this evening."

"Well, throw it out!" Gretchen snatched up the heavy glass vase and marched toward the door.

"No!" I caught up to her in two strides and carefully removed it from her grasp. "No, if you take it out the door again, it's just going to weaken the ward more."

"Well, we can't have it in here stinking up the place," she pointed out.

"Chuck it off the balcony?" Tai suggested, but Bobby nixed the idea. "We're nine stories up. If that hits someone on the ground, it'll kill them."

"Can we just pick out all the smelly leaves?" Dante peered at the pile I'd left on the bar, but was careful not to touch.

"I can't be sure we'd get them all. Or what else someone has put in this thing." It didn't feel like any magic, but was that because the horehound was masking it? I rubbed my fingertips together, wondering what effect just handling the leaves would have on Mira's protective spells.

They were all looking at me, waiting to see what they should do. I hate that.

"Okay. Okay, let's do this. Bobby, get this thing out of here. Just take it out and dump it in the trash somewhere downstairs. It's going to weaken the wards on the door some more, but I'll take the one off my room and add it to this one, after the plant is gone." Sure, that'd leave me without a secure room to fall back to, but I was here to protect Gretchen first and foremost. I'd just have to make do.

After a moment of silence, Bobby nodded. "You heard the man." He took the flowers from me and went to dispose of them.

"See if you can find out who delivered those, Bobby," I called after him.

As I'd feared, the ward was noticeably depleted by the second pass of the bouquet through its barrier. It barely registered to my senses as I crossed the threshold to go to my own room.

It took only a moment to tear down the blessed string around my own doorjamb and replace it around Gretchen's waning ward. Thankfully, that snapped the protection back to full force. Dante stood beside me in the hallway as I worked, just watching in silence, and Tai stood on the inside of the door, nodding his approval as he tested the feel of it. "Yeah, that's better. Like when you first set them up."

"It'll do for now." But I was going to need a backup plan. I could see that already. Man, I hoped I could think of one before I needed it.

Gretchen also watched the proceedings, her brow furrowed as she pondered all the implications of this interesting development. "So, is it still safe for me to go out? I mean, the spa thing and this meeting at the movie lot?"

"Should be, I would think. Might even be better to be out in public, with lots of witnesses."

"All right. Get the car, I'll be down in a second."

Tai plucked at my sleeve. "Come on, you can sweep the car or something." Hell, why not? I followed him.

The Maori kept giving me odd looks as we rode the elevator down. "Something you want to ask, Tai?"

"You really believe in all that, don't you? That string thing? What the hell is that, anyway?"

"Would you believe me if I told you a priest blessed it, and I'm using it to keep evil out?" I raised a brow at him, and grinned when he looked skeptical. "You don't really believe in this whole 'demon' thing, do you?"

"No. Not really." He looked a bit sheepish. "I mean,

no offense, but you all sound like crackpots when you talk about stuff like that."

"No offense taken. We do sound like crackpots." For some reason, this amused me. Tai, of all people, with magic almost literally flowing through his veins, didn't believe. There was some irony there. "Just remember that you can feel the ward in that doorway, Tai. Believe it or not, you know something's there. Think about why that is, sometime."

The big man snorted. "You sound like my grandma. She was always talking about magic and spirits and stuff. Bedtime stories."

"All stories gotta come from somewhere."

The lobby was dazzlingly bright as we stepped off the elevator, and it took me a moment to realize why that felt so wrong. Missouri winters were uniformly gray and overcast, punctuated only by occasional subzero temperatures or an ice storm. Here in California, the sun was shining brightly, and it wasn't even what I'd call "cool" outside. Unnatural, I tell ya.

The Town Car was waiting outside already, and I gave a small show of giving it a once-over with my mirror. There was nothing there, that I could see, but honestly, how would I know what to look for anyway? I mean, really, what *was* the demonic equivalent of a car bomb? Cam's danger disk was neutral, and I had no goose bumps or stomach cramps, so I finally deemed it safe. Tai called up and gave Gretchen the all clear.

"The heart calls to him who would listen."

The voice startled me, and I almost smacked my head on the roof of the car as I backed up in a hurry. Somehow, the eccentric homeless guy had managed to sneak up on me. Well, that wasn't promising. "Felix, right?"

The odd man nodded happily, pleased that I'd remembered. He looked just the same as yesterday, his layered clothing a riot of colors and . . . interesting odors. There was a tiny white feather tied into one of his silvery dreadlocks now, fluttering with the rest of the colorful bits of yarn and cloth as the breeze whispered by.

"I try to listen to my heart, y'know," I told him. "It's not the smartest thing in the world, sometimes, but I do try to listen."

The old man's smile grew, his weatherworn cheeks almost splitting, so wide was his grin. His teeth were half rotted, I noticed, but his eyes gleamed with a cheerfulness that was almost infectious. Up close and personal like that, I could see his eyes were an odd, pale brown color. Almost gold. Like whiskey. Considering what he smelled like, I had to wonder if maybe his liquor of choice had just filled him up that far. "Listening and obeying aren't the same. Listen when the heart calls, then let the head roll it around a bit. Sometimes, it's destiny. Sometimes, it's just a plain ol' booty call, and somebody's gonna get screwed."

Despite the serious turn the day had taken, that made me laugh a little, and I nodded. "That it is." Behind me, Bobby came out of the sliding glass doors with Gretchen and Dante in tow. "Nice talkin' to you, Felix. I gotta go now."

But I'd lost the homeless man's attention, his gaze fixed firmly on Gretchen as she passed. "And they cry out to be free, wailing in the silence that holds no souls . . ."

"Get on outta here, you freak!" Dante glared and gestured angrily at the doorman. "Can't you do something about this loony?"

With a sigh, the doorman moved to hustle Felix along as I climbed into the Town Car, riding shotgun to Tai's driving. I turned to watch as we pulled away, noticing that not once did Felix take his eyes off the car. It was like nothing else existed in his world but us, for that brief moment.

There was something in those whiskey-colored eyes, I decided. Something that just didn't belong in that jovial face. If I didn't know better, I'd say it looked like hatred.

10

Trying to get more information on Felix out of the crew in the car was worse than useless. All anyone really knew was that he'd been wandering in the neighborhood "forever" and that he was totally harmless. His origins, his current crash space, all that seemed to be shrouded in mystery. More likely, it was shrouded in "we don't really want to see the homeless guy on the corner, so we'll look the other way."

"Why, do you think he's a threat?" Bobby wanted to know.

"If I say yes, are you going to go break his kneecaps?" The look on the former soldier's face told me everything I needed to know. "No, I don't think he's a threat. He's just unusual, and in my line of business, unusual never turns out well for me."

"Felix is just eccentric." Gretchen dismissed my concerns with a wave of her manicured hand.

"Can we please talk about something other than the old skeezy guy?" Dante didn't want to have the conversation at all, it seemed. "They oughta throw his rank ass in jail."

And that was the end of that.

Did I think he was dangerous? No, not really. My advance warning system hadn't let me down so far, and there were no goose bumps, no stomach cramps around the strange old man. In fact, he'd even touched my hand without repercussions from Mira's protective spells, so I think that safely eliminated him from "bad guy" contention.

Still, I decided to watch him. Face it, Felix was one of the more interesting things to happen since I touched down in L.A., and he made more sense than half the people I'd spoken to so far.

As for our little outing, I still wasn't sure exactly what a "spa day" entailed, despite the fact that it seemed to be one of those things the women in my life enjoyed. I was also unclear as to just what I was supposed to *do* while Gretchen was doing . . . whatever it is they did.

"Mostly we read magazines," Bobby answered from the back when I asked. "Though Tai got a manicure once."

The Maori blushed, his dark skin getting even darker. "In all fairness, the girl doing it was hot. That's the only reason."

Gretchen chuckled, though it was obviously forced. She was trying to paint on a lighter mood. "We could see if she's there again . . . I'll even pay." Reaching up, she pushed Tai's shoulder playfully. The big man ducked his head and muttered to himself, but it was all in good-natured fun. "What about you, Jesse? Manicure? Pedicure?" She grinned wickedly. "Bikini wax?"

"I'll pass, thanks." It was interesting to watch the shields come down over her eyes, the walls build up around her face again. She painted on her bright and frivolous persona like an artist on a canvas. It was an elaborate show, one she had obviously practiced for a very long time. She sat in the back between Dante and Bobby and chatted until we pulled up to the salon, and you'd think she never had a care in the world.

The place we stopped at was a salon. That's really all I can say about it. Trendy, I'm sure. Everything done in black geometric shapes. The employees were all dressed in severe black clothes, and the clients seemed to be wandering around in metallic silver robes and fuzzy slippers like some clan of befuddled Martians.

I recognized the music playing softly overhead as some popular Irish-type artist Mira carried in her shop, and the air seemed to be layered with a floral scent. Freesia, I think. Or lavender. I get those mixed up, which is why I'm not allowed to help Mira stock shelves at Seventh Sense anymore.

They greeted Gretchen with hugs and squeals, and swept both her and Dante into the back with very little ado. Bobby and Tai each took up position in a couple of chairs that looked very artsy and were probably uncomfortable as hell. They both, however, were facing the front door. The nonchalance wasn't entirely authentic.

"So how long does this stuff usually take?"

"Couple of hours?" Tai shrugged, picking up a magazine to flip through it. "She's got a meeting after, so it's not likely to drag on longer than that."

Couple of *hours*? Cripes, I could get my hair cut in a couple of *minutes*! Glancing around the room one more time, I knew I was going to go stark raving mad if I had to sit here and listen to Irish tin-whistle music for hours.

I'd seen an alley as we'd pulled up to the building,

which probably meant I could find the back door to this place. "I'm gonna check the perimeter."

The back door was in the back. That's about as interesting as it got. One of the salon employees was in the alley, sneaking a cigarette, and raised a brow as I wandered through. Couple of Dumpsters, some scrubby weeds in the pavement cracks, but nothing sinister. I checked my danger disk as I passed the smoker, but it didn't react and I had to mentally mark her as clear. *Perimeter secure. Sir, yes sir.* I felt a little ridiculous.

Returning to the front, I found a place on a bench just outside the door. The least I could do was enjoy the weather. My seat was what we'll call less than comfortable, but the California sunshine more than made up for it. Seemed like everyone else was enjoying the fine weather too, a constant stream of people parading up and down the sidewalk despite the fact that it was the middle of a weekday. Did no one work here?

People-watching is fun. Well, it used to be. Now, my eyes swept over bared arms, looking for telltale black swirls. Even with the temperatures fairly cool, sun worship ruled here, and most folks had short sleeves on. Made it a little easier. I saw plenty of tans, both real and sprayed on, but no demon tattoos.

I stretched out my legs, got as comfortable as I could, and tried to clear my mind. I had some things to think on.

There definitely *was* a bad guy in play. That much was certain. Someone who knew I was here. Someone who knew I'd warded the doors. While once upon a time, that would have narrowed down my suspect list, my picture in the morning paper meant that just about anybody could have seen me. And face it, in the demon world, I'm memorable. I'd spanked too many of them for me to go unrecognized.

Hm. If I were a demon, who would I send?

Images of a handless, armless female zombie flashed through my mind's eye, and I shuddered in spite of the sun. Handless was still out there, somewhere. Prowling the Colorado Rockies, last I knew. Her master was out of the picture for the time being (I hoped) so I didn't expect to see Handless make an appearance. Besides, she didn't seem the type to send flowers.

My mirror had ruled out Scrap demons, and honestly, I had no idea what else was even on the table as far as demonic minions.

Maybe just a guy. Some poor demon-sworn schmuck, just following orders in the vain hopes of getting his soul back. I'd encountered that before too. Had the scars to prove it, though not nearly as impressive as some of my others.

Or, maybe Axel was just screwing with me. Though, I couldn't see him wasting his favor on an elaborate practical joke. That favor was a valuable asset to him, so if he was spending it now, he had his reasons.

In the midst of my deep and circular thoughts, a shiver ran through me and my head snapped up, immediately scoping for the danger. About three seconds later, I realized it wasn't my danger sense spiking. It was my cell phone, buzzing in my pocket. *Mira . . .*

But no, the caller ID said IVAN ZELENKO. *Hell.* The

phone kept buzzing insistently as I stared at it like an idiot, and I started to feel like the old man knew I was debating on whether or not to answer. I could feel that icy, blue-eyed glare across the distance, however great it was.

To pick up, or not to pick up. That was the question. Whether 'tis nobler in the mind to answer the phone and get my ass chewed out (probably rightly deserved), or to valiantly let the call roll to voice mail ... yeah, by the time I got done trying to recall my very rusty Shakespeare, the phone stopped ringing. A minute or so later, the message notification blinked on.

I still debated on listening to it. Ivan had been dodging me for three months. I didn't think he was calling just to catch up. But best to rip the bandage off quickly, right?

The deep gravelly voice forced me to hold the phone away from my ear, but there was no chance of me not hearing him. "Dawson. Am I to be understanding that you are to be working in California, and have not provided this information to Grapevine? This is to being unacceptable. It endangers you, and others. It is to be fortunate that your student is to be worried for your well-being and called me. You *will* to be returning this message." *Click.*

I decided then and there I was gonna beat the crap out of Estéban when I got home. The little twerp narced on me! I was almost thirty-three years old, dammit, I didn't need to check in with Daddy every time I set foot outside my door. And really, *Ivan* of all people was gonna quibble about sharing information? Mr. Hide-the-Champion himself? I wondered if he'd understand me if I called and said "Hi, Pot, this is Kettle." Probably not.

Feeling inordinately rebellious, I hit the DELETE button, erasing the message. He'd kept me waiting this long, I'd call him when I goddamn well felt like it.

Yeah, I'm twelve. I admit this.

Sitting there pissed off and brooding for a few hours didn't sound like a lot of fun. I eyed the bench for a moment, then managed to fold my long legs up into a close approximation of a lotus position, just resting my hands on my knees. When in doubt, meditate. And if anyone thought it strange, seeing the scrawny blond dude meditating outside the trendy salon, no one said a thing.

They did, however, stop to take pictures. I thought at first they were just getting the salon. Maybe it was the location of a famous hairdo or something. But no, when I cracked one eye open, there were people stopped, taking my picture. "I'm not him. That guy from that show. Move along." Visibly disappointed, they did, but that didn't stop the next batch. After a while, I stopped protesting. It just wasn't worth it.

Time went on, waiting for Her Highness to get her nails done or whatever, and about the time I started worrying about impending sunburn, the door opened and Tai came out, giving me a wave as he headed to get the car. "You asleep out here?"

"Not for lack of trying." I stood up, stretching muscles that reminded me how crappy my seat had been for the past couple of hours. "We all done here?"

"Yeah, with this stage at least. Dante promised her some retail therapy, so we're about to be relegated to pack mule duty."

Oh, hell. Seriously? "Shopping? Are you kidding?"

He was not.

Look, I have no idea where we went, and what I know about fashion involves making sure that the shirt I'm wearing doesn't smell bad when I put it on. But I'm pretty sure that this was the kind of store that invented the phrase "if you have to ask, you can't afford it."

It was also the store where the paparazzi found us again. We were standing around, watching Gretchen and Dante coo and squeal over their apparently amazing acquisitions, when Bobby gave a short jerk with his chin. "Heads up. Cameras."

Turning, I found the windows of the entire store front plastered with cameras, their owners pressed against the glass like land-roaming lampreys. Even as I hunched in instinctive defense, five flashes went off, dazzling my vision. Behind me, Tai tsked in disapproval. "Amateurs. You can't use a flash through the glass like that. Those shots will never come out."

Dante snorted. "Hey, it's their paycheck." He selected a shining silver shirt off the rack they were currently plundering, holding it up to the windows. "What do you think?" Four or five of the paparazzi gave him a thumbs-up, a few gave him a thumbs-down, and the rest just snapped away on their cameras.

Gretchen continued her shopping without even glancing up.

"Doesn't it bother you? Having them always *there*?" I finally had to ask, because even my limited run-ins with them were starting to grate on my nerves.

She shrugged absently. "Better to indulge them some when I can. Keeps them from climbing over my back fence and taking pics while I'm in the tub or something." Without looking, she tossed something blue in my direction. I caught it without thinking. "This would look good on you."

Upon examination, it proved to be a royal blue silk shirt, long-sleeved, button-up. Actually, it didn't look bad, except for all the zeros at the end of the price tag. "Yeah, it's cool I guess."

"You guess? It goes perfectly with your eyes, did you even look?" With an exasperated roll of her eyes, she came over to hold the shirt up against my chest, turning me to face a handy mirror. Outside, the cameras went crazy. "See? Perfect."

Okay, yeah, maybe. I guess it was a nice shirt. Did make my blue eyes stand out, sort of. "Out of my price range, thanks." I handed it back before I accidentally damaged it or something.

Gretchen tossed it negligently into one of the piles she'd started accumulating. "Boys. Never good at shopping."

That earned an offended "Hey!" from Dante, and she gave him a genuinely fond smile. "Except you."

"Better." He gave her a one-armed hug, then put the silver shirt back on the rack. "Okay, Boo, I think we've done our damage here. You got places to be."

"All right, let's go pay." The pair of them scooped up their spoils and headed for the cash register. I didn't pay a lot of attention until she thrust a shirt box into my arms. "Here. In case you ever find a need to be presentable." She marched away on her stiletto heels before I could protest.

Sure enough, the blue silk shirt was in the box. Now what in the world was I supposed to do with that?

Gretchen loaded Bobby and Tai down with bags and boxes for the trip back to the car, proving Tai's pack mule prophecy true, and I gave both of them a small frown. "How can you be bodyguards with your hands full like that?"

Bobby nodded toward the throng of photographers still following us down the street. "No one's gonna try anything with all those eyes around."

"Besides," Tai nudged me with an elbow, almost knocking me over. "That's what you're for, right?" He gave me a mischievous tattooed grin.

I just rolled my eyes at him.

As we were loading up the trunk of the Town Car, one of the paparazzi grew bold enough to call out to us. Well, to me, actually. "Hey! Hey, what's your name?"

I looked behind me, to see who they were talking to, but there was only Gretchen, giving me a small smirk. "You can answer them if you want, but it'll be all over the Internet by tonight."

"Um . . ." I glanced back at the rabid camera-bearing pack. "Jesse. My name's Jesse." Instantly, thirty cameras went off in my face and I grimaced.

"Jesse what?"

"Jesse None-of-Your-Business." The bold guy got the gift of one of my glares, and backed down quickly. It didn't faze the rest of them, though.

"How long have you been dating Gretchen?"

"Are there wedding bells in your future?"

"Where did you two meet?"

They all shouted over each other, hoping that I'd give them some sound bite they could sell to the TV tabloids. I looked back to Gretchen helplessly, but she only shook her head with an amused smile and ducked into the car.

Tai chuckled as he slammed the trunk shut. "Now you've done it. We'll never get rid of them. First rule is never make eye contact."

"Thought the first rule was not to punch them."

"Rule one-b."

"Great. My wife's gonna be thrilled to see this on the news." I retreated for the car, only to find Bobby already in the front passenger seat.

He gave me a scarred smirk. "Shotgun."

"I'll get even," I threatened, and crammed into the back of the car next to Dante, careful to keep him between Gretchen and me. Last thing I needed was a picture of me and my new "girlfriend" getting cozy.

"It's all right, they won't come to the studio. Part of the deal I made with them. They can't interfere with my job." Gretchen gave me an encouraging smile from the other end of the seat.

"Yay for small miracles." I tried to get comfortable, but soon gave it up for a lost cause.

We weren't exactly squashed, but there's really no way to sit comfortably with three adults in the backseat of a car, no matter how luxurious. And Dante was one of those people who talked with his hands. A *lot*. He almost clobbered me in the face three times in the space of driving two blocks, gesticulating wildly about whatever it was he was babbling about.

"Geez, Dante, scoot over. You're freezing." That one phrase got me smashed against the door as Gretchen grumpily pushed Dante away from her.

And you know, she was right. He *was* freezing. I shivered when our arms came into contact, his skin feeling cold and clammy.

He snorted indignantly. "Well, it's winter, and it's freezing outside too. It's a wonder I'm not a solid block of ice."

I rolled my eyes. "If you think this is cold, you guys would die in Missouri. When I left, it was like seventeen degrees that day."

That prompted a lot of questions about my home state, which carried us through to the movie lots. Odd, some of the preconceptions people have about living in the Midwest. Probably just as odd as some preconceptions about living in California.

Tai flashed some kind of ID badge at the gate guard, and we were waved through with barely a glance. I admit it, I rubbernecked just like any tourist as we drove through, checking out the place where the movie magic happened. We passed a group of nuns, standing around smoking cigarettes, an astronaut in full gear being walked along by a group of cautious attendants, and four different Elvises. Elvi? Whatever. Tai slammed on the brakes once, jolting us all in our seats as some frantic handler chased four loose chickens across the street in front of us.

Finally, we found a place to park, clambering out, and Dante made his immediate departure.

"Where are you going?" Gretchen asked.

"There's this guy . . ."

"What guy?"

Dante grinned. "Just a guy. I'll catch up with you later." And he vanished into the very strange crowd.

Bobby and Tai debated the idea of going for food for a few moments, neither man truly wanting to let Gretchen go wandering off alone despite the fact that they apparently found the studio security acceptable. She, for her part, turned to look at me curiously. "You've never seen a movie lot before, have you?"

"No ma'am."

"You come with me, then. I'll show you around, and these guys can go get lunch." Y'know, sometimes she was just as nice as a real person. This woman confused the hell out of me.

That seemed to make Bobby and Tai feel better, and so it was all arranged. I watched the guys go with a small sigh. Food would have been good, but Tai promised to bring me something. I swear, if he came back with tofu, I was gonna kick him in the shin. I gestured for Gretchen to lead the way. "After you."

On rapidly clicking heels, she lead me through a ton of identical buildings that looked like airplane hangars— "Soundstages," she told me—the streets teeming with costumed extras, stagehands, camera people, makeup artists, various and sundry machinery, and the occasional golf cart rocketing through as people scattered from its path. Several times, Gretchen saw someone she knew, waving and calling out as we passed.

"So, where are we going?"

"Oh, Barry wants to meet me at some soundstage down here somewhere. Something he wants to show me." She frowned a little in annoyance. "Normally, he pitches me new scripts in his office. Not sure what's so important that we had to come all the way out here."

Something cold slithered down my spine. I'd learned to pay attention. "This isn't normal procedure?"

"No. Why?" She walked on a few paces before she realized I'd stopped in my tracks. "What's wrong?"

"Did you speak to him? Personally?"

"No, he left a message with Dante while I was in the shower. Why?"

Nothing was wrong that I could see. We were still in sight of other people, though a few blocks back. None of them were paying any sort of attention to us. The street ahead of us was mostly empty, most of the soundstages at this end of the lot not in use for the day apparently. No danger, no threat.

The goose bumps on my arms said otherwise. "Come on." I reached to take her by the elbow, prepared to drag her if I had to. "We're going back for Bobby and Tai."

"What? Why?" She didn't exactly balk, but teetering around on those spindly high heels wasn't going to make us good time.

I was debating just throwing her over my shoulder when a cool breeze ruffled my hair, smelling of freshly turned earth. *What the hell . . . ?* Turning, I found one of the soundstage doors open. "Run." I couldn't even tell her why I'd said that, but I knew deep in my gut that we had to get the hell out of here.

"What?"

Too late. A shadowy figure filled the door, the silhouette broad shouldered and hulking. I shoved Gretchen behind me, backing slowly away. "What is going on? Who . . . ?" We both fell into puzzled silence when a Roman centurion stepped from the door.

No shit. A Roman centurion. Dressed in full battle gear, plumed helmet and all. An extra, maybe, escaped from a movie set? My finely honed danger sense said no, the goose bumps prickling up and down my arms like needles.

He lumbered toward us, not unsteady precisely, but like he was unused to where his feet belonged. His face was . . . odd, somehow, beneath his helm. Plain was the best word I could come up with. There were no scars, no dimples, no pimples, no stubble. Just smooth and blank, like his eyes. There was nothing behind those eyes. No emotion, good or bad. No soul. No life.

I was so caught up in analyzing the oddities, I almost missed the short sword he had in his right hand. When he raised it to strike at me, I damn well noticed. No movie prop, that. I recognized live steel when I saw it.

It was a clumsy overhand strike. Whoever he was, he wasn't a swordsman. A weapon of convenience, then. It was nothing to catch him by the wrist, halting the downward sweep before it landed. It jarred me to my shoulders. The dude was strong.

Gripping his wrist tightly, I aimed a kick for his gut below the breastplate, yanking him into it for some extra flavor. My teeth clacked together when it landed, and sharp pain shot through my leg. Felt like I'd kicked a block of marble, and it was a wonder my ankle didn't shatter.

The centurion didn't even grunt, merely shifting his weight to swing at me with his free hand. He clubbed it down on my shoulder, and only the fact that I was already dropping to one knee saved me from a broken collarbone. Still, it was gonna bruise like a bitch. My fingers tingled in protest. I rolled to the side even as he was lifting a foot to stomp me flat, and aimed a kick at the side of his knee.

On any human, that would have folded the joint in a way nature never meant it to go, dropping him like a stone. As it was, I'm not sure he even noticed. Dodging another stomp, my roll brought me up behind him, and I launched a hard kick at the back of his unprotected thigh with the same result. I'm not sure he even felt it, for all the reaction I got. No grunt, no gasp, no sound at all.

His back was covered in the plate armor, and while I'm sure it wasn't authentic, it still served its purpose, shielding him from most unarmed attacks. As I rolled up to my feet again, I crouched low, letting his sweeping arm go whooshing over my head. I saw an open spot, just under the arm, and jabbed hard there. Immediately, I felt the telltale signs of swelling in my knuckles as they bruised dark purple.

The thing wasn't fast, thankfully, and as long as I kept on the move, it couldn't quite get a bead on me. Sure, that kept me out of harm's way, but it wasn't going to end this fight any faster. I did one more roll, putting myself behind him yet again.

Lumbering in a circle seemed to confound him for a moment, and by the time he had me in his sights again, I was on my feet. I grabbed Gretchen's hand, giving her a yank to get her moving. "Run!" I couldn't fight this, whatever it was. Not unarmed. I could only hope, as clumsy as he appeared, that we could outrun him.

The centurion stood between us and the occupied soundstages, so we had no choice but to dart down one of the deserted streets, Gretchen's heels leaving a ratta-tat-tat trail that a deaf man could follow. I glanced back once, and sure enough, he was following us. He was also picking up speed, like he'd finally figured out what to do with his legs.

I will give the girl credit. She can freakin' run in stilettos. And not once did she stop to ask stupid questions like "What was that?" or "What's going on?"

We tried doors as we passed them, hoping to find people or, in my case, a weapon I could use. Everything on this end was locked, and I could see the wall of the lot coming up ahead of us. I didn't look back again, but the thud-thud of the centurion's steps was gaining on us.

"Fuck it." At the last possible building, I threw my shoulder against the locked door, and spilled us both into the dark soundstage. Surely there was something in here we could use. I kicked the door shut behind us, for all the good it would do, and held tightly to Gretchen's hand as we picked our way through the darkness.

The sound of the door splintering to bits behind us was amazingly loud, and Gretchen's grip on my hand tightened as she flinched. I squeezed it back, hopefully reassuring, and kept going.

There were things in the way, old equipment we stumbled against, wires and cords we tripped over. And all the while, the thing behind us was just smashing his way through, metal screeching as he shoved speakers and lights and scaffolding out of the way.

One hand stretched in front of me, I felt the wall before I plowed into it face-first, and my heart sank. A second later, I found the door. That was better. "Through here."

We found ourselves in a hallway of some kind, Gretchen's shoes echoing hollowly against the tile flooring. On the upside, there was a light at the end of the tunnel, literally. We dashed toward it. Behind us, we heard the hallway door ripped off its hinges.

The light was an industrial-grade kitchen, white and sterile. Stainless steel appliances ringed the large room, broken up with immaculate white countertops. My eyes were only for the butcher block, prominently placed on a cooking island. I snatched a French knife out of the wood, quickly testing the edge with my thumb, satisfied when it drew a thin line of blood. No movie prop here, either.

Pushing Gretchen behind me again, I turned to face what was coming down the hallway, bracing myself for whatever was about to come.

And then ninjas dropped through the ceiling.

11

I'm not kidding you. Ninjas. Actual ninjas, in their black pajamas and hoods, all harnessed into ropes and clutching a variety of weapons. Most of the "ninjas" were holding their weapons all wrong, I noted.

They blinked at us, and we blinked at them, and then someone shrieked "CUT!!!" The wall of the kitchen behind us gave a groan and slowly rolled out of the way, revealing a team of very perplexed-looking movie-type folk.

Glancing back at the hallway, I could see the shadowy figure of our centurion filling the walkway, then he slowly faded back into the darkness of the soundstage. Within moments, he, and my goose bumps, were gone.

"It took me three hours to set those cameras." The shrieking voice had quieted, but it was that quiet that said "Boy am I pissed off." "Would someone mind telling me what fucking *moron* is responsible for wasting three hours of my life?!"

The ninjas were quickly unbuckling themselves from harnesses, muttering among themselves, and the crew cleared a path for what I will assume was one pissed-off director. Frankly, as portly and round as the guy was, he wasn't physically intimidating, but his unkempt beard was bristling in all directions in his fury, and it was obvious that when he wasn't happy, no one was happy.

"Just who the fuck do you think you—" I could tell the moment he recognized Gretchen, because he nearly choked in an effort to swallow whatever curse words were about to spew forth. "Gretchen! Oh, honey, I didn't recognize you! What in the world are you doing here?"

"Lars!" Instantly, Gretchen drew herself up, pasting on a gracious smile, and exchanged air kisses with the hairy angry man. "I'm so sorry. I was showing a friend around, and we didn't know anyone was using this stage. The light over the backdoor must be burned out."

Damn. The girl lied good. While Hairy Angry Lars was distracted, I dared a glance at the small disk on my key chain collection, intended to warn me of danger. The colored surface was just settling into a deep blue, and as I watched, it faded to purple, then back to black. *Just like a mood ring.* I had to wonder what color it had been when the mysterious Roman centurion was trying to mash me like a potato.

Fidgeting with Cam's disk gave me a closer look at my hands, and I grimaced. Somewhere, no doubt stumbling through the darkened soundstage, I'd gotten into something, and it was all over my hands. Gray paint, maybe, though it flaked off as I brushed at it. Wet plaster?

"This is Jesse. Jesse, this is Lars. He directed two of the films I was in last year." Gretchen directed his attention toward me, and belatedly, I remembered that I had a rather large knife in one hand. I quickly slipped it back into the block, pretending that nothing at all was amiss. *Nothing to see here, move along.*

Lars shook my hand, but I guarantee you he couldn't

have described me to anyone later. His eyes were all for the dazzling movie star.

"If I'd have known you were coming in today, we could have arranged a tour! Listen, can I call you later? I had some interesting stuff across my desk in the last week, I wanna run a few things past you."

Linking her arm through his, Gretchen slowly herded Hairy Angry Lars off the set, picking her way through the cables and equipment with the ease of long practice. "Sure! Just call Reggie, he can set something up. It was good to see you again!"

Five minutes later, she managed to extract herself from his blatant ass-kissing, and as we walked away I heard him yell, "Well, what are you all standing around with your thumbs up your asses for? Reset!"

Gretchen made it all the way out to the street before all the color drained from her face and her knees buckled under her.

"Easy. I gotcha." I wrapped my arm around her waist before she could fall, and she leaned on me, trying to keep from hyperventilating.

"I don't . . . I don't understand . . . that man was going to kill me. . . ." Her eyes were wide, shocky, staring at the teeming street around us without really seeing anything. I debated on slapping her, but settled on some firm talk first.

"Gretchen." When that didn't work, I gave her a little shake. "Gretchen!" Finally, she looked at me. "Do you have your cell?"

"Oh . . . um, yeah. It's in my purse." She fumbled it out.

"Call Tai. Tell him to meet us at the car. We need to get back to the hotel where it's safe, okay?"

"I . . ." Nearby, someone knocked over a barrel, and she almost jumped out of her skin. I admit, I flinched too.

"Hey." I tipped her chin up with one finger, making sure I could look into her eyes. "Call Tai. Let's go."

After a moment, she swallowed and nodded, making the phone call. There was no mistaking the tremor in her voice as she spoke to her bodyguard, and I noticed that Tai never asked what was wrong.

I kept hold of her elbow as we marched back toward the Town Car, ready to bolt and run if we had to, but there was nothing there. No stomach-twisting nausea, no goose bumps, no cold wind, no smell of damp soil. Just a plain, ordinary, movie lot, full of plain, ordinary movie people. No one even looked at us twice.

"Dante's not answering his phone." Just once, Gretchen hesitated in our hasty retreat. "We have to find him."

"Do you have any idea where he was going, here?"

"No."

"Then he knows his own way home. We're not waiting." I wasn't going to be happy until I could get her back behind wards. *Sorry, Dante.* I wasn't here to protect him.

Bobby had the Town Car door open when we reached it, Tai already behind the wheel with the engine running. I shoved Gretchen inside with little ceremony, then climbed in beside her. "Get us back to the hotel."

We rode in tense silence all the way back to the hotel, Gretchen turning to look behind us often enough that I finally had to look too. Now, I'm not an expert at spotting tails or anything, but I truly didn't see anyone following us. Still, I didn't relax until we'd made it up to the penthouse and I felt the thin bubble skin of Cam's protective wards slip over my arms.

Gretchen slumped onto the couch and dropped her head into her hands.

"What the hell happened?" Bobby finally broke the silence.

"He tried to kill me." Gretchen's whisper was barely audible. "He really tried to kill me."

"Who? Who tried to kill you, honey?" Tai crouched down in front of her, gathering her hands into his, and I caught the faintest whiff of cloves. Almost instantly, I saw some of the color come back into Gretchen's face, and the trembling in her fingers stopped. She took a few deep breaths, then gave Tai a grateful smile. Did she understand, I had to wonder? Did she realize he'd just magicked her into calm? Hell, did *he* even know what he'd done? It was a mystery to be pondered another time.

"I don't think he was trying to kill you, actually." Everyone looked toward me, puzzled. "I've been replaying that fight in my head, and he never went for you. He went straight for me."

It was true. Twice, in my mind's eye, I could see openings, moments when I'd left him with a clear path to Gretchen. Mega-bad on my part, but he hadn't taken advantage of it. Either he sucked worse than I did, or he wasn't interested in her.

"So what does that mean?"

I found a seat on the back of the sofa, picking at the

leather stitching a bit. "It means this is about that." I nodded toward her tattooed arm. "Your contract. Someone wants something from you, and they don't want me in the way."

Bobby frowned, waving his hand to get attention. "So who was this asshole? Did security get him? Did you call the cops?"

Gretchen snorted weakly, and I shook my head. "The cops can't help. This thing . . . I'm ninety percent sure it wasn't human."

"What the hell do you mean, 'not human'?"

"I mean, I kicked that thing hard enough to put four ribs through a lung, and almost shattered my knee in the process. I don't care how much muscle you have, a human body doesn't stand up to that much punishment."

"On drugs, maybe?"

Again, I shook my head. "Even on drugs, bones break. Joints fold."

It took Tai, the nonbeliever, to ask the important question. "So . . . if it wasn't human, what was it?"

"No freakin' clue. I've never seen anything like it before. But I will say that this thing didn't make a sound. Not one peep, not one groan, not one hiss. In my experience, that means whatever it was, it had no soul." Voices came from the soul, offered a direct line to it even. People that I called soulless, like Gretchen, really weren't. I mean, the soul was still in the body. But if it got yanked out? Poof, voice all gone. A creature like that would be able to mimic back other voices, but their own was forfeit.

The thing had looked human. Not unusual in the demonic world, really. Much easier to slip by unnoticed if you look like one of your prey. But like most other-worldly things, it had been off slightly. That blank, man-nequin-like face, for example. Even in the era of Botox and silicone, I'd never seen a face that devoid of identifying marks. It meant something. I just had no idea what.

"Great." Bobby sighed, running a hand over his cropped hair. "How the hell do you protect against something if you don't even know what it is?"

"And there's the sixty-four-thousand-dollar question." I pushed off my seat, stretching a little. "First things first, I'm moving my gear in here. I can't do any good if I'm clear down the hall when the shit hits the fan."

"And what do you want us to do?" Bobby wasn't standing at attention, but it was a near thing. The good soldier, waiting for orders.

Despite the fact that I desperately did *not* want to be the one in charge, there really was no way around it. I was that guy. I pursed my lips thoughtfully. "If this was a normal stalker type, what would you do next?"

"Call the cops. Notify hotel security. Get a restraining order."

"Notify hotel security, then. They already know to be on the lookout for people who don't belong, so leave it vague, and tell them that only known personnel are to be coming up to this floor. Anybody else has to be cleared by one of us first." Surely, even Bobby or Tai could spot a six-foot-tall Roman centurion, right?

"I'm gonna take a shower," Gretchen announced, standing suddenly. "Things are getting too weird for me, I just need to chill out a little."

While she went to do that, I skedaddled down to my room to get my stuff. Unfortunately, someone else had the same idea.

Now, I know I'm not the most organized guy in the world, but I think I would have remembered flinging my clothes all over the damn room. "Shit," I muttered, surveying the damage.

Like any truly paranoid person, I did have the stray thought that whoever it was might still be in the room, and I stood in the open doorway for long moments, just being still. A living presence leaves a mark, something felt beyond sound or scent. A tremor in the Force maybe. But no . . . in the end, there was no one there. The door had been shut and locked. Whoever had paid me a visit was long gone.

My first thought was for my sword and armor, but both were tucked in the back of the closet right where I'd left them. What kind of robber didn't check the closet? Just to be sure, I flipped the case open, holding my palm just above my sheathed sword. Prickles rose all up and down my arm as the tiny hairs stood at attention. Yup, spells still there. Examining my armor found the same result. My gear hadn't been touched.

The only way to see if anything else had been taken was to start the process of cleaning up. I had the feeling reporting it wouldn't do a damn bit of good. *"Can you describe the suspect?"* *"Sure, he was about this tall, plumed helmet, bit on the stocky and indestructible side."* It would have been easy for the centurion to ransack my room while we were having our shopping spree, then meet us at the movie lot for our exercise in fleeing like a little girl. All the more reason for me to move into Gretchen's suite. We were too separated here, too vulnerable.

As I gathered up my scattered belongings, I was puzzled to realize that nothing seemed to be gone. The drawers had been turned out, though most were empty. The bed had been stripped with no attempt made to put it back together. The desk was rifled through, Post-its and pens tossed all over the floor. But every personal item of mine was accounted for. Even the slashed-up black T-shirt. "What the hell were you looking for?" *Worst burglar ever.* I had to be missing something.

It took me another fifteen minutes to find it, and even then I couldn't be sure it had been taken by nefarious forces. My trash can was empty. The trash can where I'd unthinkingly dropped the extra few inches of Cam's blessed string that I hadn't needed. Most likely, housekeeping had come in and cleaned. Perfectly innocuous. But I had no way to be sure.

What could someone do, with a snippet of magic string? I had no idea, and I mentally kicked myself as I dragged my repacked bag down the hallway behind me, my armor riding on the top and my sword case tossed up on one shoulder. Careless. So damn careless to just discard it that way.

"Well, either housekeeping in this place is the worst I've ever seen, or my room was ransacked."

"No shit? Anything taken?" Tai was at the bar making phone calls apparently, but he put the phone down when I came in.

"Not sure yet. But they didn't touch this," I nodded

toward the case on my shoulder. "And if they wanted to hurt me, this woulda been the thing to snatch."

"What is it?" I laid the case on the couch, opening it for him. He whistled lowly. "Daaaamn. You really know how to use that thing?"

"Yup." I lifted The Way out and handed it to him hilt first. "Watch it, it's sharp."

Tai was used to handling weapons. I recognized it in the careful way he held the sword, keeping his fingers away from the blade, not because it was sharp, but so he didn't get fingerprints on the metal. "This is too pretty to use."

"I've had the same thought myself." I packed it away, piling my meager belongings in an out-of-the-way corner. "Let's hope I don't have to."

"Bobby went downstairs to talk to security. We should tell him about your room."

"Yeah, we need to get this door rekeyed. Too many people have access, the way it is." I gave him a pointed look. "And, we'll need to re-ward the door. I can't be sure mine will hold anymore." That's all I could come up with. What better way to figure out a way through a magical ward than to steal a piece of it?

He raised a dark brow at me. "You need me to ask the kitchen for more string?"

"Um . . . no. No, we're gonna try something different. More precisely, *you're* gonna try something different."

"I'm gonna what?"

Back in the day—I say that like I'm eighty years old or something—Mira and Ivan worked tirelessly to awaken the magic ability they were sure I had. Needless to say, it hadn't worked. But I remembered those exercises. If I could walk Tai through them, get him to consciously access his magic, I was sure I'd at least be able to tell if it was working. I had to get Tai to reset the ward.

First, we had to wait for Bobby to return. I didn't want people passing in and out of the door while we were trying to do this. And while we were waiting for him, Dante returned, no worse for the wear for being abandoned at the movie lot.

"Oh, Boo! I heard what happened! Are you all right?" Gretchen, fresh out of her shower and wrapped in a big fluffy robe like armor, allowed herself to be comforted.

"Sorry we had to leave you behind, Dante." I did feel a bit bad about that, after the fact.

He just waved a hand dismissively. "Ain't no thing. You did right, protecting my girl here." He hugged her tightly and they sat quietly on the couch, her head nestled against his shoulder. Part of me felt a teensy-weensy bit jealous. Must be nice to have a best friend that didn't hate you.

Not that Marty and I would ever have cuddled like that or anything. But you know what I mean.

Once everyone was safely inside, I stripped Cameron's string ward down, carefully balling up the blessed thread and tucking it into my suitcase.

"I thought that was supposed to protect me."

"It was. It may have been compromised now, so we're gonna see if Tai can reset it on his own."

Gretchen frowned in puzzlement. She made even that look stunningly beautiful. "Why aren't *you* resetting it?"

"I can't. I don't have any magic." I shrugged, and her

confusion made me smile. Without warning, I tossed Ivan's quartz crystal at her Maori bodyguard. He caught it on instinct, and immediately the white flaw within it sent out a strobelike pulse. Hunh. So that's what it was supposed to do. "See that? Tai has more magical ability in one strand of his hair than I have in my entire body." I held my hand up when she would have asked more. "He's gonna need to concentrate, so no more questions. This may not even work." I had no idea what I would do then.

Tai toyed with the crystal for a moment, the flashing settling down into a steady glow. When he handed it back to me, it faded into inert nothingness. "I don't believe in magic."

"Pretty sure that doesn't matter now. Come with me."

Standing on the stairs, I eyed the doorway, frowning thoughtfully. Tai moved up behind me, mimicking my stance. "You know I have no idea how to do this, right?"

"'S'okay, neither do I." I wracked my brain for what little magical theory I'd managed to absorb over the years. "See, thresholds are the easiest things to ward. People have attachment to their homes. They want them to be safe. But because this is a hotel, a temporary dwelling, the attachment usually isn't there. How long have you lived here?"

"A year," Gretchen supplied.

"Hope it's enough." Next, I looked at Tai long enough that he got uncomfortable and squirmed. "How attached are you to your Maori roots, Tai?"

He shrugged his broad shoulders. "I know the stories. My grandmother used to tell them to me all the time. They're just stories."

"Okay, well, think of those stories. Think of something that epitomizes strength and protection." He opened his mouth to tell me, and I shook my head. "I don't need to know. It just needs to be something that means something to you. Hold it in your head, okay? Think of how it looks, sounds, smells. Make it as real in your head as you can."

After a moment, he nodded. "Got it."

Now, here was the tricky part. "Stretch out your hand toward the doorway. Remember what it felt like before, when the string was there? Feel that again. Feel that tingle, picture it constructing your mental image into this doorway. Build a wall, build a barrier, make it real."

I'll give the man credit. Believer or not, he tried. I extended my hand beside his, I could feel the sparks of burgeoning magic over my palm. The aroma of cloves swirled around us with enough force to ruffle my hair. It built, gathered, and just when I thought it was strong enough to become visible, Tai gasped and it all vanished with a pop of pressure in my ears.

"Shit." Tai sagged a little, bending to brace his hands against his knees. "Did . . . did it work?"

I walked through the door several times, just to be sure, then shook my head. "No. It almost did, but it slipped away." *Damn damn damn.*

"Sorry." Finally, he slumped down on the carpeted stairs. "Is it supposed to feel like this?"

"Like what?"

"Like I got hit by a truck?"

"Yeah. Unfortunately. The bigger the magic, the bigger the drain. Rest a little, you should be fine." Defensive spells were easiest to set, easiest to recover from. I watched him for a bit, but other than being wiped out, he didn't seem to be suffering ill effects.

"So now what?" Bobby came to look at the doorway. "I mean, if Tai can't do this, what do we do now?"

"Tai can do it. Even untrained, he's got the brute strength. I just gotta figure out why it didn't stick."

"Well . . . it's a hotel, right? We're not attached to it. Tai's not attached to it." When I turned to look at Gretchen, she shrugged. "You said that, just a minute ago."

She was right. We needed something to connect Tai to the threshold. An anchor. It hit me like a slap in the face, and I decided that a good old face-palm was in order. "Dammit. I even said it! Bobby, get me some scissors."

You shoulda seen the look on Tai's face when I headed at him with those scissors. "Hey!"

"Oh, quiddit. I'm just taking a couple of hairs." *More magic in one hair than in my entire body.* I was even careful and took them from the underside at the back of his neck, so it would never be noticeable. "Our anchor," I told him, displaying the four raven black hairs in my hand. "Get me some tape."

With the hairs taped at the four corners of the door-jamb, I coached Tai through trying again. "Picture it clearly. Think of all the things you want to keep safe, and picture anything else being trapped on the outside. Push that out through the palm of your hand."

Like before, the power swelled around us, stronger than anything I'd ever sensed. Even Mira, the strongest witch I knew, paled in comparison to Tai's innate talent.

I could almost follow the seal with my eyes, watch as it crawled along the jamb. There was a faint flare each time it touched a piece of his hair, and the pressure in my ears snapped like a nail being hammered home. I couldn't help but smile in triumph, even before the last of the four anchors locked in. This was going to work.

The ward hummed almost audibly when it was completed, and the hairs on my arm stood at strict attention when I passed my hand through. "Damn, Tai. We gotta get you trained." How this man had wandered around for this many years just leaking out this much magic . . . it boggled the mind.

Tai, on the other hand, was toast. Gray beneath his tan skin, it took Bobby's help to walk him over to the couch where he collapsed with a groan. "Tell me it worked, 'cause I don't think I can do it again."

"Yeah, it worked. Sleep it off, man." Part of me was proud of him. Part of me was proud of me, for being able to get it out of him.

"Here, I'll even rub your shoulders." Dante proceeded to do just that, until Tai winced.

"Watch it, you're pulling my hair."

The black man looked sheepish. "Oops. Got caught on my watch. Here, Boo, hold this for me." He tossed his watch to Gretchen, then finished rubbing the body-guard's shoulders. "Who knew we had Harry Potter right here with us all along?"

I think, if Tai hadn't been so wiped out, he might have chuckled at that. As it was, he was already sound asleep.

12

"What I don't understand, still, is why all this is happening?" Gretchen kept her voice down in deference to her sleeping bodyguard, but I'm not sure an atomic bomb dropping could have woken Tai. "I mean, they already have what they need from me. I never tried to back out, never tried to go back on my end, so why would anyone be coming for me? Why do you need to be here?"

She looked like a little girl there, all curled up in her fluffy robe, her feet tucked up under her on the couch. She wasn't that much younger than me, really, but at that moment, I felt very, very old.

I rested my elbows on my knees, trying to figure out how much to say. Did I want to admit I was here at the behest of a demon? No, not really. "From what I was told, when your contract was made, there was a loophole. Something to do with who owns those extra souls you're carting around when you die."

"What kind of loophole?"

I shrugged. "I don't know. I was told that basically whoever is around can just . . . scoop them up or something. It was your contract, don't you remember?"

Gretchen shook her head. "I didn't negotiate it. Reggie did." When I blinked at her, she shrugged back at me. "He negotiates contracts for a lot of people. Selling your soul . . . it's just another business transaction." She sat in silence for a few moments, nibbling her bottom lip. Mira did that when she was thinking, too. It made me miss her. "It has to be decided somehow. I mean, if there were four demons standing around the moment I die, do they all get a cut, or is there a way to choose?"

"I'm sure the wording is in the contract. Do you think he'd remember exactly what was said?"

Gretchen hopped to her feet, nudging Dante off the couch in the process. "He doesn't have to. He keeps a written copy on file in his office. Come on, we're going to Reggie's."

Everyone was wrangled in pretty short order, with the exception of the sleeping Tai. Gretchen turned her big baby blues on Dante, fluttering her eyelashes. "Could you stay with him? I don't want him here alone when he can't defend himself."

Dante snorted. "What do you expect me to do if someone breaks down the door? Style their hair while we wait for Tai to wake up and kick some ass?" Still, he agreed to stay. I had the idea he'd have agreed to walk into Hell in Gretchen's place if she asked him.

With Tai out of commission, Bobby had to drive, which left Gretchen and me alone in the back. "Y'know, we could have just called him."

"No." She shook her head firmly. "No, I want the document before he has time to alter it."

I tilted my head, looking at her thoughtfully. "You don't trust him."

"Of course not." She looked at me like I was stupid. Maybe I was. "I don't trust anyone, except Dante. That's how you survive here."

"That seems . . . very lonely."

She shrugged. "I knew what I was getting into when I asked for it. I don't regret anything."

"Was it worth it?" Some perverse part of me had to know.

She smiled a little. "I guess we'll see."

Reggie's office was somewhere very . . . office-y. "Century City," Gretchen told me when I asked where in the hell we were.

Some big high-rise, taller than anything you'd see in Kansas City. It reminded me of the office building from *Die Hard*, which honestly creeped me out a little. Anybody said "yippy-ki-yay" and I'd be the first one out the door.

We pulled into the parking garage, but when Bobby went to get out of the car, I stopped him. "Stay here."

He frowned. "Why?"

"Because if we have to come out of here hot, I want the doors unlocked and the engine running." Did I really think we'd be attacked in the middle of office cubes, copiers and fax machines? No. But it wasn't impossible.

After a moment, Bobby nodded and settled back into his seat.

Gretchen had to check us in at the security desk, then we waited a few moments for the elevator. If anyone else passing by recognized her, they were professional enough not to remark on it. How strange her life must be, I realized, when just simple anonymity was a luxury.

Reggie's office was one of many in an agency full of agents and lawyers. The receptionist at the front couldn't have been more than twenty, and her skirt was hiked up so high I could almost see things I shouldn't have even been paying attention to. Maybe it makes me a bad person, but I'm guessing she wasn't hired for her intellect. She barely looked up from texting on her phone to nod us in. Apparently Gretchen had an all-access pass.

Reggie himself was behind his desk when we walked in, preening in a hand mirror, and he stood up with a broad smile when he saw who it was. "Gretchen honey! What are you doing here? Did I miss an appointment?"

"No no, we're just dropping in." She exchanged hugs with him, then plopped herself in one of his comfy leather chairs. "We're actually here because I need a copy of some paperwork."

"Of course. Which?" He perched himself on the edge of his desk, but he couldn't help darting a glance toward me. I smirked in my head, but kept it off my face. He was trying to figure out why I was here, what this was all about. Good. Let him wonder.

"My contract."

He chuckled. "More specific? You have a lot of contracts, honey."

"This one." She held out her arm, displaying the writhing black tattoo. "I need to see some things."

He raised one sandy brow, but nodded and walked to one of his file cabinets. "Are you . . . thinking of backing out?"

"I don't know yet. I just want to see it."

Reggie shot me a venomous glance at that, like somehow it was all my fault. Well, okay, it was. Suck it, just like my shirt said.

It took him a few minutes of flipping through files to find it. I didn't believe for a moment that he didn't know exactly which document it was. He was stalling, trying to figure out what we were doing and how to undo any damage I'd done. "Ah, here we are. But I don't know how much good it's going to do you."

Gretchen took the offered document from him. Somehow, I'd expected it to be scrawled in blood on parchment, or human skin or something, but it was just a regular old contract, printed on legal-sized paper. Unfortunately, it was written in the scrawling demon script, and it wriggled as we looked at it. The only legible thing was Gretchen's signature on the final page, along with a smaller version of the tattoo on her arm—the demon's signature, so to speak.

Reggie stood silently, letting her flip through the pages—there had to be at least twenty of them. Long, detailed contract—before he cleared his throat. "Can I ask what you're looking for?"

"The loophole." Gretchen had her head down, so she didn't see Reggie go a little gray under his tan. I did. "You remember the loophole, don't you, Reggie?" She fixed him with a piercing stare when she finally raised her eyes to him. Maybe she hadn't missed him going pale after all. Y'know, I had to admit. The girl kinda impressed me.

"It's been a long time since I negotiated that one, Gretchen. I don't recall any particular loophole."

"Read it to me." She stood up from her chair, thrusting the papers at him. Somehow, she managed to tower over him despite the fact that he had a good four inches on her, even with her in heels. "Find me the part that explains exactly what this loophole is, and why something tried to kill me today."

His gaze shifted back and forth between Gretchen and me. I just crossed my arms over my chest and did my best to look intimidating. She had this under control, apparently. When he got no reaction from me, and Gretchen continued to stab him with her frosty baby blues, he sighed and leaned against his desk again.

"I can't read the language, Gretchen. But, if I had to guess, the other assets that you've gathered over the last five years—"

"Souls," Gretchen interrupted. "Souls I've gathered."

Reggie nodded reluctantly. "Souls. I believe that the original intent was for those to go to the demon who offered you your contract. However, if there is anything in that contract that might leave ownership . . . ambiguous . . . well, that might be worth killing over, don't you think?"

"Ambiguous how? How is ownership decided?"

Reggie shook his head. "I don't know, honey. I don't remember any such phrase when I negotiated this one. It may all come down to some interpretation in the language."

Gretchen frowned. "We need someone to translate this, then."

"There I can't help you. I'm sorry." He shrugged. "But if someone wants those surplus assets—"

"Souls!" We both looked at Gretchen in surprise when she raised her voice. "They are *souls*, Reggie! Not assets, not commodities, they are people's *souls*. And someone is willing to kill to get them from me. And while I know I'm not going to *get* old, the idea of being tortured or something is pretty high on my list of things not to do before I die!" She shook the contract in his face. "You did this. You're the one who fucked up this contract, and now something is after me. We all know I'm gonna die young. Live fast, leave a good-looking corpse. Leave a tragic legacy behind. That was part of the *plan*. This? This was not."

For a moment, I thought she was going to slap him in the face. Personally, I kinda wanted to see that. Instead, she just shook her head. "I'm going to go make a copy of this. I'm gonna find someone who can read it." She stalked out of the office, leaving me and Reggie to eye each other warily.

"You did this. She didn't give a shit about that damn contract until you showed up."

"You really wanna go there? Start pointing out who is to blame for what?" I raised a brow at him, and ultimately he couldn't meet my stare. He looked down first. In man-speak, that meant I won. With a smirk, I started walking around, exploring his office. Golf trophies. Autographed celebrity pictures for just about everybody who was anybody in Hollywood. Framed press releases. Everything displayed in very careful order, very neat placement.

There were also some old books, the bindings so faded I couldn't even tell what they used to say. I picked one up and flipped a few pages, just to hear Reggie hiss in caution. They were practically ancient, whatever they were. Handwritten in fading ink, the paper thick and yellowed. The words in it were English, but not the version we speak now. The kind where they put an e at the end of random words. Olde. Towne. Taverne. There were a few sketches on some of the pages, not professional drawings, just little idle doodles. I fancied that this was the journal of some medieval student, bored in his classes. On the next page, surely I'd find the equivalent of "Kilroy was here."

"That book is priceless. Please be careful."

I raised a brow at him, and toyed with the idea of dumping the old tome on the floor. But being a fan of old written works myself, I relented and put the book back on the shelf. "How many, Reggie? How many souls have you bargained away at the behest of your clients?"

"It is my job to do what the client wants, regardless of how ill-advised I think it is. And really, most of the time, it works to their benefit. At least in the short term."

"And yours?" I picked up one of his trophies, turning it over in my hands then replacing it on the shelf crooked just because I could and I'm petty. "I notice you haven't sold your own soul in one of these very profitable arrangements."

"Of course not. Do I look stupid?"

"Then what do you get out of all this?"

"As their representative, I get a small percentage of their earnings. If I can enhance that earning potential with this kind of contract, so much the better. That's not evil, Mr. Dawson, just good business."

"And if it gets you in good with the forces of Hell, then maybe you'll get a little compensation on the back side, right? Should you ever need it?"

He was quiet a while before he answered. "That possibility hasn't been addressed yet."

I snorted. "Not out loud, maybe, but you have it all worked out in your head. Who to ask for a favor, what leverage you have where. All planned out neatly in that tiny, oily little brain of yours. 'Cause that's the kind of guy you are. You're a planner." I finally turned to look at him. "You're disgusting."

Reggie smirked at me. "Glass houses and stones, Mr. Dawson. Remember, I know who sent you here. An interesting . . . side job you have going, there. Could be lucrative in the future, if you play your cards just right."

That stung. Bad. Mostly because he wasn't wrong. "My business is mine. And at least I'm not dragging other people down with me." Except my wife. My daughter. My friends, family, loved ones. Yeah, I'm a real freakin' hero.

"To each his own then." He shrugged, smiling at me as if we were old friends just chatting about the weather.

I don't think I've ever wanted to punch somebody in the face so badly in my life. Luckily, Gretchen came back about then, keeping me from devolving to my baser nature.

She slapped one copy of the contract down on Reggie's desk, and thrust the other one at me. I rolled it up and crossed my arms over my chest again. "If you can't tell, Reggie, I'm really unhappy about this. I'll be reviewing my contract with you as well over the next few days." She gave him a cold smirk. "I already have a copy of that one at home."

"Of course, honey. As you see fit. Let me know if

there are any points you want to renegotiate." He gave her a smile too, charming and poised. Somewhere in all this, he'd gathered himself, recovered from his upset earlier. I didn't like that. Somewhere in that slick, sleazy mind of his, he'd come up with something, something we didn't know. And if it made him happy, it wasn't something I wanted to see happen.

"Come on, Jesse." She turned on her heel and stalked out, leaving me to follow. My skin itched, right between my shoulder blades, the entire time my back was turned to Reggie. Pretty sure that was the exact spot the daggers from his eyes were landing.

Back in the car, Gretchen stared at that contract until I thought her eyes might pop right out of her head. Finally, she tossed it into the floorboards, rubbing at her temples with a pained sigh. "There's no way to read this. Feels like my head is going to explode."

"Well, there *might* be a way." She raised her head to give me a curious look. "There's one other person who was there the night you made this contract, right?" I reached over and tapped the tattoo on her arm with one finger. "What if we ask *him*?"

She thought it over, but finally shook her head. "Even if I could get him to show up, you think he'd tell the truth? He's a demon."

"You call his name, he'll show up. I promise that much. As for truth ... well, we got a fifty-fifty shot, right?" Oh, how I hated this idea. Hated it with a freakin' passion. You don't summon demons. You just don't. I'd done it once, just once in the five years I'd known about them, and it still felt like slimy ants marching all over my skin every time I thought about it. Something like that, it leaves a stain in your mind.

"But he won't." She gave me a perplexed look. "I've tried to call him again, and he doesn't show up."

"Wait. You mean to tell me you called a demon *by name* and it didn't show?"

"Yeah. Does that mean something important?"

I had no idea. I'd never heard of it happening before. I mean, a demon's name was power. One whisper of it could get their attention in whatever Hell they existed in, no matter how far away. Call it out loud, and they would ride a human voice across the veil, materializing in our world with all their powers in full effect. Why one would miss that opportunity was beyond me. "Well, we're gonna try again. You got some place you suggest for this? The hotel room is off limits." It was the one stronghold we had, if we could even call it that. I wasn't going to invite a demon right in.

"Reggie has a place he uses. Says it's special. We could try that?"

I nodded. "Sounds like a plan."

"Bobby. Take us to the observatory."

"Actually, Bobby, I need to stop off and grab some stuff. You guys got a Wal-Mart out here somewhere?" I wasn't going to mix it up with a demon without a bit more ammunition. And it's amazing what you can pick up at your local stop-n-shop, if you know what to look for.

The supply run took no time at all, and dusk was coming on as we drove toward the observatory, the winter sun setting into the ocean somewhere behind us. Night was a good time for demon summoning. They tended to avoid the sunlight, and if we were dealing with a reluctant demon, I wanted to make sure the widdle fellow felt right at home.

Bobby pulled the car through the gates of a park and on up the winding street. It felt like we were the only ones in the world, trundling up toward the observatory that I could already see lighted against the night sky. "Are you sure this place is open?"

"Until ten. And this time of year, there shouldn't be too many people here. I hope."

It seemed like we drove uphill forever. And while my brain knew that this wasn't technically "the mountains," little me, born and bred around Missouri's river bluffs, thought it looked pretty damn impressive. Below us, I could see Los Angeles spread out like a Christmas tree, the lights of the city gradually taking the place of the light of day. I was forced to admit, if only to myself, that Kansas City looked nothing like this.

"If we were here during the day, you can see the Hollywood sign from certain places along here," Gretchen supplied, perhaps tired of the silence. She even sounded a tiny bit apologetic. "But they don't light it at night."

"I'm sure I'll be fine without seeing it." Sightseeing was *so* not the top priority on my list right now, but it was nice of her to think of it. I think.

At the top of the hill sat the observatory building, pristinely white against the darkening sky like a reversed silhouette. A few evening sky watchers were trundling in and out as we parked, but all in all I was satisfied with our "innocent bystander" quotient. I held Gretchen's

door as she slid out of the car, then gathered up my plastic bag of supplies. Bobby moved up behind us like a big,
menacing shadow, and I was suddenly glad he was on
our side.

"Where to now?"

"Just out on the lawn. Reggie said the city spread out
below us lends power. Something about all the hopes
and dreams gathering in one spot." Gretchen stopped to
slip off her heels as she left the asphalt lot and started
picking her way gingerly over the lawn. "He said it would
be better to do it at the Hollywood sign, but the cops
come too quick up there."

I put my hand on Bobby's chest when he would have
followed Gretchen across the grass. "Have you seen this
before? A real demon?"

He shook his head. "No. But how bad can it be, right?"

I shook my head in return. "You're staying here."

That got me a serious frown. "I've seen actual combat,
man, I think I can handle a little hocus-pocus in the
dark."

"Look." I lowered my voice, mindful that there were
civilians nearby. "Once you hear a demon name, you
can't unhear it. It winds through your brain in a way I
can't even describe, and it will sit there in your skull, fes-
tering for the rest of your life. Ask me how many I have
in my head."

The scarred marine hesitated a moment before asking. "How many?"

"Thirteen. Thirteen of those nasty, slithery things
swimming around up here." I tapped my temple. "And
I'd give anything in the world to be able to scrub them

out. So take what I'm offering. Stay here, make sure we're not disturbed. 'Kay?"

After a few moments, he nodded. "All right. You want my weapon?" He shifted his coat aside, displaying his holstered gun.

"Nah, I'm set." I shook my plastic bag with a rustle. "Guns are usually no use anyway." For fighting a demon, which had no vital organs to disable, a bullet just didn't cause enough damage. And the bullets that would, well, those were too dangerous to the bystanders. Better to stick with the tried and true. To that end, I popped the trunk of the car and fished out the tire iron. Trust me, I could beat the crap outta a whole lotta demon with a good piece of metal.

Armed and supplied, I trotted to catch up to Gretchen, and she gave me a faint smile. "Thank you for that, by the way. I don't think Bobby would have stayed behind for me. He respects you."

I gave her some noncommittal man noise. I wasn't sure Bobby respected me. I was just glad he'd listened to me.

We found a place far enough away from the building to be deemed "out of sight" but close enough that the faint light still provided some clarity. Gretchen turned to look at me expectantly. "What next?"

"Well, first we're going to make sure you're safe during all of this." Out of my little shopping bag, I produced a box of salt. "Find a place to stand where you'll be comfortable. I don't want you moving after this."

She obeyed, and I took great care in pouring a solid line of salt in the grass around her bare feet. No doubt, I was going to kill this section of lawn here, but better that than risk Gretchen's soul.

I'd seen what demons could do to the people they'd bargained souls from. The handless, armless zombie creature flashed through my mind again, and the skin down my back crawled even though I knew she was far away. If a demon owned your soul, he didn't have to wait for you to finish with it before he came to collect. Yank a soul out of a living body, and poof . . . instant zombie. I wasn't taking that chance with Gretchen.

"No matter what happens, you stay in this circle, understand? If it comes down to it, you stay in this circle until the sun comes up, and then you run for the car."

The starlet frowned at me. "You talk like this is going to turn into something bad."

"It never turns into something good." Next out of the bag was a plain bottle of water with a wide mouth. From my collection of key chains, I took the plastic carnival token and dropped it into the bottle, giving it a good shake. Voilà, instant holy water. "Hang on to this for me. Don't drink it."

"I thought you said you don't have any magic."

"I don't. But I have a lot of friends who do. They hook me up." Last but not least, I unhooked my mace canister from my belt loop. I thumbed the cap off and sprayed a bit off to the side, just to be sure it was working. The odor of cayenne and cumin cut through the chilly night air.

Now that the sun was down, California remembered that it was late December. I spared a small moment to wish I had one of my jackets with me, but I was also pretty sure my goose bumps weren't entirely from the cold. We were about to do something colossally stupid, and my danger sense wanted to make damn sure I knew it. Sure enough, Cam's little warning system was also swirling, the color a muted blue-green.

"All right. Let's do this thing." I picked up the tire iron and rolled my head on my shoulders to loosen up the muscles. Ready as I'd ever be.

My starlet companion took a few deep breaths before attempting the call, which I couldn't fault her for at all. The one and only time I'd said a demon name aloud, I'd choked and puked my guts up, all at once. That she could do it at all told me what kind of tough cookie she was. "_____!"

My vision swam, and the hillside we stood on tilted at alarming angles. My ears felt like I'd flossed them with razor wire, and my stomach did dangerous flip-flops before the world righted itself. Five years, I'd been hearing such things, and it never got any better. Such is the power of the demonic language. There are just some things humans aren't meant to hear, much less say.

And then we waited. And waited. And waited some more. Though I kept my senses open, waiting for that faint hint of sulfur to betray its location, the demon failed to show itself. I'd seen some wait to make grand entrances, sure, but as the minutes ticked on, it was going from fashionably late to totally gauche. "I don't get it. Why isn't it coming?"

"Should I call it again?"

"No! Do not do that."

"I told you. I haven't seen him in a couple of years now."

"No. No, something's wrong. It has to be here." Careful not to get too far from Gretchen, I started walking a spiral in the grass, edging my way outward in a search for . . . something.

When I found it, it was not what I expected.

13

I nearly stepped on it, and only a faint mewling sound kept me from planting my heavy boot right in the middle of it. In the darkness, in the damp grass, it was easily mistaken for a lump of mud, or a great oversized slug, about the size of a football. "What the hell . . . ? Gretchen, come look at this."

"You said not to leave the circle."

"I think it's safe." Against my better judgment, I crouched down to get a better look, poking at the strange blob with the end of the tire iron. It shrunk from the touch of metal, curling in on itself, so I poked it again, this time with my finger. It bleated like a tiny goat, and wriggled at my touch. Warmth spread from my fingertip, spreading up to my wrist, then faded away. Mira's protection spell, barely triggered.

"Ew, what is that?" Gretchen leaned over my shoulder to look, careful to keep me between her and the slimy thing.

"I think this may be your demon." I poked it again, and it squirmed, helplessly trying to flee my harassment.

"No. No, this can't be. My demon looked like a man. Tall, handsome. He had red hair." She scooted closer, and the puling thing in the grass thrashed as best it was able. One end of it—I'll assume it was the head—reached up toward her, almost begging. "God, do you really think it is?" She reached out to poke it as well, and I caught her wrist. Yes, I was pretty sure it was safe for her to leave the salt circle, but why push our luck?

"Demon strength is measured by how many souls they own. Maybe someone got to him. Took all his souls away. Drained his power, knocked him down a peg." Or fifty. I'd never seen a demon so weak, but even as we examined its pathetic little form, I knew that's what it was. A demon that had lost almost every trace of power. It was barely existing.

"How does that happen?"

"Don't know. Maybe it ran afoul of a champion, like me. Maybe someone fought it, beat it." There was a part of me that felt some satisfaction at that thought. Maybe this is what happened to the demons I'd fought. Maybe right now, the Yeti was in Hell, oozing through some other demon's summer garden or something.

Because part of me is still a little boy, I poked it again, just to hear it whine. It curled up in a little hurt ball, making piteous whimpering noises. "It's so weak, it can't even speak. We're not going to find out anything from it."

"What do we do now?"

I glanced around, then back at Gretchen, shrugging. "This is your chance, you know. If you want your soul back. If I can get it to negotiate somehow, pretty sure I could take it out in this condition. This would all be over." Hell, I was pretty sure I could stomp it flat with one boot. Squish. Or better yet, dump that bottle of holy water over it and watch it sizzle.

She thought about it for long quiet moments, before shaking her head. "No. No, this is what I chose. If we undo this, I'll lose everything I've worked for. It's all I have to give to my mom and sister. I can't let that happen."

Quite frankly, that was not the answer I'd expected. From my crouched position, I looked at her for a while, trying to solve the puzzle she'd become in the short time I'd known her. Finally, I stood, brushing my hands off on my jeans. "Whatever the lady wants. Let's go then."

"You're just going to leave it here?"

"You have a better idea? The odds of it hurting anyone are fairly slim I'd say. It'll either find its way back across, or it'll fry when the sun comes up. Either way, it won't break my heart."

"It's suffering." Even in the dark, her blue eyes were accusing, reminding me that I was supposed to be a better person than this. *Dammit*. Why do women do this to me?

"Step back. You don't want this in your eyes." When she had removed herself to a safe distance, I crouched down again, shaking my mace canister a little as I spoke to the tiny blob in the grass. "Understand that if I had my way, I'd be dumping holy water on you right now. As it is, you get a reprieve. If you ever get a chance, thank the lady." I gave a small spritz of the spiced-up water, holding my breath and leaning back to keep my own concoction from choking me. The slug-demon gave a small "meep!" noise and vanished. It didn't even have enough oomph to leave a sulfur smell behind.

I stood again, offering my arm to Gretchen. "Come on. Let's go home."

Back at the hotel, we briefed a now-conscious Tai on

the events of the day, and both bodyguards took their try at reading the demonic contract. I had some brief hope that Tai's innate abilities would allow him to miraculously translate it, but no such luck.

Given that his protégé had spent most of the day unconscious, Bobby declared it was his turn for a nap, and retired to the spare bedroom. Gretchen followed suit, disappearing into her own room shortly thereafter, leaving me alone with the Maori masher.

He didn't seem to be any the worse for wear, despite his earlier exertions. His eyes were bright, his color good. Definitely better than Mira looked after some of her spell castings gone wrong. "I'm freakin' starving. I'm gonna order some Chinese takeout. You want?"

It occurred to me that I hadn't eaten all freaking day. "Oh, hell yes. Order one of everything." I was *starving*!

He chuckled, and after he ordered he went downstairs to wait for the delivery, leaving me alone for the first time in days.

The suite felt strange with everyone asleep. I'd never heard dead silence in this place that usually seemed so full of drama and noise. Though you'd think a little peace and quiet would be a relief, I actually found myself wishing for Tai's return, just so I wasn't all alone with my reading.

While I'd have preferred to be reading something with explosions and riveting action, instead I pulled out the much-crumpled copy of Gretchen's contract. I didn't have the foggiest idea how to read it, of course, but that didn't stop me from trying.

It occurred to me that I'd never actually seen a written demon contract. Tattooed into my skin, yeah, but never on paper. A small part of me wondered if my wife, language whiz that she was, could pick up Demonic. Would these wavering black scribbles mean anything to her, if I could find her a teacher? Do they advertise for that on Craigslist?

Half an hour, a huge carton of General Tso's chicken and a raging freakin' headache later, I was forced to admit that there was nothing on that paper I was going to be able to interpret. I could think of only one person who might be able to, and *man* I didn't want to call him.

He picked up on the third ring and there was no trace of sleepiness in his gravelly voice at all. God only knew where he was, or what time of day it was there. "Dawson." No hello, no hey, just *"Dawson."* Ivan was pissed at me.

"Hey, Ivan, how's it going?" That too went unacknowledged.

"Is there to being a reason you are not following protocol? A reason that your student is to be calling me, instead of you?"

I knew I was gonna have to take my ass-chewing before I could get to the real reason I'd called him, so I sighed and took it like a man. "I'm not out here for a soul challenge, Ivan. I'm just . . . repaying a favor I owe."

"And this favor is to being more important than your safety? This favor must to being very important indeed." His voice dripped with sarcasm, and the part of me that would always be a teenage boy standing before the judge wanted to curl up and die of shame. It wasn't that he was mad, it was that he was disappointed. I guess we never outgrow that particular aversion.

"It was a favor I couldn't refuse to pay back. And that's all I really feel like saying on the subject." He snorted, obviously not satisfied with my answer. "Listen, I called you for a reason. I'm looking at a contract here in front of me, and I'm having some trouble reading it. Do you think you could look it over?"

"What language is it to being in?"

"Um . . . Demonic."

There was a long pause at the other end of the line. "You have . . . a written copy?"

"Yeah. It's a long story. Do you have time?"

"*Tak*, I can to be looking at it. I could to be arriving in two days."

"I need it sooner. You have a fax machine handy?"

"*Tak*." He gave me the number and I jotted it down on the back of my hand. "I am not certain if I can to be reading this, but I will to be trying. Regardless, you and I must to be talking, Dawson. Much is to being unsaid between us."

"Yeah, I know. I'll quit dodging your calls if you'll quit dodging mine." Again, he snorted, but he didn't deny it. "I'll fax this now. Gimme a call back when you've had a chance to look at it."

With Gretchen's contract flying through the ether to Ivan, there was nothing left for me to do but sleep.

As comfortable as that leather couch was to sit on, sleeping on it is not advisable. I woke with aches and pains in places usually reserved only for post-combat injuries, and my face plastered against the slick leather with my own sweat. I peeled myself off the sofa to find Tai sitting at the bar, still wearing sweats and a T-shirt.

"Morning, sunshine." I flipped him the bird and he laughed. "Breakfast is on its way up. Tread softly though, I just woke Bobby up and he's cranky in the mornings." When was Bobby *not* cranky?

I suppose I should have been disturbed that I'd slept so deeply, but I'd come to rely on my early warning system so much. If I wasn't all cold and goose bumpy, I was safe. Even in my sleep.

There were no messages on my phone, and a part of me was disappointed. Somehow, I thought I'd wake up and Ivan would have this all figured out for me. What else was I supposed to do now, besides hobble around like a broke-down horse?

"There's a garden on the roof, right?" I asked Tai, who nodded. "I'm gonna go up, do some exercises and stuff. Holler if you need me."

A few katas should work the rust out of my muscles. That was my first excuse for riding the elevator up to the roof. The second was that I needed a little bit of privacy for the next call I was going to make. A call that didn't require my phone.

The garden on the roof was stunning. It was easy to believe I'd suddenly stepped back in time to feudal Japan, walking through some shogun's carefully sculpted courtyard.

A path had been formed of white river stones, carefully sealed down so they wouldn't scatter underfoot. The trail was bordered by large bonsai-style shrubs and low bamboo posts containing solar-powered lights. There were small alcoves carved out, with benches for sitting, and if you followed the path far enough, it opened up into a large gathering area. Already, there were tables and chairs set up, paper lanterns hanging, preparing for the New Year's festivities to come. A small stream wove in and out through everything, adding a soothing music to the morning air, ending in the reflecting pool at the center of the roof. I peered over, looking through the rippling water all the way down into the hotel lobby.

Like any true child at heart, I fought the urge to drop a rock on the glass, just to see what would happen. Surely, it had been designed with just that impulse in mind. Breakable glass would be a pretty big design flaw.

No one else seemed to be around, this early, which was good for me. I really didn't want anyone to see what I was about to do.

"Axel." I whispered his name into the morning air, then waited. Sure, I'd never tried to actually get his attention before, but I firmly believed he could hear me, wherever he was. When I got no response, I tried louder. "Axel!"

A few minutes went by with no response, and I tried one last time, yelling as loud as I could. "AXEL!!" On a nearby roof, some birds took off, squawking in protest, but that was all I got. No blond demon. Not even a possessed squirrel. I guess he meant it when he said he couldn't be caught here.

"Dammit." Then I felt stupid for expecting otherwise. He was a demon, after all. He'd protect his own ass before anything else.

When my phone rang, I almost jumped out of my skin and part of me wondered what the area code was in Hell. But no, it was just Ivan. "Dawson."

"Mornin', Ivan. How goes it?" I found a seat on one of

the benches bordering the stream, just letting the sun soak into me.

"This contract is to being very interesting."

"You were able to read it, then?"

"*Ni.*" Not one for small talk, our Ivan.

I sighed. "Great. So we're no closer to finding out what the hell is going on."

"Hm. *Ni.* But do not to be despairing. I am to be knowing a few people who may be able to help. I will make phone calls." We were both quiet for a few moments. "Will you to be challenging for this, once it is translated?"

Would I? That was a good question. "I asked her. She doesn't want me to. And I wouldn't feel right, challenging for her soul against her will, y'know? That's a kinda personal thing to do."

"Perhaps if I was to be speaking to her, I could convince her to accept our aid." That thought made me smile. I wondered what the Hollywood starlet would think of my gruff Ukrainian mentor.

"You can try, I guess. She's still sleeping, though."

"That is all right. I will speak to her when I arrive."

"Um . . . you really don't have to do that, Ivan. I have this under control." I had nothing under control.

"Regardless. I will arrive tomorrow. Where are you to be staying?" I told him. There was no point in arguing once he'd made up his mind. "Until tomorrow." He hung up on me.

"Do you often talk about people when they're not around?" Gretchen's voice might have startled me, if I hadn't caught a whiff of her perfume a couple of minutes before. She stepped out of the little alcove where she'd been hiding—poorly—wearing yoga pants and a tight T-shirt, her feet bare on the river stone path.

"Well, yeah." I spun around on the bench, flipping my feet to the other side so I could face her. "They tend to get upset when I talk about them to their faces."

"I told you, I don't want out of my contract." She frowned at me, crossing her arms over her chest. She looked very much like her mother at that moment.

"I know. And I won't do anything without your say-so. I'm just trying to get the damn thing translated for you." I stood up. Having her look down at me was too much like being scolded by my mom.

"Who were you talking to? You sent my contract to him."

"His name is Ivan. He's another champion, like me." He was more than that, but . . . need to know basis, and she didn't need to know. "He can't read it either, but he might know some people. He's gonna call back." I tilted my head at her. "You know, your demon was the weakest one I've ever seen. I wouldn't want to jinx myself and call the fight a sure thing, but . . . if you wanted it . . ."

"Don't you dare." She advanced on me, poking one finger into my chest, and I held my hands up defensively. "I told you, I hold up my end."

"Hey, whatever you say. Just pointing out your options is all." I glanced around. "Where's Tai? He let you come up here alone?"

"I told him I was coming up to work out with you." She shrugged. "I wanted to see what you were doing. And I find you poking your nose in my business where it isn't wanted." Once more, she jabbed her finger into my chest, which was one more time than I intended to tolerate.

Her eyes went wide when I snatched her wrist away, and but she recovered quickly and struggled against my grip. "Let go, asshole!" When that didn't work, she tried to kick me in the shin, which was gonna hurt her way more than it was me, with her feet bare.

"Bobby and Tai never taught you how to get out of this hold? Seriously?" As short as she was, I may have even been able to pick her up and dangle her from that delicate little arm, were I so inclined. "Here, quit tugging, you'll never get loose that way."

Her eyes wary, she stopped fighting against me, and watched as I explained. "Look at how I have you here. When someone has you like this, the weakest part of the grip is the thumb, okay?"

"Okay . . ."

"So all you have to do is give your arm a quick twist, toward the thumb, and you'll come right out of it." I released her, and offered my own wrist. "Grab me, I'll show you."

After a moment of hesitation, she did as instructed, squeezing my wrist as hard as she could. With a quick yank, I was free. "Well, yeah, you can get away. You're stronger than I am."

"Has nothing to do with strength. My six-year-old daughter can break away from me like this. You try it." This time, I simply offered my open hand, waiting for her to place her wrist in it. When she did, I gripped as hard as I could without bruising. "Now, turn toward the thumb." She did, and I clamped down harder, preventing her escape.

She frowned. "See? You're too strong."

"You grab me now."

"What?"

"Grab me in return, then yank against the thumb. Double the force, see? I promise you, you *will* come loose."

"I feel stupid."

"If I were some crazed stalker, and you had to use this, at the end of the day you'd just feel glad to be alive. Do it."

Her brow creased in concentration as she jerked against my grasp just like I'd instructed. Her look of amazement was priceless as she freed herself. "I did it!" Then she looked at me suspiciously. "You let me go. It can't be that easy. Hold tighter this time."

We practiced a few more times, with me holding her as tightly as I dared. Even then, I could feel the tiny bones in her wrist grinding, and I hoped I wasn't going to leave a mark. Once she felt she'd mastered that, I showed her a few more. How to get out of a two-handed grab. How to get free from a choke hold from behind. How to get loose from a hold on her hair. She picked it up pretty fast, really. I was kinda impressed if I did say so myself.

"Okay, so . . . I get loose, then what do I do?" She bounced a little on her toes, grinning at me. "Can you show me how to kick some ass?"

I snorted. "If it comes to you using this to get away from an attacker, you scream your head off and run like hell. That's the best thing you can do."

Gretchen pouted, turning on the full force of those deep blue eyes and full lips. "Oh, come on, show me something. Just one punch. Anything."

I sighed as I debated with myself. When confronted with an attacker, most people are just going to get themselves hurt if they try to fight back. The best thing to do is get away, run to a safe place. Your garden-variety street mugger isn't going to chase.

Still . . . I couldn't deny any woman the right to defend herself. I'd taught Mira. I was slowly teaching Annabelle. First person to lay a hand on one of my girls was gonna be damn sorry.

"Okay. Make a fist for me." She did, bringing her hands up in a really bad boxer's stance. "No . . . thumb on the outside. You punch someone like that, you'll break your thumb." Automatically, she corrected herself.

I grabbed her by both wrists, like we'd been rehearsing. "You have choices here. Your best choice is to break the hold and run, like I said. But, you can also do the last thing he expects. You will only get one chance to surprise a man, so you have to make it count. From this position, you can yank him into a head butt." I demonstrated, slowly. "I advise against this, mostly because you're gonna knock yourself senseless if you don't do it right. Still, as a last resort, it's an option. Aim for the bridge of the nose. Broken and bloody makes it damn hard for a guy to see.

"You can also break the hold"—I slowly walked her through what we'd been practicing—"and then punch. I'd advise going for the throat if you can, or the eyes." I showed her how to jab with stiff fingers. "If you do it, *mean* it. Put your shoulder behind it, roll your hips, try to punch through the back of his head. You're only going to get one shot."

She watched me intently as I demonstrated, then carefully followed through, copying my motions. Damn, I wished I had more time to really teach her.

"What about kicking him in the nuts?"

I shook my head. "Every man in the world expects a woman to do that. He'll be ready. If you wanna go that route, you wait until he's yanked you close in, then grab him where it counts. You have those long fingernails, put them to use. Dig in, twist, turn, try to yank them off. Even through jeans, that's gonna hurt like a bitch." Even the idea of it made me wanna cringe and hold myself. "If you have to kick, go for the side of the knee, or rake your shoe down the bony part of his shin. Or even better with the heels you wear, stomp on his foot. It'd be just like stabbing him. Unless he wears steel-toed boots."

"And then?"

"And then you *run*, Gretchen. You're not a superhero, you're just a woman who wants to live to see the next sunrise. You run like hell and you make as much noise as you can. Understand?"

"Yeah, I guess so." She sulked a little, mostly for show, then brightened. "Okay, let's do it again."

I wasn't sure how long we worked up there in the roof garden, but it was long enough that Tai came looking for us to see what was up. With a bemused smile, he joined in as a target dummy, and even added a few moves of his own, proving that the big man was more than talk. While we were evenly matched in height, he outweighed me by a good chunk, and he was almost as fast. I didn't like to think what a fight between the two of us would be like. I'd be pretty unhappy running into him in a dark alley, that's for sure.

Finally, Gretchen declared that she was starving and called a halt to our impromptu class. Despite my late dinner the night before, I was pretty damn hungry myself, but as we rode the elevator down, I had to admit I also felt pretty damn satisfied. Hopefully Tai and Bobby could keep teaching her after I left, and then Gretchen would be able to take care of herself. Somehow, that made me feel better.

14

Later, I didn't feel so much better. "But I don't understand *why*."

Gretchen raised a brow at me as Dante zipped up the back of her teeny tiny little dress. I had to wonder if she got a discount, since they used so little fabric. "Would you hide in a hole, if someone was after you?"

"Well, no, but I'm well known for not being too bright." That got a laugh out of her, at least. "Seriously, going to a party is important?"

"Like I said, this is how I pay my rent. There will be people at this party. Important people that I need to keep connections with."

I looked at Tai and Bobby and got zero support. Dante was no help either. He just shrugged and patted her on the shoulder when her dress was zipped. "There you go, Boo."

"Come help me with my hair." Taking him by the hand, they disappeared back into her room.

Once again, I looked at the two bodyguards. "This is nuts."

"It's not as bad as it sounds," Tai insisted. "We'll be at someone's private home. They have their own security, plus probably some extra for the party. There'll be a whole herd of other bodyguards there, just like us. The groupies were disinvited, so it'll just be celebs and their dates. Even Dante isn't coming. If she has to go out, the only place safer would be the White House."

I eyed Bobby, sitting in dour silence. "And you? You're okay with this?"

He shrugged. "I do what I'm told. I don't have to like it." Privately, I thought Bobby was only encouraging this so he could get a shot at whatever this thing was.

Tai looked me over and shook his head, tsking. "If you're going, you need to change. She'll totally leave you behind if you're not up to snuff."

I failed to see what was wrong with what I was wearing, but apparently an I SEE STUPID PEOPLE shirt wasn't elegant enough. Bobby and Tai were already dressed in black slacks and white button-up shirts. I was pretty sure that if either of them stretched too much, both shirts were going to rip right down the back. Big men were just not meant to wear stuff like that.

I had a plain white dress shirt too, stuffed in the bottom of my suitcase. It was, of course, wrinkled all to hell, and I grumbled as I set up the ironing board. Okay, yes, I know how to iron. Doesn't mean I like it.

"No!" We all jumped as Gretchen poked her head out of her room, her hair half done and Dante clucking behind her like a mother hen. "No, you wear the one I got you, the blue silk." And then she was gone again.

Both bodyguards gave me amused smirks and zero help. With a sigh, I traded out shirts and set about ironing the blue silk.

Bobby watched me for all of two minutes before he came and shoved me out of the way. "Oh, for fuck's sake. You're gonna take all night." With the speed of military efficiency, he had my shirt ironed and tossed at me in a matter of moments. "Damn civilians."

When I stripped off my T-shirt to change, Tai whistled lowly. "Damn, man! What'd you do, dance with a lawn mower?"

I looked down at my bare chest, eyeing the interesting collection of scars that dotted my pale skin. Burn splatters down one forearm. Some quarter-sized horseshoe-looking marks on my shoulders. And my crowning achievement, the vicious claw marks raking my left side from armpit to hip. All presents from demons I'd faced, some more formidable than others. "Pretty sure that's one of those questions you're happier not knowing the answer to, Tai."

Even Bobby looked impressed. "That one had to puncture a lung there," he mused, pointing to my Yeti scars.

I ran my fingers over them, feeling the rough ridges along my ribs. "Lung, stomach, intestines, nicked the liver, broke almost every rib on that side, and just barely missed my kidney and my heart." Yeah, Jesse had been a tore-up boy after that one. Sometimes, I wondered why I lived.

"Jesus Christ!" Gretchen's exclamation startled us all, followed by Dante's almost whispered, "Wow." None of us had heard them return.

Suddenly self-conscious, I shrugged into my new shirt. "It's no big deal. I lived."

"Were all those from demon fights?" Gretchen tried to get another look as I buttoned up my shirt, and I frowned and turned away to block her view. Of course, she immediately followed me in a circle until I batted her hands away from my collar with an annoyed growl.

"Yes."

"And you keep doing it?" There was no mistaking the awe in her blue eyes. "Are you nuts?"

"Like I said. Not too bright."

She looked at me like I'd suddenly grown two heads until Dante cleared his throat. "I'm gonna go, Boo, if that's okay. You look great, you don't need me."

"Oh yeah, Dante, thanks." She walked him to the door, kissing his cheek as he left.

He was right, though. She was stunning. I couldn't even tell you what he did to her hair, except it was all piled up on top of her head and falling down in these little wispy tendril thingies. Her dress was a dark teal that brought out a hint of green in her eyes, draping to bare her back and reveal her shimmery soul tattoos again. Her shoes, of course, were high enough to require a building permit.

She turned to face us, giving us a critical once-over. "Well, as soon as Jesse tucks his shirt in, we're ready to go." All eyes in the room looked at me expectantly until I'd done as instructed, but before we could head out the door, I stopped them.

"Wait just a sec." In the pack that contained my armor were my leather bracers. I slid them on, using my teeth to fasten the buckles, then rolled my cuffs down over them. The shirt sleeves would hide them, and at least I felt like I had a bit more defense with them on. Invisible snowflakes peppered my skin as the spells on them settled into place. Joint work, that, Mira's carved symbols combined with Cameron's prayer.

My demon mace went on my belt loop, with Mira's pentacle and Cam's danger disk. I patted my pockets down, trying to think if I could carry anything else inconspicuously, but that really was the sum total of my concealable gear. Demon fighting isn't really what you'd call subtle. I didn't offer an explanation of my actions, and no one else asked, so when I was done, we were off.

I had no idea where we went, exactly, but the street was lined with huge house after mansion after castle. They all had high walls and gated drives, most with little guardhouses to the sides. Some of those had people in them. Most did not.

The sprawling house we pulled up to was designed with a Spanish flavor, and the only reason I knew that was because I worked in an open-air mall with the same decorator. Terra-cotta slate roof, stucco walls, fancy mosaic tiles under our feet. Fountains. That kinda stuff.

I spent more time scoping out the security than the architecture, though. They were easy to spot. First, we had the security force that belonged to the house. You could tell them because they were all wearing identical gray sport coats with a teeny little logo emblazoned on the left breast. They had earpieces and radios clipped to their belts. I counted six before we turned the car over to the valet.

The cops, of course, were outside directing traffic. Two cars, one officer apiece. Probably there to keep the neighbors from calling in complaints.

And then we had the bodyguards, dressed in black slacks and white shirts just like Bobby and Tai. Some of them had jackets on, hiding shoulder rigs just like Gretchen's two bodyguards, but most of them were just big, bulky thugs, so muscle-bound they couldn't have touched their hands behind their backs. Sure, they looked impressive, but when it came down to it, they'd be worse than useless. Mostly because they didn't *know* they were useless. I spotted fifteen I was sure of, and another four or five who were "maybes." Given the size of the crowd, it was obvious that very few people came with personal muscle.

There had to be a hundred people there, easy. A few I recognized. TV personalities, music stars of various genres, couple of football players. Most I didn't. Probably important behind-the-scenes people or something.

"Jesse, come here and meet Alec." Gretchen beckoned me over to greet one of the few people in the world skinnier than me. "This is Alec's house, he's a dear friend of mine."

Alec—his painted-on tan only serving to accentuate the age lines he was trying to hide around his eyes—shook my hand with a clammy touch, and gave me an obvious up-and-down look that was more than friendly. "Well, hello."

"Married." I wiggled my wedding ring at him.

"Pity." He turned a raised brow on Gretchen next. "And you, you hussy. Running around with a married man?"

She rolled her eyes at him. "He's a new bodyguard, Alec. Strictly professional."

"Again, pity. Now, follow me, my dear. Adrian's here and you *must* see what a mess they made of his hair."

Gretchen gave me an apologetic smile as she was whisked away, Tai following at a distance like a big tattooed shadow.

That left me and Bobby, and the odds of witty conversation there were next to nothing. We looked at each other for about two seconds, then turned and walked in opposite directions. Luckily, mine took me toward the hors d'oeuvres table.

I had no idea what I was eating by the handful, but they were at least tasty. I ignored the glares from the catering staff as I camped at the table, and just let my gaze scan the room. Whaddya know; I was rather surprised to spot a face I knew. And not just in a "Hey, that dude is on TV" kinda way. More in a "Hey, I once punched that guy in the face" kinda way.

The last time I saw Travis Verelli, he was in a YouTube video being hauled out of a hotel room in his tighty whities and sock garters. He was an agent, and one of his clients beat him with a phone and tied him up with cords from the window blinds. Considering that he was trying to have me arrested at the time, it made me grin every time I thought of it.

"Travis! Hey, buddy!" You shoulda seen the look on that man's face when I walked over and threw my arm around his shoulders. "Wow, you're looking great!"

"Erm . . . Hi, Jesse. Been a while." There was a deer-in-the-headlights look as he tried to decide how to react in front of his friends and colleagues. I'm guessing screaming and running like a little girl wasn't on the list of acceptable solutions. "Didn't know you were in town." There was a distinct green tinge under his tan. I'll assume he was recalling the sound of his nose crunching under my fist. That's what *I* was doing, anyway.

"Only here for a few days, seeing the sights and all that. We should totally get together before I go. Catch up and all that." Under the guise of a manly one-armed hug, I squeezed his shoulder. Hard.

"Oh yeah. Totally. I um . . . I still have your number, I think." His tone said, *I would rather eat a plate full of maggots*, but he kept that perfect, slightly sick smile plastered in place.

"Rockin'! I'll talk to you soon then." I clapped him hard on the shoulder, enough to stagger him a couple of steps, and walked away, pretending like I hadn't just wiped my greasy hand off on the back of his coat. That gave me a warm fuzzy feeling. Sometimes, evil is fun. I totally get that now.

Other than that, the party was a party. I mean, aside from the fact that no one was wearing entertaining and snarky T-shirts, it could have been a barbecue in my own backyard. Folks mingled, drank, ate. They gossiped and whispered and told bad jokes, just like my buddies, but instead of kilts and cutoff cargo pants, they did it in designer dresses and immaculately tailored suits and tuxes. Same, but not same.

A while later, as I made my way back from the restroom—which was bigger than my kitchen, I might add—I had the distinct pleasure of walking into Travis Verelli again. This time, without his cronies around, his eyes almost shot lasers in my direction. "You." He made the word sound like the vilest of curses. "What the hell are you doing out here?"

"I think that's none of your business, Trav." I leaned against the paneled wall, hooking my thumbs in my pockets to give the air of total indifference. "What about you? Schmoozing more clients to beat you up?"

"I told them all about you, you know. Everyone standing out there. No one's going to hire you. I told them just what kind of things you do." He poked his finger in my chest. "You cost me three clients. Good money!"

I had to smirk at that. "You sure it was me? Wasn't that Internet video of you looking like a total chump?"

I swear, he had froth coming out of his mouth he was so pissed. He got right up in my face to make sure he could spit all over me. Ugh. "You just wait. I have the right connections now, you'll be getting your comeuppance." *Comeuppance? Who talks like that?*

When he tried to jab me again, I caught his wrist, sliding his shirtsleeve up to his elbow. The damning black tattoo was there, as I knew it would be. "Shame shame, Travis. You've been making bad business deals."

He didn't try to jerk free of me, almost proudly showing off his demon brand. "You have no idea the power behind this mark. They'll be coming for you, you know. All your kind. You're all dead men."

I gave his arm a yank, jerking him right up close and personal so he could hear what I had to say. "They already tried, and failed," I growled in his ear. "You wanna try next?"

I don't know what he would have said, because at that moment, a woman screamed. That scream was followed by more, some of fear, some shouts of anger. Something had gone very wrong out there.

The second my attention was diverted, Travis jerked free of my hold and bolted, vanishing into the recesses of the house. I had the choice of chasing him, or finding out what the hell was going on. Of course, I chose to run headlong into unknown danger. It's what I do.

The party was in chaos when I got back out there. I saw at least three fistfights, the combatants rolling on the ground in their nice suits as they tried to pummel the crap out of each other. To my left, a finely coiffed woman reached out and snatched a handful of hair off the head of the woman next to her. The pair of them disappeared in a flurry of sequins and rage-filled screeches, the crowd around them absorbing the brawl with an air of hungry anticipation.

What the hell *was* this? One fight at a party I could see, but four? And where the hell was security?

Only once before had I seen something like this, a rage that spread from person to person like wildfire. A demon had caused it, last time. My demon. *Axel, if this was you, I will find a way to kill you myself.* In a large crowd, the hysteria could cause a riot. People could die.

Cam's danger disk was boiling orange and red swirls when I glanced at it, and I started shoving my way through the seething throng. "Gretchen! Tai!" There was no way they were going to hear me over the shouting.

Some idiot in a tuxedo tried to take a clumsy swing at me as I crossed the room, and blinked stupidly when he found himself flat on his ass instead. After that, they cleared a path for me without really seeming to know why. Maybe in this haze of dog-eat-dog, I was the wolf they'd let pass.

I spotted Bobby first, his broad-shouldered frame clearly marking another empty space in the madness. Another wolf the little dogs were shying away from. Tai was behind him, sheltering Gretchen and Alec against the wall as all hell broke loose.

I hastened to join them when it occurred to me that Alec was the host of this party. And yet not once did he seem concerned for his guests, his property, nothing. He wasn't on the phone, calling the cops, wasn't trying to bring order. He wasn't giving commands to his own security guards.

He was just looking at me, clawing my way across the battlefield that used to be a dinner party. He smiled at me once, the wrinkles around his mouth suddenly failing to follow any natural contour of his face. Even as I shouted "No!" he turned, drew back a fist, and clubbed Tai in the back of the head.

The Maori dropped like a stone, but was almost instantly on his knees again, shaking his head groggily. Down, but not out.

Gretchen stared at her friend in astonishment. "Alec, what are you doing?!"

Alec didn't seem to hear her. With another shove from behind, he sent Bobby sprawling and made a beeline for me. Even then, it took me a few moments to realize that the man's face wasn't Botoxed to hell, it was smooth. Even the wrinkles were artificial-looking, placed there rather than being earned. Artfully carved into a semblance of humanity.

"Get Gretchen out of here!" Without waiting to see if the other guys obeyed, I flicked the cap off my demon mace with my thumb and released the palm-sized canister in his face the moment he got close. It didn't even faze him, and I was forced to retreat out of the cloud of cumin and cayenne. *Okay, not a demon then.*

Whatever this thing was, it was faster than the last one I'd faced, more coordinated. Not-Alec lunged for me, and I only barely ducked under one grasping arm. Somehow, I knew I didn't want that thing getting a grip on me. As I moved past it, I kicked it square in the kidneys (if it had kidneys), using its own momentum to send it careening into the crowd. By the time it turned around, I had Mira's pentacle charm in my hand, and the next time it grabbed for me, I caught its arm, mashing the blessed star against its bare wrist.

Nothing. No reaction at all. *Not a zombie.* And now I was within reach. It hammered a forearm down on my shoulder like a freakin' anvil, and the leather bracer on that arm flared white-hot for a second. I'd almost forgotten I was wearing them. I was left with a dull ache instead of a shattered collarbone. Mira's spells, saving me again.

My fists found its ribs, landing blows that would have dropped a human this size, but I felt only a dull thud under my knuckles. No ridges of ribs, no tight muscles, no squishy guts. What the hell *was* this thing? And of course, the punches had no effect. It kept advancing, like Frankenstein's monster, inexorable. I could only dodge those grasping arms so long, and I dared one last elbow to the face before I darted out of reach again.

Again, my bracer flared hot — cooler than before, how much longer would the spell last? — and Alec's perfectly formed nose smashed sideways . . . and stayed that way. The thing paused, blinking as it found one eye partially blocked by a blob of what used to be a nose.

"Oh, I got you now." Normally, I wouldn't kick that high. Leaving your feet in a fight is the best way to get knocked on your ass. But nothing else had made a dent, until that moment, and I needed to exploit that weakness.

With a two-step run-up, I launched a jumping side kick square into Alec's formerly normal face, the thing staggering back a couple of paces as I landed light on my feet.

My boot left a perfect print, like I'd walked through soft mud.

Before I could ponder just what that meant, Bobby did something monumentally stupid. I'd forgotten he was there, actually, taking it for granted that they'd spirited their charge out like they were supposed to.

His arm snaked around the tall creature's throat, putting it in a choke hold that would have meant lights out for anything else. As I'd discovered already, this thing wasn't going to go down that easily.

"Bobby, don't!"

My warning was too late, of course. The thing spun in Bobby's hold, wrapping its arms around his rib cage and bodily lifting the big marine off his feet. Still, Bobby refused to let go, smashing his forehead into the thing's mangled face twice, even as his own face was going blue.

God, I could hear his ribs cracking as the thing

squeezed. The sound was louder, it seemed, than Gretchen's screams and the distant sirens outside as help finally arrived. "Let him go!" It was me the thing wanted, dammit, not Bobby.

The only thing I could think to do was hit it until it stopped moving. The spells on my right bracer lasted exactly one hit, and caved the back of the thing's head in. The left one lasted two more before it flared into ordinary, scorched leather, and by that point, the creature's head was a lopsided mass of ... I have no idea what. One ear was on top of what remained of its pulp of a head, the other was caved so far in I couldn't even find it. What had appeared to be hair was now a solid mess of brownish paste, and one cheekbone jutted out at an impossible angle to the rest of the face.

Staggering on its two feet, it dropped Bobby, which was really all I'd needed. The bodyguard fell to the ground and didn't move, blood trickling from his nose and mouth.

I expected the thing to turn and come at me again, but apparently having its head mashed into a Picasso painting was causing some problems. It turned to look at me once with its one functional eye, the other smashed closed by Bobby's forceful head butts, then lumbered off into the chaos, tossing people from its path like they were so much kindling.

I wanted to follow. Everything in me ached to chase it down and kill it. But I didn't know how, still, and I was pretty sure I couldn't take it one-on-one. And we had a man down.

Gretchen was leaning over Bobby, tears streaming

down her face as she tried to wipe the blood away, smearing it more than anything. "Oh God . . . Oh God . . . Bobby . . ." Her phone was in her hand, though, smart girl that she was, and I could tell she already had the paramedics on the way. Tai towered over them, gun drawn but pointed safely down, standing grim guard, but the lunacy that had overtaken the party guests seemed to be fading. It left behind a room full of the broken and the bleeding.

The source of the rage-inducing spell wasn't hard to find, once I got a moment to focus. The faint hint of sulfur lead me back to the buffet table and the cans of flaming Sterno. Someone—our mashable friend if I had to guess—had placed little wooden coins in the blue flames. Most of them were destroyed already, but I managed to find one that was only half charred. On it, a demonic sigil had been etched. It was half erased by the chemical flame, but I could still feel the prickle of magic as I swiped my thumb over it. With the design altered by the burning wood, it was harmless now, but I stuck it in my pocket anyway. It was too dangerous to just leave things like that lying around.

15

Hospitals look very different when you're not the one in the bed. The chairs are uncomfortable, the vending machines are full of stale food, and I'm pretty sure that time passes there according to no known law of physics. It might have even been running backward, and wouldn't that be helpful? Rewind the evening and start over?

Bobby apparently didn't have any next of kin to call, and Gretchen refused to leave until she knew if he was going to be all right. So we sat in the waiting room, watching white coats come and go, surrounded by some of the other party casualties. Someone brought Tai an ice pack for his head, once he'd made it very clear he wasn't leaving Gretchen's side, and after I snarled at a few of the nurses, they steered wide around me too. I guess I looked bad, but none of the blood was mine, I swear.

The most interesting event was the moment they wheeled Alec through the emergency room doors. Alec, the party host, whose head was notably *not* pulped beyond recognition, though he had a couple of black eyes and some swelling going on.

Sneaky thing that I was, I managed to overhear the paramedics as they handed him over to the attending physician. "Found him stuffed in a closet, beat to crap. Freakin' crazy rich people. Probably had the whole party hopped up on something."

They weren't wrong, exactly. The whole party had been hopped up on something, but it was nothing that would show up in a drug test. I flipped the warped piece of wood over the back of my knuckles as I pondered it. *Where did you get this, hm?*

Alec—the real Alec—had been beaten and stuffed in a closet so Not-Alec could take his place. That I was pretty sure of. Impossible to know if that had happened during the party, or long before any guests arrived, but the idea had led me to several conclusions.

One—I was pretty sure Not-Alec and the centurion were one and the same creature. So, while the thought of only one enemy was comforting, the thought of an enemy that could change shapes was not. I needed to find out how to detect it sooner, since it seemed to be getting better at taking human form.

Two—My hands were covered in dried blood—Bobby's, I was sure—but they were also covered in a layer of gray . . . something. It flaked off as it dried, turning to powder, just like the muck on my hands at the movie lot. I wasn't sure what it was. It didn't smell like anything, and tasted faintly like chalk (yes, I know that tasting it wasn't smart, but . . . you do what you gotta). I saved some of it in a folded piece of paper for examination later. Whatever it was, it was connected to the creature.

Three—It wasn't a demon. The mace would have sent him scrambling. It wasn't one of the Yeti's zombie pets. The blessed pentacle would have seared it like a hot brand. As the centurion, it hadn't spoken, but as Alec it had. Unless that had been Real-Alec, instead of Not-

Alec, and . . . a person could hemorrhage something trying to follow all the twists and turns.

When I'd touched it, there was no spark of magic, nothing I could sense. No cloves, no sulfur. Almost like it was as dull and neutral as I myself was. Inert. So it couldn't have created the little riot-inducing coins. Not on its own, anyway. It had to have help. Something controlling it, or at least partnered with it. Something that had known, long before we arrived, that Gretchen would be at that party.

I scribbled all my thoughts down on a yellow legal pad that I'd stolen from the nurses' station, scratching out false starts and dead ends with enough force to rip through three layers of paper. Anyone who found it would think they were the ramblings of a madman, but I had to do something to organize the buzzing in my head. I still felt like there was something missing. I had all the pieces, but they just weren't connecting in a way that would point a big flashy arrow at the bad guy.

On the other side of the room, Gretchen shook a doctor's hand, then came back to her seat, gathering up her purse. "Bobby's sleeping, and probably will be for quite a while. They think he'll be all right, but they're still not sure what internal injuries he has. Something about watching him for crush syndrome or something. The doctor says we should go home and get a little rest, come back in a few hours."

Since sunrise had passed about an hour ago, rest seemed like the best course of action for all of us. But the thing had known we were at that party. We couldn't go back where we were expected. "Where would be the last place someone would expect to see you? Someplace you never go."

"Um . . . the beach?"

"Tai, take us to the beach. Doesn't matter which one."

As we drove, I briefed them on what I'd deduced about our shape-shifting friend. Neither of them had any ideas on the matter, but I felt better keeping them informed.

It was early morning in late December, so I wasn't sure how many people would be at the beach. Luckily, aside from a few joggers and dog walkers, we seemed to have the place largely to ourselves. Gretchen kicked off her shoes and walked down toward the water's edge, Tai sticking close to her side.

I just watched up and down the sands, gray in the early morning light, listening to the faint pulse of the ocean somewhere in the back of my ears. I pulled the hair tie from my ponytail, letting the light breeze ruffle my long hair. The seabirds called, already swooping low to see if we had any treats to offer, but it was still a sound that belonged. Something right and natural. It was like meditating, and I continued to breathe in time with the tide until my phone rang.

"Dawson." At the sound of Ivan's deep, gravelly voice, relief coursed through me so hard I almost sat down in the sand. "I am here."

The old man was here, and suddenly, it didn't matter if I was pissed off at him or not. He was here, and he'd fix this shit. I told him where to find us, and waited.

By the time Ivan got there, Gretchen was sacked out in the backseat of the Town Car, sleeping as best she could. Tai had the radio on softly, his eyes closed as he rested in the front seat, but I didn't think he was sleeping. In fact, his head came up when he heard me stand, his eyes watching my every move until he was sure things were okay.

"Ivan!"

The enormous white-haired man strode across the sands, his black trench coat flapping around him like wings. I had to wonder if he knew he still looked like death walking. Probably the kind of death that would grind your bones to jelly and eat it on toast. Ivan's a big boy. "Dawson! There you are!"

"Man, it is *so* good to see you." We did the one-armed manly hug thing, Ivan pounding me on the shoulders like he was trying to mash my back through my front. "You have any trouble getting here?"

"*Ni.* I have visited Los Angeles before." Ivan then leaned back to look me up and down. "You are not to be looking well. What has happened?"

"Christ, where do I even start?"

We found seats on the beach, far enough away that we wouldn't disturb Tai and Gretchen. First, I turned over the half-burned demon sigil. "Destroy this somehow. Don't burn it." The old man took it grimly, tucking it away in a coat pocket with no further questions. Next, I poured out the little envelope of gray dust into my palm. "What do you think this is?"

The old man wet his finger then dipped it in the powder, first sniffing then tasting it. (See? It's not just me!) "Hmph. It is to be tasting like clay."

"What, like . . . Play-Doh?" Anna had Play-Doh, it

came in bright colors, had a distinctive smell, and was salty tasting. (Oh, don't even act like that. You ate it when you were a kid too.) This powdery stuff wasn't Play-Doh.

Ivan was apparently familiar with the concept, and gave me a scathing look. "*Ni*, clay. Like ... dirt. Soil. From the earth."

"I smelled damp soil, at the movie lot." Freshly turned earth, in fact. Like a new grave. How's that for a somber thought? "Why would he be coated in clay?"

"Perhaps you should be starting this story from the beginning. Explain to me what is to be happening." Yeah, seemed logical, so I did. I think I included all the pertinent details in a way that made sense. Helped to have them scribbled down on my yellow legal pad. Except for that part where I was out here doing a favor for a demon. I kinda threw that in at the end, hoping he might miss it. That didn't go over so well.

In fact, I don't think I ever saw the old man speechless until that moment. His craggy face turned red all the way up into his snowy hair, his jaw clenched until I could hear his teeth grinding, and even the birds overhead suddenly found a different place to be.

"You are to be realizing that this is *foolish*, *tak*?" Funny how he could make "foolish" sound exactly like "suicidally insane."

"I know. Believe me, I know. But it had to be done."

Ivan let out a long breath through his nose, clearly still pissed but trying to be calm. "Often, we do things that must be done, regardless of whether they *should* be done." He shook his head, then ran a finger through the gray dust in my hand again. "I am having a thought about this."

"Oh?"

"Mm. When I was to being a small boy, many years ago, I lived in a little town, very far from any city. In those days, the old ways were to be existing beside the new. Magic and science all at once. Superstition alongside diagnosis.

"As always in those times, there was to being a powerful man who wanted more."

"More what?" I was fascinated. Ivan had never spoken of his past before. At least not to me.

"Everything. Power, supplies, land. Fear. And he would send the soldiers. We had little. Barely enough to live, not enough to spare. The elders of the town, they were to be knowing when the soldiers would come again. They went to the priest, and asked him to pray for protection."

With one thick, gnarled finger, Ivan drew a symbol in the sand between us. It wasn't one I recognized.

"He found this in an old book. No one knew where the book was to be coming from, it was just always to being there in the church. Following it, they shaped a man from the very dirt of the fields. A great man, taller than I am to being now, twice as wide. The legs were like tree trunks. And with this sigil, they said to him 'live.' And he did."

"Wait, I know this legend. You're talking like a golem, right? Isn't that a Jewish myth?" Right there, I'd exhausted my golem knowledge. I had a vague memory of one being connected to Prague, somehow, but that was it.

Ivan smiled faintly. "Many peoples of the world have shared stories. And magics."

"So did it work? This golem, did it protect your town?"

"Mm. To start. The powerful man eventually lost power, and another took his place. And another, and another. Always they came, the soldiers, just wearing different colors. Always, the clay man would kill them. But something dark was to be happening. With every death, the clay man gained more will of his own, as if the blood fed him life.

"There was to being a day when he would no longer obey, when he turned on his creator. It was decided then to be destroying him, and to never build such a man again."

"So did they? Destroy it, I mean?" *And please oh please tell me it was easy to do.*

"*Tak*. They erased the sigil, and he fell to dust."

Erase the sigil. Oh sure, lemme just strip the thing naked while it was pounding on me and look to see where someone had carved on it.

"This thing, could it change shapes? Look like real people?"

Ivan shrugged. "I am not to be knowing. It did not, in my memory."

"Could it speak?"

The old man frowned a bit in thought. "It did not, at first. When they came to destroy it, it did then."

"What did it say?"

"It said only 'Please, do not.'"

Specific details notwithstanding, Ivan's golem legend sounded like my best bet. A biddable minion, strong, almost indestructible. That's the kind of errand boy I'd send, if I were a demon. A moldable clay man, capable of impersonating anyone.

"If it *could* look like someone else, how would I tell? Is there some kind of test?" Not-Alec had been human enough to fool my eyes, and my danger sense.

"A real man will bleed, Dawson. A clay man will not." Ivan looked disappointed that I hadn't figured that out myself. "And he will bear something belonging to the one who created him. A token, binding his will to his master."

Well, hell, that could be anything. I rubbed my forehead, trying to ease the slight ache there. "So even if I kill this thing, I gotta worry about who's pulling the strings behind it."

"It would to be seeming so." Ivan erased the sigil from the sand with a swipe of his hand. "You should have been informing me of this before. This is not to being a defensible position." He gestured around the nearly empty beach.

"Do we really want to get into who did and didn't tell each other what?" I raised a brow, challenging, but it was aimed at the frothy waves a few yards away. Still couldn't quite bring myself to stare the old man down.

He sighed. "Perhaps it is something to be 'getting into.' It is impossible to be knowing when we may have another chance, *ni*?"

"Okay. You go first." I brushed the golem dust off my

hands and leaned back on my arms, prepared to listen at least. I mean, how long could I really hold a grudge anyway? "You lied to me about how many champions there are. Why?"

"Because information that you do not have cannot be taken from you. I have long feared that the forces we fight would rise up against us, organized. If each of you believed that there were but few, perhaps our enemies would believe it also." He shook his head a bit. "It is only now, when we are to being under attack, that I worry I have made the wrong decision. When they come for me—and I am to be believing that they will—much knowledge will be lost. Things I cannot enter into Grapevine, memories and skills that cannot be put into words."

A samurai welcomes his death, if it is a good and honorable one. Still, Ivan's fatalistic tone made me squirm uncomfortably. I didn't like to think about it. "You're talking like you'd lose."

He smirked a little. "I am to being old, Dawson. Sometimes I wonder if I have not outlived my purpose."

"So how many of us are there, really?"

"At last count, one hundred and twenty-three. Not to be counting our comrades within the Catholic church. I have been attempting to recruit more, in recent years, but so few believe in such things, in these modern days."

Damn. A hundred and twenty-three champions. Way more than I'd ever dreamed. "Who else knows? You, Viljo . . . who else?"

"You." He traced idle designs in the sand, just to give his hands something to do. I understood, I often did the same thing myself in uncomfortable situations. "No one else is to be knowing the whole of it. I am to be giving instructions to Viljo. Grapevine is to be wide open to you. Learn them all. It may to being important at some future day."

I frowned. "Sounds like you're planning a sudden retirement, Ivan." And like he was picking me to be his replacement. Um, no? I was gonna retire after this myself, remember?

"I fought my first demon when I was to being younger than your Estéban. I have seen the best and the worst that our kind offers to others. I loved a beautiful woman, and lost her. I fathered a daughter and have seen her grow into a fine woman. I have brought men together who work to make this world a safer place. I think I am entitled to my rest, when it is to be coming. But I will not rush headlong toward it, either." His grin was a little lopsided, and he poked me in the shoulder almost hard enough to shove me over. Either that, or I was way more tired than I realized. "You worry much, Jesse Dawson."

With that, he heaved himself up off the sand, straightening his long coat. "Am I correct in believing that you are not to be having a safe place to retreat to?"

I stood and brushed myself off too. "Not sure. This thing, someone's telling it our moves, someone who knows where Gretchen will be. It could be waiting for us back at the hotel."

Ivan looked me over again, reaching out to pluck at the sleeve of my blue silk shirt. Only then did I realize that it was charred in places, revealing where the spells on my leather bracers had scorched through the cloth. "You are to be needing sleep. And weapons. I will return to this hotel with you, and we will see what may to be waiting for you."

That actually made me feel a little better.

Luckily for us, there was nothing waiting for us at the Masurao Grand. Ivan inspected Tai's newly set wards, declaring them remarkable. He checked over The Way and my armor, declaring them passable. In that suite, we were as safe as we could possibly be. At least until we could arrange something else, something no one could trace.

"Walk with me, Dawson." I escorted him down the elevator to the lobby, where he stopped to hand me a folded piece of paper. "This is to being the address of a local woman. She may be able to help you translate the contract."

I looked it over. The name said Cindy Lee. "Do you trust her?"

"*Ni*. And she will require payment for any work she is to be doing. But she is to being the best I could find." He busied himself buttoning up his coat, though there was no way he needed it as nice as the day was turning out to be. "I will to be remaining in town for a few days. If you are to be needing magical assistance, call me. I understand it is to being unsafe for your Mira to be working her magics." Christ, I was gonna kill Estéban for his big mouth.

"Yeah, I'll give you a holler." We clasped forearms, and I held his in my grip when he would have pulled away. "When I'm done here, Ivan, we need to talk more. I think . . . I think I'm done." There, I'd said it. Saying it out loud makes it true, right? I was committed now.

Whatever plans Ivan had for me, if I walked away, that was the end of it. He owed me that much.

After a moment, he nodded. "We will to be seeing."

To my sleep-deprived eyes, the sunlight outside was garishly bright, reflecting harshly off the windows of the cars parked out front. I stood with Ivan while we waited for the valet to bring his around. Neither of us could seem to think of anything else to say.

"And he will be a king among kings . . ." The moment the doorman was distracted, Felix appeared, shuffling along in his brightly colored rags. His whiskey-colored eyes were fixed on Ivan, and he smiled broadly, the wrinkles in his face deep and jolly. Even his dreadlocks seemed bushier today, a reflection of his apparently jubilant mood. "He will walk with his head above other men. His arm will protect the weak, his hammer the innocent. And he will be rewarded for his duties on the happiest of days."

Ivan looked down at the old homeless man, and I was struck by the odd juxtaposition. Towering Ivan, frost-haired and severe in his black coat, standing over stooped, wizened Felix, who seemed to walk along in his own personal rainbow. I couldn't help but watch curiously as Felix reached out a hand to rest on the bigger man's chest, his fingers too gnarled to lie straight. The black man's smile faded a little, becoming a bit sad around his already worn edges. "I am sorry."

Ivan nodded. "I am not."

Felix patted him a few times, fidgeting with Ivan's shirt buttons like he would tidy them right up, then shuffled away as the doorman came to hustle him off.

I raised a brow at my mentor. "What was that about?"

He didn't answer me.

It didn't occur to me at the time to wonder how Felix had known that in his youth, Ivan fought demons with a hammer. A maul, to be precise. And by the time I did think to wonder, I already had my answer.

16

Upstairs, I found Tai crashed out on one couch, his arm draped over his eyes, and Gretchen on the other, her head pillowed in Dante's lap. No idea just when he'd shown up, but his presence seemed to be doing her good. He smoothed her hair gently, giving me the "don't you dare wake her up" glare. I just held my hands up. I fully intended to find myself a horizontal position pretty damn quick too.

But first . . . my conversation with Ivan on the beach kept trickling through my head. *A clay man will not bleed, Dawson.* For my own peace of mind, I had some testing to do.

Tai wasn't the golem. That I knew. I mean, magic just oozed out his pores, and the golem had none as far as I could tell. Not to mention that he'd been there tonight when the thing attacked, so that let him out.

Gretchen wasn't, obviously. Even fully clothed, the tattoos on her back were there, and my skin itched just thinking about it. Almost like I could see them swirling through her T-shirt. Almost like I could hear them crying out.

Dante . . . well, I suppose I should test him just to be sure, but surely someone would have noticed if he'd been replaced. His expressive face held none of the smooth waxiness I'd come to associate with our centurion friend, and Gretchen was his best friend. If he wasn't himself, she'd be the one to know. Still, if I tested one, I'd have to test them all. It was only fair.

"Dante, does she have some pins or something around? Sewing kit, maybe?"

He gave me a puzzled look, but nodded toward Gretchen's room. "On her dresser, should be some. Don't touch anything."

I rolled my eyes at him as I went to find something sharp and pointy. Like I was gonna do a panty raid or something, geez.

Gretchen's room was not nearly as decadent as I'd been imagining. Her bed was covered in stuffed animals and pillows, done in shades of tan and pale blue. Her clothes were strung all over the floor wherever she'd dropped them, and her closet doors stood wide open, revealing heaps of shoes beneath a kaleidoscope of gowns and other garments. Other than the sheer volume of it, it could have been any girl's room, anywhere.

A huge mirror surrounded by lights crowned a low table on one side, and curiosity made me go check out the pictures tucked around the frame. Gretchen and friends, mostly, Dante appearing in more than half of them, the only sign of the passage of time being the changes in his hairstyle and color. Tai and Bobby were there too, though usually standing sternly in the background, only caught on film by accident. Other people, some famous, some not, all with plastic smiles for their best friend of the moment.

One picture, down toward the bottom, was a school photo of a young blond girl. At first, I thought it was an old one of Gretchen, but looking at the year on it, I realized it had to be the sister. The one who was getting married. Because I'm pushy at heart, I moved the picture up higher on the frame, letting it set at eye level. Maybe seeing that would change Gretchen's mind about her sister's nuptials.

On the low table, practically hidden in all the tiny pots and cakes of makeup and hair frillies, I found a small box of safety pins. That'd do nicely. And in her private bathroom, I found a box of bandages and some antiseptic. Perfect. First Aid Man, that's me.

Gretchen was sitting up when I returned to the living room. "What are you doing?"

"Little test. Just to make sure we're all who we say we are." I fished a safety pin out of the box, opening it. "Who wants to go first?" No one was gonna volunteer, but Gretchen and Dante watched closely as I crouched at Tai's side and jabbed the big Maori in the pad of his thumb. He twitched, grumbled, but didn't wake up.

A drop of dark red blood welled at the pinprick, and I swabbed it and bandaged it like a good little nurse. "Me next." Grabbing another pin, I gave myself the same treatment, showing off my bleeding finger to Gretchen and Dante for verification. "See? All human here."

"Why exactly are we doing this?" Gretchen offered her hand, and I stabbed her with a fresh pin.

"Because I think I know what that thing is that's been attacking us, and if I'm right, it shouldn't bleed. Shouldn't be *able* to bleed." A droplet of blood welled up on her finger, and she stuck it in her mouth in lieu of a bandage. We both turned to look expectantly at Dante.

"Really?" When we just kept looking at him, he grumbled and held out his hand. "Why is the black man always the suspect?"

Gretchen chuckled, resting her head on his shoulder, and I jabbed him in the finger. For a heartbeat, nothing happened, but just when my adrenaline was about to kick in, a tiny bit of blood seeped to the surface. "Congrats, Dante. You pass." I blotted it away with a tissue, then handed him a bandage.

A knock sounded at the door, which brought Tai immediately awake. "Oh good, room service is here."

I blinked at him. "I stab you in the hand, you don't wake up. But one hint of food, and you're bright-eyed and bushy-tailed." He just grinned and shrugged at me as I got up to answer the door. "Hey, Dante? Burn those tissues, okay?" Blood wasn't something I wanted just lying around for any old demon or spell caster to pick up. Even I knew that much.

"Yessir."

Spencer was waiting at the door when I opened it, and he grinned as he pushed the cart in. "Hey, Jesse Dawson! How's it going?"

"Not bad, man, yourself?" I stuck my hand out to him, and when he reached to shake mine, I stabbed him in the back of the hand with the safety pin I'd palmed.

"Ow!" I held him until I saw blood, then let go. "What was that for?"

"Amusement." I could be nice, though. I handed him a bandage.

Instead of being pissed off—and if someone stabbed me with a safety pin, that's exactly what *I'd* be—he got that look again, like he'd just seen a glimpse of the real Santa Claus. "You're testing for something, aren't you? Taking DNA maybe? Ooh! Implanting me with a microchip! No, wait, vaccinating me against an alien virus! Man, I gotta write this down . . ." He patted down his pockets until he found a pen, then scribbled some notes on our ticket. "I can totally use this, this is good stuff."

There are so many kinds of crazy in the world. Spencer was his own unique brand. "Just park the cart over there, man." I pointed generally in the direction of the dining table.

There was a tiny whoosh from the fireplace as Dante incinerated the bloody tissues, and Tai barely let Spencer get the cart stopped before he started pawing through the plates.

"We weren't sure what you'd want, but I figured bacon was a safe bet." He handed me a plate heaped with it, and my stomach gave a loud growl. It had been a long time since the mushroomy things at the party last night.

"Bacon is perfect." I stuffed several pieces in my mouth, then realized that Spencer was still standing there, staring at all of us. "I'm still not tipping you. Get the hell out."

With a sigh, he departed.

"You know that guy?" Tai asked, and I just mumbled something around my mouth full of bacon. I wasn't claiming responsibility for Spencer, no how.

Before I could gorge myself completely on my breakfast, something buzzed in my jeans pocket. I hadn't thought about my phone in so long, I'd forgotten I even had it. I'd also forgotten to call my wife for like two days. Oops.

Taking the bacon with me, I retreated to the spare bedroom. "Hey, baby!"

There was a long pause at the other end of the line, and then Mira sighed. "I'm guessing from the sound of your voice that you're perfectly fine. So now I don't know if I should be relieved, or furious."

"I vote both. I deserve it." I flopped on the bed, munching on my breakfast. "I am *so* sorry, baby. Things got a little nuts out here and I completely lost track of time." Come to think of it, I wasn't even sure what day it was. Not good, when we had a mysterious New Year's Eve deadline breathing down our necks.

"Yeah, we saw."

"What?"

"You've been all over the tabloid shows this week. Beating up paparazzi, going in and out of hospitals and dance clubs. . . . That was a nice silk shirt she bought you, by the way."

Inwardly, I cringed. I could only imagine how those pictures looked. "Would you believe I've destroyed that shirt already?"

"It wouldn't surprise me any." She hesitated a moment. "You *are* okay, right?"

"Fine and dandy. The hospital trip wasn't mine."

"Oh. That's good, I guess."

There was something important I was supposed to ask her, but it took me a few minutes to remember what it was. "Oh! Hey, do you know any more about . . . y'know."

"No. Test is still negative. I'm still late."

"Maybe you should go see Bridget. I mean, what if something's wrong?" That thought chilled me clear down to my core. What if something *was* wrong with Mira? What if it was something really bad?

"She knows. We've talked about it. If it goes on much longer, we'll do something. Right now, it still falls into the realm of stress or just plain getting older."

"You're not getting older. You're what, like twenty-two?" That at least earned me a chuckle from my thirty-something wife. "Hey, you know I love you, right?"

"Yeah, Jess. I know. I love you too."

We spent a few minutes catching up on Annabelle's antics and Estéban's high school drama. I hadn't realized until that moment how homesick I was. God, I wanted to see my family, smell my little girl's hair, kiss my wife. I didn't want to be out here in La La Land anymore.

My phone started giving me the sad little chirp to remind me that I hadn't charged it in forever. "Baby, I gotta go, my phone's dying."

"Okay. Jess, please be careful out there. It's making me nervous."

"Hey, you know me. I'm always careful." I'm not sure she heard me, though, as that was the moment my phone gave up the ghost. *Dammit.* I didn't get to tell her good-bye. At least I'd snuck an "I love you" in there before it croaked.

Not saying good-bye felt like bad juju, and I couldn't shake the feeling as I returned to the living room.

"So what do we do now?" Gretchen looked at me expectantly.

"*We* do nothing. *I* am going to go wander through the hotel and stab more people with pins."

Tai raised a brow. "Seriously? You think they'll let you do that?"

"It's Hollywood, right? And I'm with Gretchen Keene, right?" I nodded toward the movie star in question. "According to her, that means I can do anything I want and no one will say anything."

And apparently, I could. You'd think someone would object to a random guy strolling through the hotel kitchens, poking people with safety pins, but I got surprisingly little resistance. Well, until I got to the head of hotel security. I guess poking him with a pin was probably not high on my list of smart acts.

The nice security men delivered me back to the suite, and Tai, who answered the door, promised them I would be on my very best behavior from then on. Before I could come in and take my lumps like a good boy, Gretchen came out the door, obviously dressed for a trip out.

"Um . . . where are you going?"

"Your friend Ivan gave you the address, right? For the translator?"

Tai gave me a look that said he'd been trying to talk her out of it for some time now, obviously with zero success.

"You realize that there is a big mud man out there who seems to know your every move, right? You're safer here."

Her jaw firmed obstinately. "Look, whoever sent this golem thing, it's because of my contract. If I'm going to defend myself against whatever this is, I have to know first and foremost why it's here and what it wants."

Dammit. When the girl's right, she's right.

"Okay, but we're all running on fumes right now. Let us get some rest and we'll go this afternoon. Fair?"

I think she still would have balked if Dante hadn't backed me up. "He's right, Boo. You look like death warmed over. A few hours of peaceful sleep in a safe place . . . you'll thank me later."

Finally, Gretchen relented, allowing Dante to slip her purse off her shoulder. "Okay. But I'm setting an alarm. Four hours, then we go."

That, I could live with. Hell, I'd lived on a lot less for a lot longer.

Dante left, mumbling something about appointments or something, and everyone else fell into a coma. I didn't even mind that I was once again plastered to the leather sofa.

My dreams, though . . . I hadn't had too many bad ones since I banished the Yeti last fall. And this one wasn't bad, per se. Just . . . odd.

It was night, that much was certain, and as I took long strides out of a tunnel, the stars seemed unusually bright. Almost like they were fake, or like there were too many of them in the night sky for reality.

Semi-conscious-me noted the oddity, but dream-me didn't seem to care. I stepped out of the tunnel, feeling concrete give way to hard-packed dirt beneath my boots. The air still smelled of the heat of the day, of sweat and breath of people only recently absent. Dream-me was glad they were gone.

I stepped from the tunnel (again, like I was on a perpetual loop) into an enormous open space. The dirt field spread out before me, silent and waiting. I was waiting too, I realized. Waiting for someone, or something. Deep down, I knew that whatever it was, it wasn't coming.

I stepped from the tunnel, and I could feel palpable fear beating at my back. Weariness, pain, anger ... whatever was behind me had given all it could, and there was simply nothing left to wring out of it. It was finished.

I stepped from the tunnel, and across the great open area, someone stood. Even with the unnatural starlight, it was too far away to see who it was. It was tall and slender, a black shadow against the blacker night (and I had to wonder, how could such a brightly lit night be black?). The next time I came out of the tunnel, the hard-packed dirt was empty again.

I think I must have stepped from the mysterious tunnel a hundred times. A thousand, maybe. Over and over again in that endlessly looping dream, out onto an open field of dirt, beaten solid under thousands of tramping feet. I never figured out what I was waiting for, or if the distant shadowy figure was it. I never figured out what was waiting in the tunnel behind me, or if it was enemy or friend.

I do know that when Tai's hand grabbed my shoulder, jolting me awake, I came up swinging. My fist slapped into his hand with a resounding smack, and we both just blinked at each other for long moments.

"Bad dream?"

I played it over in my head again, then just shrugged. "I honestly have no idea." My dreams had come true before. Well, just one dream, but it was enough to set a precedent. What the hell did this one mean? I had the last one for four years before it finally happened. I had to wonder if and when this one would pop out of my brain and into reality. Somehow, this one scared me more than the Yeti dream ever had, and I didn't even know why.

17

I didn't even know L.A. *had* a Chinatown, but sure enough there was one, and that's where Ivan's horribly scrawled directions sent us. We had to park the car and walk, and as we threaded our way down the crowded street, I felt like a tourist, gawking around at the ornately decorated buildings. Oddly, instead of it marking me as an outsider, I fit right in with the rest of the sightseers, everyone around us craning necks and snapping pictures in front of local landmarks. Like most things out here, Chinatown was geared toward the almighty tourist dollar, with flashy colors and music, gold leaf and neon. Twice, we had to dodge frantically dancing Chinese dragons, their puppeteers' feet moving in sync beneath the thick fringed edges, and there didn't even seem to be any special occasion warranting the display.

I had a hard time picturing Ivan walking down this street, all severe in his black trench coat, a black mark on the carefully choreographed gaiety. Of course, I was rapidly coming to realize that I knew very little about the man himself. It was impossible to say what had drawn him down here to find this person he'd now sent us to locate.

"Here. I think we turn here." Gretchen led the way as we left the clamoring street behind. Tai and I spread out some, flanking her protectively as the voices behind us dwindled to nothing within a few yards. Now this, this was somewhere I could picture Ivan frequenting.

I couldn't tell if it was supposed to be a street or an alley. It was narrow, and clogged with Dumpsters and discarded paraphernalia from the surrounding businesses. No one would ever be able to get a vehicle down it. A thin trickle of water (we'll hope it was water) ran from a gutter, down the middle of the uneven paving stones, and vanished into a sewer grate with a sad little tinkle of sound.

No one was here, I realized. No employees sneaking out back for a cigarette break, no homeless people scrounging in the trash. No lost tourists, except for us. Goose bumps whispered along my shoulders, and I rubbed my thumb over the disk hanging from my belt loop. Around the edges, it was faintly purple.

The doors along the walls were mostly padlocked shut, blank and anonymous, until we reached one that was not. A sign hung on the wall, written in Asian characters I didn't recognize. It was a rather utilitarian sign, generic in its plainness. No hint of "welcome" about it, but no sense of "fuck off" either.

The metal door itself was ajar a few inches, allowing the thick aroma of incense to escape into the dank alley. There was a light on inside, dim and flickering. Candles, maybe?

"Do we knock?" Gretchen looked at me questioningly.

"Oh, hell yes." I didn't know what kind of person might specialize in reading demonic script, but I was willing to wager that barging in on such a person unannounced would be hazardous to everyone's health.

Reaching past her, I rapped my knuckles on the metal sharply, and was rewarded with the faint tingle of a ward flaring. I had to smirk a little. The heady incense almost drowned out the distinctive scent of cloves, and I had to wonder if that had been done on purpose.

Within, a voice answered in a language I didn't speak, but the sound of "coming!" is pretty universal. Within moments, an elderly Asian woman opened the door, smiling when she saw us. Her head barely reached my bicep, even petite Gretchen towering over her. Her graying hair was nearly white, pulled back into its tight bun, and her clothes were some kind of traditional garb, a small jacket and long skirt in simple fabrics. Not Japanese, I knew that much, but it didn't look like Chinese either.

"Um . . . hi. Ivan Zelenko sent us?" The old woman gave no indication that she recognized his name, or that she even spoke English. The deep wrinkles around her eyes only served to make them glitter merrily as she gestured us inside, and babbled something at us in her native language. I don't think she cared that we couldn't understand a word she was saying. Or, maybe she wanted it that way. For all I knew, she could be saying "Come inside, we'll feed you to the monster in the back room."

Inside the small shop—at least, I assumed it was a shop; either that, or a junk heap—we picked our way gingerly through the narrow aisles, trying not to knock things off overburdened shelves that seemed to take up every spare inch of space. I saw greasy car parts on those shelves, mingled in with half-woven baskets, ancient, cloudy bottles of indeterminate contents, and several old rotary telephones. There were busted-up video games from years gone by thrown in with old canned foods that bulged ominously. The shelves were stacked to the ceiling, and I eyed several precariously balanced fans on the top as we made our way through. That'd be a helluva booby trap, for the unwary.

Tai, as broad-shouldered as he was, was reduced to edging his way along sideways, and even I was having problems. The path had obviously been designed for someone much shorter than either of us. Glancing back over my shoulder, I told him, "If anyone offers to sell you a mogwai in this place, don't buy it." He laughed.

Unfortunately, Gretchen's smaller stature wasn't holding her up as much, and as she got farther ahead of us, I cursed myself for not putting her between us where we could keep an eye on her. "Hey, slow down. . . . Listen, we're trying to find Cindy Lee—"

Either she didn't hear me, or Gretchen just wasn't listening to me, because she kept right on following the tiny Asian woman until they both disappeared through a beaded bamboo curtain up ahead. "Dammit . . ." I quickened my pace as much as I dared, finally bursting out of the clutter into an open room with a rattle of peeved bamboo.

The three women in the room turned to look at the ruckus, each of them throwing an identical look of disappointment at me. Gretchen, at least, I could stare down in return, and once Tai stumbled through the narrow doorway behind me, the heat was directed elsewhere.

The third woman in the room stood out in the strange surroundings just by means of her normalcy. She was tiny, just like the other woman, but young, Gretchen's age maybe, her silky black hair drawn back in a plain ponytail. Her sneakers were worn, her blue jeans were dirty, like she'd been sorting through the clutter in the other room, and her T-shirt was from UCLA. In fact, I could easily believe that she'd just come from campus, if I hadn't known that most schools were still out for the winter holidays.

Smiling, she patted the old woman on the back, speaking to her in the same musical language, and the elderly woman shuffled off through yet another beaded curtain. "Hi, I'm Cindy. You must be Ivan's friends?"

"He sent us, yes." She didn't look like she wanted to shake hands, and I didn't offer. Though she looked petite and delicate, something just told me not to. For no apparent reason, the thought of touching her hand filled me with a cold dread. "I'm Jesse. This is Tai and Gretchen." She nodded to my companions as I introduced them, then turned her gaze back on me.

"Have a seat, all of you, while we discuss our business. Would you like tea? Soda? Something stronger?"

"Some water, maybe?" Gretchen asked as she found a seat on a low futon-type sofa. Tai sat with her, and I kept my standing position near the door. Always cover your way out.

"Of course." Our hostess crossed to the other beaded curtain, calling out to the elderly woman I presume.

While her back was turned, I shook my head subtly at Gretchen. Maybe I was being paranoid, but I didn't want her eating or drinking anything that came from this strange woman's hands.

As Cindy turned back, she gave me a faint smirk, and I got the idea that somehow she'd seen my signal to Gretchen. She didn't remark on it, though, and I wasn't going to bring it up if she didn't.

She took a seat on the opposite side of the low table in the room, the creaking of her wicker chair sounding almost like the furniture was complaining at being put to work. "Now. Ivan told me little of what you are needing. Perhaps you could explain?"

"Before we get to that . . . I have a request, and it's kinda strange." I had no idea who this woman was. But before we went any further, I needed to make sure who she wasn't.

She raised a dark brow at me curiously when I showed her the safety pin. "Do you always stab women you've just met?"

"You'd be surprised." I gave her half a grin. "Would you prefer I get to know you a bit more? Cindy, that's not a Chinese name, right?"

"I'm Korean, actually. And no, it's not. It's short for Cinderella."

"Your name is Cinderella."

"At the moment." She held her hand out to me. "I think we've become good friends now, yes?"

Despite my inexplicable aversion to touching her, I held my hand out, and allowed her to place hers in mine.

I don't know what I expected to happen, but nothing

did. Her hands were soft, unmarred, obviously not into heavy manual labor. There was a faint tingle up the hairs on my arm, the telltale traces of magic on her skin, but nothing like Tai could produce. Hell, I'd felt stronger signs from my wife. I couldn't even tell if this strange woman was a practitioner, or had just brushed up against something recently. And still, everything in me screamed to let her go, to put distance between me and this tiny, harmless-looking little girl.

I pricked the offered finger, releasing her as soon as the blood welled up, and she wrapped it in a tissue. "You'll understand if I ask you to leave the pin, of course."

"Sure, whatever you want." I snapped it shut and tossed it her way. Practitioner, definitely. A layman would have let the safety pin go, and then I'd have had a trace of her blood if I needed it later. She knew what she was doing.

Gretchen glanced briefly at me to see if we were ready to go on, then took the rolled contract out of her purse. "We need this translated. I understand that you're an expert with this language." Good girl, smart girl, she displayed the paper to our new friend, but didn't hand it over right away.

Cindy tilted her head, a small smile curving the corner of her mouth. "I don't know that I'd say expert, but I'm familiar with it, yes. May I ask, where did you get it?"

Before Gretchen could offer up her story, I stepped in. "No. We just need to know exactly what it says, in minute detail." With demons, every word has a dozen different possible meanings, all of which can drastically change what you think you're agreeing to. If we were going to find this loophole, I couldn't risk a vague translation.

The young woman held out her hand, and when I nodded, Gretchen passed the thick paper over. Cindy pursed her lips as she looked over the contract. "This is a lengthy document. It will take some time."

"How much time?" New Year's Eve was fast approaching. I had no idea what was supposed to happen then, but I didn't think we had a lot of time to waste.

"A few hours? Three or four, I would think." Her dark eyes flitted over the page as she spoke to us, and I could tell she was already translating in her mind. "There is a very good restaurant across the street if you want to get something to eat while you wait."

That actually wasn't a half-bad idea. I didn't want to sit here in this oddity shop for three or four hours. "You wanna give us a price quote on the translation?"

Cindy looked up from the pages and gave me a sly smile. "I have no way of knowing that until the job is done. We'll discuss payment when you return, all right?"

Man, I didn't like that. It felt eerily like the favor that had gotten me into this mess in the first place. But who else did we know that could read demon script? She had us, and she knew it.

The restaurant across the street was Chinese—go figure—and was actually *very* good, as promised. The three of us ate with a minimum of conversation, either lost in our own thoughts or simply watching the people as they moved around us. It wasn't the same before-Christmas hustle and bustle that I'd seen just a week ago.

Now, they were people on a mission, with a destination. Going to parties, picking up supplies, spending Christmas loot. They were smiling people, people who weren't worried about the credit card bills that would be coming next month, or anything really beyond what they were doing in the next few minutes. They had the happiness that comes with momentary blindness.

I think Gretchen picked up on it too. She seemed pensive, a faint crease drawn between her brows, and I almost asked her what she was thinking about. Almost. I wasn't sure we were up to the touchy-feely-deepest-darkest-secrets phase of our relationship yet.

By unspoken agreement, after two hours had gone by, we all got up to return to Cindy's little clutter shop. At least, I think it was a shop. Come to think of it, I hadn't seen a single cash register or anything there. No customers, either, except us. Maybe it was just junk she put in the way to keep people out.

The elderly woman answered the door again, escorting us back through the shelves as they swayed ominously over our heads. Cindy herself was curled up on the futon when we reached the open room, her sneakers discarded and her bare feet tucked under. She looked like a college student, hitting the books for some prefinals studying. She didn't even glance up when we came in, typing one-handed on a small laptop as her other finger marked her place in the demonic script.

Tai and I let Gretchen take the chair, and while he stood guard over her, I explored the room a bit more.

The floor beneath our feet was plain cement, not even smoothed out properly in some places, but the majority of it had been covered with old rugs. Layers and layers of old rugs, actually, the ones on top worn through enough to reveal the patterns of the ones underneath. It made for uneven footing at best, and a fire hazard at worst. I wondered how the little old lady made her way through here on a regular basis without breaking a hip.

Aside from the furniture, which looked like it had been rescued from Goodwill at some point, there was very little else to see. A few lamps hung from the ceilings, their low lights almost drowned out by dark shades beaded heavily just like the curtains that marked the doors. In one corner, a small set of shelves stood, displaying various knickknacks, and one ancient portable TV, the kind with the black-and-white six-inch screen and the antenna half broken off. I found a small Buddha on the top shelf, carved out of jade or a good replica of it, and smiled a little. He looked just like the one that sat by the waterfall in my backyard, and it was like finding a friend in a strange place.

I might have even reached out to dust him off, but I caught the slightest hint of cloves in that corner. It wasn't fresh, by any means. Old, musty, faint. Whatever the spell was, it had been cast so long ago that it had almost faded away to nothing. Most likely, it would no longer be functional at all, no matter what its intention had been. Of course, there was also the very rare chance that the old magic had soured over time, becoming something other than what was meant entirely. In those instances, the results could be . . . unexpected, and highly unpleasant.

Best to follow my mother's advice, and look with my eyes, not my fingers.

"And there. Finished." Cindy gave a few sharp taps to her keyboard, then closed the laptop. "This was an interesting job, to say the least." A few moments later, the elderly woman entered, handing Cindy the pages from some unseen printer. She nodded to us all, her cheerful smile still in place, as she disappeared into the other room again.

"So what does it say?" Gretchen leaned forward, suddenly eager now that all the answers were within our reach.

The translator gave her a small smile, but turned her dark gaze toward me. "I believe there was the matter of payment?"

"What's your price, then?" It hadn't escaped me that Ivan said he didn't trust this woman. I almost dreaded what was going to come out of her mouth.

She pursed her lips thoughtfully. "Hm. I think about five thousand dollars will suffice."

"Done." Gretchen whipped out her phone. "I can transfer that now."

"Wait . . . what?" I blinked at the seemingly innocuous Asian woman.

She smiled at me, and while it was still saccharine sweet, there was something behind it. Something darker. "What did you expect me to ask for, Jesse? A lock of hair? Drop of blood? A soul? I can get those things easily, should I want them. But money for rent, for supplies, that's a bit harder to come by. It turns out I really am a material girl."

Gretchen did whatever it was she had to do, and Cindy handed over the printed pages. "You can read through the entire thing if you want, but I highlighted a few sections I found interesting. Page seven, paragraph three was one of them. It seemed . . . important."

I crouched down next to Gretchen, looking over the printout as she flipped to the indicated paragraph. "Upon death, the additional souls collected will become the property of the collector's master." Oh yes, that was definitely the clause we needed to see. How very kind of Cindy to guess just what we were about. Kind, my ass. She knew too much on such a short acquaintance, and I was really starting to not like it.

Gretchen looked at me, puzzled. "I don't understand. Is the demon that made this contract my master?"

"I think that's the loophole, Gretchen." I flipped a few pages forward and backward, skimming for the pertinent words, but I wasn't surprised when I didn't find them. "Your 'master' is never defined. So I think what happens is, these souls go to whoever you name as your master. The decision lies with you." And that's why that thing was after me, not her. They couldn't risk killing her until she'd passed her cargo on to someone else. They needed it to be someone on their side. They needed to get me away from her, lest I influence her choice. Axel's master plan was starting to become clear to me. The bastard.

"Is there anything in here regarding a New Year's Eve date?" I flipped through again as I asked, but I was already pretty sure I wasn't going to find anything.

"Nothing that I saw, no," Cindy answered. "Momentous date, though. Turning of the year and all. Things happen on a date like that."

"Why?" Gretchen fixed her sharp blue gaze on me. "Why ask about New Year's?"

I hadn't told her. I should have, but I hadn't. I think that makes me some kind of asshole. "The person who sent me out here said that everything would be settled one way or another by New Year's Eve."

"That's tomorrow. Settled how?"

"I don't know." She gave me a suspicious look, and I took her hand. "I swear, Gretchen. Even the person who said that didn't know what it meant."

"Y'know, it might have been nice to know that the world was gonna end in twenty-four hours or something." She stood up, snatching her translated contract out of my hands. "The original. I want it back too."

Cindy handed that over with a rueful smirk that said she'd have kept it if we'd have conveniently forgotten about it.

"I'm getting goddamn tired of you people playing chess with my life." Gretchen shot me a glare of pure venom, then whirled on her heel and stalked out of the room.

When I tried to follow Gretchen as she stormed out, the translator caught my wrist to stop me. "Hang back a moment." I really, *really* didn't want to be alone with this woman, but good manners required that I stop. Cindy waited until she heard the alleyway door slam before she continued. "I see things, Jesse Dawson."

"Like dead people?"

A flicker of annoyance crossed her face. "You don't have time for snark. Listen to me. That girl's light isn't much longer for this world. You mentioned New Year's Eve . . . I don't expect her to see the new year."

"And you would know this how?"

"Like I said, I see things. I see the thin golden threads on you, stretching back to the East over so many miles. Protection spells, from a woman who loves you very much. I see the shadows left behind by contracts you've made. I bet you never knew that they left ghostly little marks. I see how long your light stretches for. Would you like to know?"

"No." A man shouldn't know the hour of his own death. It's just not right. Not that I believed she'd tell the truth anyway. "These things you see . . . are they certain?"

"Of course not. Nothing is ever certain until it's passed, and even then it's negotiable." She smiled a little, finally releasing my arm to sit back on the futon again. "My own light should have ended . . . well, longer ago than you've been alive."

"You expect me to believe that you're older than me?" I'd have bet money that I had a good decade on her.

Cindy smiled sweetly again. "The woman who let you in here? She is my great-granddaughter."

"Why would you tell me this?" I mean, if she really was what she said she was, you'd think that kind of thing would be a little more hush-hush.

"Because someday, you're going to come to me, Jesse Dawson, and you're going to want to know how it was done. And if you're very, *very* unlucky, I might even tell you." She grinned then, showing teeth, and a shiver went down my spine.

"You see that too?"

"No. We'll call that one a hunch."

I shook my head. "Does Ivan know what you are?" I had a hard time believing that he'd have sent us here, knowing that she was . . . what the hell was she?

The strange woman chuckled softly. "Ivan and I have known each other for a *very* long time. You'd better be going. She's going to take off without you in another few moments."

That, I believed.

18

"I'm going to die, aren't I?"

We'd ridden back to the hotel in stony silence, Gretchen's pique with me obvious just by the set of her lovely jaw. It was only after we were alone, Tai retiring to the spare bedroom for some much needed shut-eye, that the movie star deigned to speak to me again.

"Everyone dies, Gretchen." I looked up from my place on the couch, my armor in my lap as I lightly oiled the leather straps.

"Yeah, but soon. I'm going to die soon." On the other sofa, she sat with her feet curled beneath her, her legs bare in a pair of tiny shorts, but the rest of her almost lost in the huge sweatshirt she'd thrown on. A man's shirt, that much was certain. Dante's, if I had to guess. "You said it's all going to be over by New Year's."

How to answer that? If Mystic Cindy was to be believed, Gretchen had just over twenty-four hours to live. New Year's Eve was fast approaching. The thing was, I didn't trust Cindy any more than I trusted Axel. Neither were what I'd call a reliable source. "The ancient samurai believed that death wasn't a thing to be feared. It wasn't the dying that was important, it was how you died."

"Do you believe all that?" She sat forward a little, watching as I worked with my mail armor. "The whole samurai bit?"

"Yes, I do." Since she seemed so interested, I shifted my position so she could see what I was doing, laying the piece out flat. "These are chausses. They cover my legs when I fight."

She reached out to touch the tiny links of chain. "So if you think that dying is nothing to be feared, why do you wear armor?"

I chuckled. "Just because I'm not afraid of it doesn't mean I wanna jump into it. Besides, there are worse things than dying." Excruciating pain came to mind. Picking your own intestines up out of the dirt. Things like that.

Her curious hands went next to the rest of my gear, poking through the pile of supple metal. "How does this all work?"

"You want me to put it on and show you?" Honestly, giving an armor how-to was much preferable to debating mortality. When she nodded, I got up, laying all the pieces out flat so I could get them on correctly. "First, the padding. 'Cause this stuff is heavy, and the links pinch when they move." Getting chain mail caught in leg or chest hair? Like I said. Excruciating pain.

The padding part of my armor was easy to get into. It was the rest of it that required long hours of practice. Gretchen watched me for a few moments, then got up to help with the buckles. "So you have a handler that helps you get into this stuff for a fight, right?"

That made me laugh a little. Yes, I had a companion along for most of my fights. Usually my buddy Will. But he was there mostly to put the pieces of me back together at the end, rather than dress me at the beginning.

"Normally, I'm on my own for this part." On my own save for my client, often standing in the dark in some deserted location. Waiting for the fitful scent of sulfur on the wind. "But yeah, I have buddies who help out when they can. My best friends." Well, singular now. Just Will. It was hard to remember to remove Marty from the list.

I held my arms up parallel to the ground while Gretchen worked on the buckles down my sides. "It's good to have friends. Sometimes, one good friend can make all the difference."

"Like Dante?"

She smiled a little, still fumbling with the thick leather straps on my armor. "Yeah. He's the one person in the world I trust above all else. He's my best friend."

"Tai said you grew up together?"

"Mhmm. His mom lived next door to us. She'd watch me and my sister sometimes, when Mom had to work. We've always been inseparable. I honestly don't know what I'd do without him."

"What about all those other people? The ones at the party, the ones you waved to at the movie lot. Aren't they your friends too?"

"They're just ... people I see sometimes. If I drop dead tomorrow, most of them will show up at my funeral just to be seen by the cameras, and then they'll never think of me again."

"That's a bit grim, isn't it? No, here ... that attaches to my belt." I could have buckled everything on myself faster, but I didn't think this was all about her seeing me in my armor. She needed to talk, apparently, and this was her excuse.

We got the chausses settled, and I slipped my burned-out bracers back on just for the full effect. I bounced a bit on my toes, jingling as the mail settled into its proper place. Gretchen stepped back to look me up and down, lips pursed thoughtfully.

"Isn't that stuff heavy?"

"Yup. That's why I work out to be strong enough to carry it."

"I can't imagine being able to move in it, let alone fight." A ghost of a smile flashed across her face, but it was gone in a heartbeat. "You think I'm a bad person, don't you? Because of these." She reached over her shoulder where her shirt had drooped to bare skin, her fingers no doubt touching the upper edges of the iridescent soul tattoos on her back.

"I . . . I don't agree with it." There, that sounded tactful. "I don't know that I'm really in a position to judge who is 'bad' or not."

"They weren't always good people themselves, y'know. I mean, what kind of guy offers his soul up to bang a girl thirty years younger than him? A guy with a wife and kids at home . . ." Before I could answer her, she went on. "I know that doesn't make it right. You were gonna say that, right?"

"Something like that, yeah."

"Just . . . in the beginning, at first, I thought they maybe really cared for me. I used to think I was in love. But I wasn't, and they definitely weren't. They got bragging rights or whatever, and I got their souls." She kept feeling over her shoulder for the tattoos, her eyes distant.

"Can you feel them? I mean, do you know they're there?" I'd been dying to ask that since I got here.

"Sometimes. The newer they are, the more I'm aware of it. Then after a while, I just get used to it again, and I don't think about it anymore." She turned around, moving her shirt to show off more of her back. "These here at the top, they're the oldest. If I didn't see them in the mirror now and then, I wouldn't remember they were there. The ones down at the bottom . . . those are newer. Sometimes . . ." She shook her head, though with her back to me, I couldn't guess at the look on her face. "You'll think I'm crazy."

"Takes a lot for me to throw the crazy card. Sometimes what?"

"Sometimes, when they're new . . . I think I hear them. And that's stupid, 'cause they're not *real* souls. I mean, if they were real souls, the people I took them from would be dead. They're just . . . liens, I guess. Markers for souls. But sometimes when they're new, I think I hear them saying things. Whispering. Crying sometimes."

Later, when I looked back on this, here is where it all started going horribly awry. But at the time, it seemed like the nice thing to do. I reached out and put my hand on her bare shoulder, squeezing a little to offer comfort.

She spun around, throwing her arms around my waist and burying her face against my mail-clad chest with enough force to back me up a couple of steps. "Erm . . ." Okay, so what do you do there? Awkwardly, I petted her hair a little, not quite sure what to do with this turn of events.

"I don't want to die," she whimpered, and I could hear

the tears in her voice. Oh boy. I don't deal well with crying women.

"Hey, look, no one said you were gonna die. And ...
that's what I'm here for, right?" I coaxed her to lift up
her head, and rapped my knuckles on my mail. "Armor
and all. Serve and protect or whatever."

Gretchen sniffled a little, blue eyes swimming in tears
even as she tried to smile for me. "You're a good person,
Jesse. Better than I am."

"Hey no, you're a good person—" I'm sure I had really profound stuff to say here, but it's kinda hard to talk
(or think) when a gorgeous woman suddenly kisses you.

Her lips were soft and she smelled like coconut. Those
were the first two things I noticed. I could taste the salt
of her tears, and the hint of cherry from her lip gloss.
Honestly, I was so stunned, it took me a few precious
seconds to react. It had been years since I'd been kissed
by anyone other than my wife.

My wife ... Oh shit, Mira ... I caught Gretchen's arms
as she tried to slip them around my neck, and gently held
her in place, stepping back out of her embrace. She
blinked at me with huge glimmering eyes, obviously
never expecting me to stop her. "I'm married, Gretchen.
And I love my wife very much." I said it as gently as possible, 'cause ... well, mostly 'cause I didn't want her to
cry anymore. I'd have promised anything (well, *almost*
anything) if she'd just stop leaking from the eyes.

It ... didn't go as well as I'd hoped. The diamond tears
welled up in her eyes, spilling down her cheeks, but she
nodded with a tiny hiccup of a sob. "And ... I'm sure she's
a good person too ... just like you. ..." Finally, she turned

away, flopping down on the couch again to hide her face in her folded arms. Her entire frame shook with silent sobs.

Crap. I was seriously close to waking up Tai, just to see if he knew how to deal with this better than I did. Or Dante. Where the hell was Dante when I could really have used him? "Hey ... um ... you want like ... some ice cream or something? Chocolate?" That's what women liked when they were upset, right? "I could go down and get some. . . ." Yeah, room service would deliver, but that wouldn't get me out of the room, now, would it?

After a few moments, she nodded, and just as I was about to slip out the door, she called after me, "And whipped cream! Lots of it!"

The door shut behind me and I sagged against it for a moment. *Holy crap* ... This was ... what ... how ... "Holy crap!" I muttered to myself. I was gonna get ice cream for her, and seriously debate a strong shot of whiskey for myself. And I'm normally not a hard liquor kinda guy.

The elevator dinged, and I hopped on without waiting to see if anyone was getting off. Unfortunately, that resulted in me mowing down poor Dante. He sprawled on the floor of the elevator, and it took us a couple of moments to get our legs untangled from each other. I think I even stepped on his hand once, and he snatched it back with a pained hiss.

"Oh damn, sorry, man." I offered my hand to help him up, and he gave me the uninjured one so I could pull him to his feet.

He looked me up and down with a puzzled tilt to his head. "What the hell are you wearing?"

"Armor," I answered, like it was the most natural thing in the world. "She's crying. Go fix it." The elevator doors closed on the puzzled look on his face.

Down in the kitchen, no one commented on my armor. They were too busy insisting that the kitchen closed at ten, which was an hour ago, and giving me dirty looks when I kept insisting "No, *bigger*!" But seriously, how hard is it to understand that I wanted a *big* ice cream sundae? I finally took the can of whipped topping away from the flustered cook and emptied it over the top of the biggest bowl of ice cream and hot fudge I'd ever seen. And I still wasn't sure it was big enough. "You got any strawberries? And cherries too, lots of cherries."

A quart of strawberry syrup and half a jar of maraschino cherries later, I was making my way toward the elevators again (and dammit, the ice cream was already dripping into the links of my armor), when I noticed a commotion in the lobby.

A group of black-coated hotel staff had surrounded someone near the front door, either denying them entrance or ... well, I don't know what the "or" was. An angry voice rose from the center of the circle. "No, I don't need a fucking ambulance! You just gotta tell me if she's here!"

If I didn't know better, I'd swear that was Dante's voice. Curious and more than a bit confused, I went to investigate.

Being tall has its advantages. When I got close enough, I was able to see over most of the heads to find that sure enough Dante was there, leaning heavily on Homeless Felix's tattered shoulders. Dante's bright red hair was dingy, the dye having mostly washed or grown out, and there was an ashy grayness to his dark skin. His cheeks were hollowed out, eyes fever-bright, and his clothes were so grimy I almost couldn't tell the color of what used to be a preppy-looking sweater vest.

"Dante! What the hell happened?" I shouldered my way through the crowd, not caring who I slathered with whipped cream.

Dante frowned, looking me up and down. "Who the hell are you?"

This is the point where I started thinking "Oh shit." I looked to Felix for answers, which should probably tell you how confused I was. "What happened to him?"

The eccentric sage shook his head sadly, his dreadlocks swaying with a clatter of beads. "Things are not always what they seem, warrior. I tried to tell you . . ."

"I'll tell you what happened. Some fucking psycho snatched me off the street and locked me up in a dark room for weeks, draining my goddamn blood like a fucking vampire! That's what fucking happened!" Dante thrust a hand at my fact, showing me a wrist rubbed raw and blistered by some kind of restraint, and multiple needle-stick sites. "He took my goddamn face! How is that even fucking possible??"

Half an ice cream sundae shifted and slid off the heaping bowl to splatter on the floor around my feet. The melted slop almost covered up the graying clay, drying on my combat boots. I'd tripped over him, I realized, in the elevator not fifteen minutes ago . . . I stepped on his hand, and there was drying gray mud in the tread of my boot when I checked the sole.

"Gretchen ..." I dropped the bowl and heard it shatter into a thousand wet, sticky pieces behind me as I dashed for the elevators. A businessman was just getting into the first open car, and I grabbed him by the collar of his nice suit, tossing him to the side like a rag doll. "Hey!"

I didn't have time to make stops on the way up. The guy would thank me later. I fumbled as I swiped my keycard for the penthouse, and was faintly relieved when the light flickered green and the doors slid closed. *Come on, faster, faster ...*

It was up there with her. I knew that now. It had been with us all along, maybe. Longer than I'd been in L.A., anyway, 'cause Dante—the Dante downstairs—had no idea who the hell I was. *But he'd passed the test!* The blood test, he passed. Dante passed through the wards, passed the pin test ...

The blood, I decided. Had to be the blood the creature had taken from the real Dante. Made it easier for him to hold the form, maybe allowed the soulless construction to steal the voice. Maybe it let him bleed, too.

"Fucking come on!" I slammed my fist into the wooden paneling in the elevator, as if that would make it climb the floors any faster.

At the penthouse level, I squeezed through the elevator doors before they'd fully opened, startling Spencer who was standing in the hallway with his food cart. The wannabe screenwriter blinked at me in surprise. "But ... I just saw you get on the other elevator with Gretchen ..."

"You're sure?" I grabbed his jacket, shaking him once. "You're sure they got on the elevator?"

"Yeah, completely." I released him, dashing for Gretchen's suite. Spencer called after me, "I think it went up to the roof, if that helps . . ."

I was intent on getting my sword first and foremost. No way was I facing that thing empty-handed again. We were gonna see how well he liked being in giant clay chunks. But I was brought up short by the sight of Tai's body sprawled facedown on the floor between the two sofas. The remnants of the glass coffee table littered the carpet and crunched underfoot as I scrambled to get to him.

"Tai!" Pulse, pulse, where was the damn pulse . . . I found it, thankfully, slow but steady in his thick neck. My hands came away stained with sticky blood though, and I found a nasty gash in his raven hair, just behind his left ear. He'd been attacked from behind, clubbed like a baby seal. And his gun holster was empty.

"Holy shit, what happened?" Spencer stood at the top of the stairs, eyes wide in shock. "Is that blood?"

"Don't just stand there, call 911!" At my sharp command, he seemed to snap out of it, and lurched for the phone.

I carefully rolled the big Maori over, checking him for other injuries, but there didn't seem to be any. Tai was breathing. There wasn't a damn thing I could do for him. My sword case was still under the sofa where I'd left it, and I snatched up The Way, headed for the door.

"I called 911!" Spencer reported, like he expected a treat for being such a good puppy. "The ambulance is on the way. Now what do I do?"

"Stay with Tai until they get here. Tell them he has head trauma."

"And then what?"

"If you value your life, go home, Spencer. Go back to Chicago." I slammed the door behind me and ran for the elevator again.

19

The roof was deserted, as it should be this late at night. The paper lanterns had been supplemented with string after string of party lights in preparation for the New Year's festivities, but for now everything was dark.

I stepped out of the elevator, cursing inwardly at the cheerful "ding" I couldn't prevent. My presence was known, whether I wanted it to be or not. Still, I took care to step softly on the white stone path, straining my ears for signs of where Gretchen and the thing had gone.

It wasn't hard to find them. Above the sound of the distantly trickling waterfall, all I had to do was follow the sound of Gretchen's outraged protests. "Get your hands off me! Let me go!" Her strident voice carried through the darkness. I tracked the sound through the narrow pathways until I arrived at the open area where tables and chairs had been clustered around the central reflecting pool.

Dimly, I knew that Spencer said he'd seen *me* get on the elevator with Gretchen, but I hadn't truly thought about what that meant until that moment. A tall, slender man held Gretchen by the arm, not even budging as she struggled against his grip. His clothes . . . well, those weren't mine. In fact, they'd been on Dante, last I'd seen. The few inches difference in my height from Dante's made the blue jeans a bit high-water, and the difference in our weight made the shirt hang loosely on the wiry frame. His blond hair was unconfined, hanging at shoulder length, but the last few inches were fire-engine red, the remnants of the dye in Dante's short dreads. When he turned, I caught a glimpse of his face. It was mine, sort of. The right nose, kinda pointy. Sharply angled cheeks, but they were smooth, my newly acquired scar only a faint blemish on the surface. The jaw was strong, but without the reddish stubble I'd started to grow. Me, but slightly off. Only someone who didn't know me well would mistake this thing for the genuine article.

Gretchen jerked against his grip again, and only then did I see the gun held in his free hand. That should have been the first glaring clue that it wasn't me. Yes, I can shoot. No, I don't. "I will scream my goddamn head off if you don't let me go."

"Go ahead." Now the voice . . . the voice he had down. I was used to hearing my own voice out of Axel's mouth, I knew what I sounded like. "No one will hear you up here."

"I will." Seemed like a good line to make an entrance on. I stepped out of the overhung path, dropping The Way's scabbard in the bushes. I angled the blade just right so the scant light would reflect down it. Melodramatic, yes, but I wanted him to know it was there.

There was a soft gasp from Gretchen as I appeared out of seeming nowhere. "But . . . ." Her eyes were wide as she looked between her captor and me. Okay, so apparently the fake me was more convincing than I'd thought. Obviously, Gretchen hadn't known the difference.

The golem was a bit less surprised. "Stop where you

are." It leveled Tai's stolen gun at me. "This has nothing to do with you."

Slowly, I kept moving forward, one step at a time. "First off, you stealing my face and my voice, that has everything to do with me. Second, you happen to be threatening someone I promised to protect. Again, to do with me. And third, I think you got caught midtransformation. Your hair's a bit muddled there, your face isn't quite right. So I think the odds of you hitting the broad side of a barn with that gun are slim to none. I'll take my chances." I'd seen this thing be clumsy before, and my guess was that it happened when it had to change form quickly.

Apparently I was right, because it quickly rethought its strategy. It yanked Gretchen closer, jabbing the barrel of the gun into her ribs. "At this distance, I won't miss."

Yeah, I stopped advancing then. "You can't kill her. You need her to name her master. Presumably *your* master?" I tried to catch Gretchen's gaze, promising her with my eyes that this was all going to be all right, somehow. Even in the darkness, I could see how pale she was, but she nodded to me faintly. She was at least trying to hold it together.

"I don't need to kill her. I only need to hurt her." It shoved harder with the gun, and she winced at the dig into her ribs. "The outcome is already decided. She only needs to say the words."

"I'm not saying shit . . ." That earned her another gouge in the ribs, and she whimpered, but stood firm. "If you knew me at all, you'd know that."

"He knows you better than you think. He's been with you for . . . weeks, maybe."

Gretchen turned startled eyes on me. "How is that possible?"

"Dante. He's been impersonating Dante."

The creature smirked. My smirk. "It took you long enough to figure it out. Even your little test failed. I bled his blood for you, easy enough."

"Dante's blood . . . ?" Gretchen looked back at the creature holding her captive. "You killed Dante?"

"He's alive," I quickly assured her. "Hurt and sore, but he's fine. He's downstairs. The thing kept him alive, because he needed the blood to take Dante's form, his voice." And my blood, he'd gotten from the tissue I'd told "Dante" to burn. At least, that's what I'd have done in his place.

Golem-Me grimaced. "As well that this masquerade is over then, if he's escaped. He wouldn't have kept much longer at any rate."

"You *hurt* Dante?" Despite the darkness, I could see angry fire flare in Gretchen's blue eyes. "You *hurt* him?" As scared as I knew she was, only one thing would override that, and it was sheer rage. Women in protective mode are probably the scariest things I've ever seen, bet you me. "Fuck you!"

Damn, the girl was quick. Before I could yell at her not to, she swung, jabbing her stiff fingers into Golem-Me's eyes. The thing recoiled as she raked her fingernails out, taking huge gobbets of clay with it. In the scuffle, it dropped the gun and Gretchen snatched it up. The golem lurched in her direction, and she fired, the flash bright in the darkness. A good chunk of the golem's shoulder disappeared. "Stop! Don't you make a fucking move!"

I'd been on the move myself, and we both came to a screeching halt. Always do what the lady with the gun tells you. I didn't think she could kill the golem with it, but a stray bullet was definitely not going to be healthy for me.

The pause gave the golem time to fix its eyes, the creature smoothing away the gouged clay with its fingers until it could see again. Definitely no chance of mistaking it for me now, the eye sockets hollowed out and lumpy around the edges. The clay orbs rolled like real eyes, but there were no pupils or irises to be seen. Just flat, matte gray marbles in the deep, dark sockets.

Gretchen climbed up on the edge of the reflecting pool so she didn't have to look up at the both of us. Her bare feet shuffled for balance on the precarious stone edge, but her aim with the gun never wavered. It was enormous in her small hands, but she held it like she knew which end was the dangerous one. She looked like a child up there, lost in her huge sweatshirt, hiding behind someone else's gun. "You pretended to be my best friend. You sat there and listened to me spill my guts. I told you stuff nobody else knows. I trusted you!"

If I didn't know better, I'd almost say the golem looked sheepish, but his voice was flat. "As you were meant to."

"You were supposed to trust him, Gretchen." The thing was still between me and her. I slowly circled, trying to put myself at a better angle if I had to rush the golem. Man, I hoped I didn't have to. "You were supposed to trust him enough to hand over those souls."

"And you?" The muzzle of that gun swung my direction, and I froze again. "Some mysterious person sent you here to 'protect' me? I was supposed to trust you too, right?"

Girl had me there. I could totally see that as part of Axel's plan, and he'd have known that I'd never go along with it if he laid it all out beforehand. "Doesn't matter what the person who sent me here wanted. I said I'd protect you. I meant that." I motioned with my free hand. "Come down, come this way." If that thing went to grab her, I was pretty sure I wasn't gonna make it in time. I needed her closer.

"No. Screw you both. I'm done being told what to do and when to do it." I think Golem-Me must have moved, because she swung the gun back around in his direction. "Did it ever occur to anyone to just *ask* me? I mean, what am I gonna do with them? I'd have *given* them to anybody who asked. But no, you gotta mess with my head, mess with my life."

The golem blinked at her a little with his malformed eyes. "Then . . . can I have them?"

She laughed bitterly. "You know . . . I might have given them to you. Except you hurt Dante. Nobody hurts my friends."

I was trying so hard not to pay attention to the sharp, icy goose bumps marching up and down my spine. Something was going to happen in the next few moments, I could feel it. Something not good. "Gretchen, come here. Give me the gun." I stretched my hand out to her, trying to will her to step down and take it.

Her gaze swiveled to me again, and she gave me a ghost of a smile. "I believe you, you know. I think you'd have protected me, if you could. You're good people. You don't belong out here with people like us. You don't belong working for whatever asshole sent you out here."

"Gretchen, don't . . ." I had no idea what she was about to do, but I knew I desperately didn't want her to do it.

She shook her head, her blond hair falling in wisps around her face. This high up, the wind was starting to pick up, tugging everything in the direction of the ocean. "They're not gonna stop coming. If you kill this thing here"—she gestured toward the golem—"they'll send something else. Bobby almost died. Tai might be dead. They're gonna kill you too. Until I give these things over to somebody else."

Golem-Me moved again, and she calmly aimed and blew another hole through its shoulder. I heard the splat this time as the lump of clay went flying through the air and plastered against a nearby light fixture. "I said don't move."

With one arm half-detached and dangling, the golem had no choice but to stop again. It held up its one good hand defensively.

I leaned closer, as if that one or two inches closer to my hand would make her suddenly want to grab it. "I'm harder to kill than you think. Just come to me, and we'll figure out how to deal, okay?"

Gretchen shook her head, her hair flying around her face in the chill breeze. "Nobody's invulnerable. That's just in the movies. But I've seen your scars. I know you're damn hard to kill. You'd have to be, doing what you do, right?"

"Right. Not a job for desk jockeys." Just keep her talking. It was all I could think to do.

She nodded, then raised the gun. For a heartbeat, I just knew she was going to aim it at herself, and I jumped forward to stop her. "Stop!" Her barked command jerked me to a halt again, and I watched as she pointed the gun instead into the reflecting pool.

I couldn't see the glass in the pool, but somewhere around the fourth or fifth shot, I heard the glass start cracking, and by the time she emptied the entire clip into it, the snapping and popping of spiderwebbed glass continued like more gunshots in the night. It would be a matter of moments before it collapsed under the weight of the water, spilling into the lobby so many stories below.

"They'll never stop. They'll come after me, they'll come after the people I love. And frankly, I'm not the kind of person who can deal with this. I'm not strong enough." She tossed the now-useless gun aside. "I hope you are."

The world went into slow motion there, I swear. The golem and I both lunged for Gretchen at the same time. I saw one of her bare feet step back, hovering in the air over the rapidly draining pool. Even as she teetered, her balance shifting backward, she smiled at me. "I name Jesse James Dawson my master."

And she fell.

The fractured glass in the pool exploded as she hit it, dropping her nine stories down to the marble floor far below. I knew the instant she hit, because the sensation of two hundred and seventy-six souls slammed into me with the force of a tsunami. It took my breath away, drowning me in the scent of cloves, crushing my chest under the pressure of so much power. My vision went white, and my ears were deafened by the sound of distant screaming, words I never could quite make out.

I came to—at least, I think I came to—on my knees with my forehead pressed against the white stones on the ground. I could feel them under my splayed hands, every little ridge, every tiny imperfection in the rock. I could have told you which ones had quartz in them, a few with fossils, some with flecks of granite. I could have picked out the tiny forms of dead insects, trapped under the sealant.

The night breeze passed over my skin, and I could have named every bit of contaminant in the polluted air, and underneath it all, the hint of sea salt. Someone three floors down was smoking weed on their balcony, and I could taste that too, like they were standing next to me. Tiny particles in the wind rasped over the backs of my hands, my cheeks, like I was being sandblasted by things people normally never noticed.

Under my supersensitive touch, I felt the rooftop ripple infinitesimally as the golem shifted its weight, turning to face me. "And so I will simply take them from you instead."

His voice, stolen from me, jangled in my head like a thousand fire alarms. Even as expert as the mimicry was, I could tell the difference now, and the forgery of it grated at my senses like jagged chunks of glass.

"No. You will simply kiss my ass." My own voice wasn't much better, rough-edged with anger and grief. It raked my senses like steel wool.

The Way's bone hilt was within my grasp when I reached for it, and I could feel every thin porous hole in the carved femur as I wrapped my fingers around it. The bone warmed instantly, like it was happy to be in my hand again.

As I forced my way to my feet, I could feel the outlines of each and every rock through the soles of my heavy boots, and when I was finally able to focus my eyes, every light in sight—from the streetlights far below to the stars so many zillions of miles away—pierced straight through my corneas and seared in the back of my brain. It should have been agonizing, but instead it was just . . . pure. Like I was finally seeing things as they really were, with all the filth and the grime stripped away.

I could see the thin veins running through every leaf of every plant that surrounded me. I could see the water pulsing through them, bringing life. I swear I could see the plants breathing, absorbing our castoffs to produce life-giving oxygen. I almost got lost, watching those wisps of gas wafting off into the night sky. Might have, even, if the golem hadn't lunged for me then.

The roof dipped and swayed and I moved with it, countering with The Way before the golem had even committed to its charge. My sword passed through the clay fingers on one hand, sending them spinning off into the dark.

It was hard to concentrate on what I was doing. Part of me just wanted to watch the bits of light, gleaming and bouncing off my blade as we moved. I could have stared at the layers and layers of magic that coated the blade for hours, picking through each tiny bit of Cameron that remained on the metal. Because that's what it was. Every bit of magic on my sword was a piece of Cameron's soul, freely given, and I could smell him on it now.

That same Cameron-taste permeated my armor, and beneath that, on my body itself, I was wrapped in delicate golden threads, just like Mystic Cindy had said. Those tasted like sage and strawberries. Like Mira.

Again, I felt the ground beneath me lurch and ripple, and though I felt like I was moving in slow motion, part of me knew I was striking impossibly fast, dropping under the reaching clay arms to slash at the knees. The Way passed through the first, and halfway through the second before I lost momentum. I threw my shoulder into the golem's stomach, sending it careening off balance with only one leg left to support it. The severed calf stayed where it had been left, the flesh color melting into gray from the cut downward. *From dust to dust* . . . With my strangely enhanced vision, I could see the threads of magic stretch to the breaking point between the severed pieces of the limb. And then, like a rubber band extended to its max, the golden strings of power snapped back, yanking the lumps of clay back into one piece.

Bit by bit, the lost pieces of it snaked across the rooftop, plastering back together with a wet sucking sound. In no time at all, the thing was struggling to its feet again, turning to face me.

Any other time, this would have been cause for concern. How do you destroy the indestructible? But my vision was dazzled with the glimmering web of magic, with the intricate connections that protected and animated the clay. I could see the spell, wound tightly around its clay flesh, anchored into a sigil etched between its shoulder blades. *Erase the sigil*, he'd said. . . . But why? Why do that when I could just . . .

Okay, I admit I have no idea what I did that night. At the time, it was all just so . . . logical. The golem bared its teeth at me, hatred gleaming from what used to be my eyes. Within one of its palms, I could see the snippet of blessed thread glowing, a piece of my wards. That was how it had passed in and out. Inside the other palm, the single piece of Tai's hair shone like a beacon, ten times as bright as Cam's blessing. Taken when the Golem-Dante had been rubbing the big man's shoulders. And embedded at the back of its neck, a piece of paper, no doubt the token from the creature's maker and master.

The web of magic that bound it up was complex, delicate but strong. Lace made of steel. But as such, just one small snip would unravel it all. So that's what I did. I gestured with one hand, flinging my will away from me, and every thread of magic in its path snapped with an audible pop.

The golem itself burst into a cloud of dry dust, drifting all around me, glittering like fairy dust as it slowly sifted down to earth. The piece of Cam's string turned black and shriveled, withering like it had been burned. Tai's hair, almost pure magic in and of itself, was immolated entirely. And the piece of paper, the token, poked out from the pile of dust and ash, one charred and curled corner visible.

The rooftop swayed as someone else's feet took careful steps, and I whirled, The Way poised to strike. What I found there was nothing that I had ever expected. It was Felix. I knew, deep down inside, that it was Felix. But the mental image of the eccentric homeless sage with the colorfully ribboned dreadlocks just would not hold together in the face of . . . I can't even describe it. With my vision practically boiling over with magic, I could see straight to the truth of it, and I dropped to my knees, pressing with the heels of my hands at my burning eyes. And still I could see it.

There was only one thing in the world that could be so beautiful and so terrible all at the same time, and if you'd have asked me ten minutes before, I would have sworn that I didn't believe in them.

Felix was an angel. Contrary to popular myth, he did *not* have a halo, or a white robe and feathery wings, and I was pretty sure he didn't know how to play a lyre. There aren't even words invented yet to describe what he looked like, and even just glimpsing him like I had, I knew the image would be burned behind my eyes for days. Maybe forever.

"It is best to keep your eyes averted, warrior."

"Yeah, no shit," I mumbled, feeling the scorching-hot salt of my tears coursing down my cheeks. It felt like lava, searing straight into the bones of my skull. Thankfully, Felix's voice just sounded like Felix. I was pretty sure hearing an angel actually speak would have liquefied what was left of my brain cells.

"The sensitivity will pass soon. Your body must adjust to so much power." I felt every step he took as he approached me, and I shied away, scuttling over the ground like one of the lesser demons I had fought so often. I couldn't risk glancing at the edges of his toes or something. I didn't want to see, couldn't stand to see.

"Adjust, or go stark raving mad, is that it?" 'Cause oh, I could feel it. At the edges of my thoughts, this little gibbering voice usually reserved only for reacting to demonic speech. The part of my mind that would run away and never come back, given its choice. If I let my guard down, even for a second, I wasn't sure I'd ever get control back. A rather frightening thought.

"That is correct." Felix crouched just out of my arms' reach, thankfully. I think, if he'd have touched me, that'd be all she wrote. I'd have been done.

"So . . . you've been here, this whole time. You knew what Dante was . . . you knew what he was after. . . ." It explained the raw hatred I'd seen in the old man's face — God was that just a couple of days ago? It felt like centuries.

"Yes. We knew."

"Then *why*?" Really, that's the only thing I wanted to know, the only thing I felt like I could wrap my mind around. "Why didn't you do something? Why didn't you protect her?" Because he could have. Surely he could have. If there were demons, and they were bad, then the angels, they were good, right? They did good things, like save people and grant wishes or some shit, yes?

Felix sighed, and I felt the ground beneath me sway as he stood up. "Because this is not our war, warrior. Our fallen brothers, they battle amongst themselves, but it has nothing to do with us. So we only watch."

"Bullshit!" I dared a glance up, without thinking, but luckily some of the dazzle in my sight seemed to have worn off. Felix looked almost like himself again, though his rags and dreads were wreathed in a faint golden glow.

"What is that quote? All evil needs to triumph is for good men to do nothing?"

He smiled a little, his whiskey-colored eyes absorbing the last of the glow to shine like polished gold in the darkness. "We are not men."

"Then why make yourself known now? If God's not going to send us help, why are you here?"

"Who says He has not sent help?" With a faintly sad smile, he melted back into the narrow pathways and I knew the moment he was gone. The weight on my chest, the mere pressure of his presence, was gone.

I sat there for a few more moments, rocking back on my knees and balancing my sword across them. I could still feel the minute texture of everything I touched, but it was no longer threatening to overload my circuits. Another few minutes and I'd be almost normal, I thought. If I had another few minutes. Gretchen was down in the lobby and inevitably, someone would come looking up here to see what had happened. Being caught here with an empty gun and a bared sword probably wasn't going to end well for me.

"Man . . . man, are you okay?" Spencer's voice was not nearly as harsh in my ears as I'd been fearing. I wondered that it had taken him this long to talk, when I'd been aware of his presence almost from the beginning. Mercifully, the rooftop no longer buckled when he approached me. I turned my eyes on him, mostly just to see what he looked like in my vision, and I was relieved to see that he was just . . . him. Somewhere in the last few minutes, I think I'd forgotten what normal looked like.

"I'm all right." Gingerly, I got up, feeling my mail sitting against my back like it was so much raw meat. Under the padding, under my T-shirt, iridescent white tattoos writhed and slithered as they settled into their new homes. I could feel each one intimately, could point out where one ended and another began, though it would be invisible to the naked eye.

"Man . . . I saw everything." There was awe in his voice. Funny how seldom we hear genuine awe in this day and age. "What . . . what was that?"

"You know what it was." Moving to the pile of golem dust, I dug through it until I found the slip of paper. A business card, more precisely. I had a matching one in my wallet, belonging to none other than Reginald Goldman. *Well, hello, Reggie.* I wasn't surprised. Maybe I should have been, but I think I'd lost the capacity. I tucked the card into one of my bracers, and brushed my dusty hands off.

"What . . . what do we do?"

I finally turned to face Spencer, and he backed up a step. I can only imagine what it was he saw in my eyes. "We do nothing. You tell no one, because they'd never believe you anyway."

"But . . . Gretchen Keene?"

"Gretchen Keene took her own life tonight." For just one moment, I was tempted to look over the edge of the pool to the lobby far below, but I squelched the urge. Some things I just didn't need to see. Not really. What I'd already seen had been bad enough.

20

Gretchen Keene was declared dead at 12:15 a.m., New Year's Eve morning. Just like Axel and Cindy said, it was all over by New Year's. Stupid me, I'd thought she had at least another day, twenty-four more hours to put things right, but . . . you see what happens when you assume.

Spencer's presence turned out to be fortunate. When security and the police came storming out of the elevator, he was able to back up my story, swearing that yes, Gretchen had held me at gunpoint, then jumped to her own death. He didn't mention golems, or angels, or the fact that my sword was tucked away under a bench far out of sight. Because really, who would have believed him? I was there, and I wasn't sure *I* believed it.

Still, the police held me for hours, asking the same questions over and over again, mostly centered around why in the hell I was wearing a full suit of mail armor. I used my one phone call to ring Ivan up, and by the time the old man arrived, the cops gave up trying to make me say something different. I gave them my contact information in Missouri, and they let me go.

"I am to being sorry, Dawson." That was all Ivan had to say, and I was glad for his stoic silence. There was too much going on in my brain to make small talk.

My ticket back home wasn't good until tomorrow, so that gave me an entire day to kill in L.A. First, Ivan took me to retrieve my gear, and inspected my back closely as I changed into a clean T-shirt. "I have never to be seeing the like." One thick finger touched my shoulder blade, and the ridges of his fingerprint rasped like sandpaper. I hissed, jerking out of his reach. It was too sensitive, still. Tender.

"Now what are we to be doing?"

"Now I need you to help me play bad cop–worse cop." Apparently, he got the reference, 'cause he didn't ask me any more questions after that.

Tai and the real Dante had been taken to the hospital, and though I wanted to go check on them both, I just couldn't make myself. I'd failed to protect Gretchen and I just couldn't face either of them yet. If ever. There were, however, two people I very much wanted to visit before I left town. I chose the more pleasant—if you can call it that—of the two first.

With Ivan and a phone call to a faraway Viljo on my side, it wasn't hard to find the address for Gretchen's mother, and I knew we'd found the right place when we pulled up to find the house surrounded by a veritable army of paparazzi and news vans. They snapped pictures and tried to thrust microphones in my face as I got out of Ivan's car, but one look from the big Ukrainian had them backing up a good couple of yards. Someday, I wanna learn to do that, just back people off with a look.

I didn't know the woman who answered the door. Family friend, if I had to guess, and acting as a gate-keeper in this time of tragedy. She was ready to do battle, that much was clear. "If you don't get off this property, I'm going to have the cops on your ass so fast . . ."

"I'm not a reporter. I'm ... I was one of Gretchen's bodyguards. I just came to talk to her mother."

The fierce expression on her face faded into a bit of doubt, but I still don't think she was going to let me in until a voice came from inside. "Let him in, Rebecca." Reluctantly, the self-appointed guard let me pass, then made a show of slamming and locking the door behind me.

The house itself was ... average. Everything was average. Seventies-era wood paneling, threadbare and scuffed furniture, a few dusty doilies, some knickknacks on the shelves. It could have been my mom's house. It could have been anybody's mom's house. Part of me cringed to be walking across the rug in my dusty boots, expecting to get smacked upside the back of the head for it.

Rebecca escorted me to the room on the left, where two other women were seated on the worn sofa. I recognized Gretchen's mother, sitting with her back ramrod straight, her face severely composed to hide her grief. The other was lying with her head in Patty's lap, and sat up when I entered, brushing her blond hair back out of her face and hastily rubbing the tears off her cheeks. Gretchen's sister. Older than the picture on the mirror, but I'd have known her anyway. The resemblance to Gretchen was eerie.

It occurred to me as I went to introduce myself that I didn't even know Patty's last name. I settled for "Ma'am. I'm Jesse Dawson." Patty stood to shake my hand, offering me a smile because it was the polite thing to do. "We haven't really met, but I saw you the other day at the hotel."

Patty nodded. "I remember. You're fairly new to her employ, yes? I don't remember seeing you before."

"Yes, ma'am. I've only been here a week." Christ, really? A week? Not even that. Five days. So much chaos in just five days. "Um ... may I sit?" When she nodded, I found a place on a small ottoman that had seen better days. I sat gingerly, afraid the whole thing would collapse under my weight.

"Would you like some coffee or something?" It was an offer made out of etiquette, not any real desire to see to my comfort. Still, the thought of caffeine did sound suddenly enticing.

"Um, yes please. Black." Rebecca disappeared into the kitchen. We all sat in awkward silence, looking at anything but each other, until I realized that I was about to be hypnotized by the pattern on the carpet. The power of Gretchen's souls lingered. "Um ... I just wanted to stop by today to tell you how sorry I am."

Patty seemed to relax a bit, then. Condolences, those she was prepared to deal with. "Thank you. If you leave your number, we'll make sure we get details of her services to you, once they're decided." The little sister hiccupped at that, biting back a sob.

I shook my head, my hair falling down around my face. It was easier to look at the carpet, than at this woman. I'd failed her too. "No ... I mean, I'm sorry I couldn't stop her. I was with her. I tried ... I should have tried harder. I should have done ... something."

The feel of Patty's hands as she took mine in hers surprised me. Rough from a life of washing dishes by hand,

I could almost taste the lotion she'd put on. Jasmine. I forced myself to look up and meet her eyes.

"Gina was a stubborn girl. Once she'd put her mind to something, there was no changing it. Even . . . even this. The police told me she hurt one of her other bodyguards last night. I don't know that there was anything else you could have done, if that was her aim." Her voice was steady, her blue-gray eyes clear. Behind them, I could see the agony she was so carefully holding in check. No mother should have to bury a child.

I turned my hands to grasp hers instead, searching for the words to explain the unexplainable. "I came today, because I wanted you to know that she was a good person. What she did . . . I don't know that I can ever explain it to you, fully, but what she did, she believed she was doing for the greater good. In her mind, it was a sacrifice, not a suicide."

Patty's brows creased in puzzlement, the first emotion I'd really seen from her. "I don't really understand."

"And I can't explain it any better. But I know that she was a good person. I just need you to know that, too."

The older woman smiled a little, and I caught the first hint of tears in her eyes. "I knew that already." She patted my hands, and sat back on the sofa.

I stood then. I wasn't sure there was anything else to say. "Thank you for having me in your home."

"Thank you for coming."

I passed Rebecca in the entryway as she returned with the coffee. She gave me a stiff nod, and seemed relieved just to see me departing.

"Wait!" It was Gretchen's sister who caught up to me,

stopping me before I could open the door. "I'm . . . I'm Chelsea, Gina's sister."

I nodded. "I saw pictures of you." She was twenty-two, if that, and just as stunningly beautiful as her sister had been. Younger than Gretchen, but old enough to be getting married, apparently. I saw the flash of the engagement ring on her hand.

Chelsea hesitated a moment, debating on whether or not she truly wanted the answer to the question she was about to ask. I'd seen that look before, on a lot of people. "Did she . . . did she say anything? About me or Mom, I mean? Before . . ."

"She said she wanted you to all be safe and happy. She said you were going to make a beautiful bride." A good man shouldn't lie, but when Chelsea smiled through the tears that spilled down her cheeks, I couldn't feel bad for it. "She was very proud of you."

"Thank you." After another moment's hesitation, she hugged me with one arm, then darted back into the living room.

Outside, there seemed to be some kind of standoff between Ivan and the cameras. The big man leaned against his car, arms crossed over his broad chest, like he was just daring one of them to snap his picture without his permission. For their part, they seemed to be pretending he didn't exist, except for furtive glances in his direction.

As I walked across the lawn, one of the photographers tried to jump into my path, only to have his camera fizzle out in a shower of sparks and the smell of burning electronics. I raised a brow at Ivan as we got into the car, and he gave me a flat look in return. "That wasn't very nice."

"I have no idea what you are to be talking about."

Our next stop took us back to Century City. Apparently, we were expected, because the cute little receptionist went pale and reached for the phone the moment we appeared. Ivan gently placed his big hand over hers, stopping her in her tracks. "*Ni*. This is not to being the job for you."

After a moment, she nodded with wide eyes, and scampered for the elevator on her spindly high heels.

"You totally have to teach me that," I muttered, and the big man snorted.

"You are either to be having it, or you are not."

Confronted with the closed double doors to Reggie's office, I deferred to my elder. "After you."

Ivan smirked and with one well-placed boot, kicked the doors open with a crash of shattering wood. Maybe I'd have to rethink calling him "old man."

Reggie's hand was reaching for the panic button (at least, I assume that's where it was going) under his desk, but a shove from Ivan planted him back in his high-backed leather chair, rolling it all the way to the windows behind him.

"Hiya, Reggie!" I hopped up on his desk, crossing my legs and giving him a slightly manic grin. "Reggie, this is Ivan. Ivan, Reggie." My enormous Ukrainian mentor rested a hand on the agent's shoulder, pinning him into his seat. I was pretty sure it would take more strength than Reggie had to budge it.

"What do you want, Dawson? As you can imagine, I'm a bit busy today."

"I'm sure you are. I'm sure that Gretchen's death has opened up all kinds of lucrative income opportunities for you." I idly picked up items from his desk—his name plate, a glass paperweight, a stapler—and entertained myself by dropping them on the floor. The paperweight exploded quite nicely, scattering shards all over his hardwood flooring.

Reggie shrugged—or tried to, with Ivan leaning on his shoulders. "What can I say? She's worth more dead than alive when it comes right down to it."

"You're a great humanitarian, you know that?"

"Again, is there something you wanted?"

I flipped his charred and wrinkled business card into his lap. "Found something of yours."

He picked it up, examining it, then tossed it to the floor with a negligent flip of his wrist. "I give out thousands of those, you realize."

"Yes, but this one is special. This one was buried in the neck of a rather well-constructed golem, who has since, sadly, just gone to pieces on us."

"And just what does that have to do with me?" His smirk lasted until Ivan squeezed the nerve cluster at the base of his neck, then his face crumpled in agony. I let it go on for a moment, then nodded, and Ivan released him.

"Reggie, I want you to understand something. Last night, I had what we'll call a moment of perfect clarity. Got to see the world and all things in it as they really are, that kinda thing. And you, sir, are a lying sack of shit."

I hopped off the desk and continued my random breaking of things, just because I could, and because all Reggie could do was watch me and fume. "See, I know you created that golem. Got quite a bit more magical talent than you let on, don't you?" His lacrosse trophy cracked into four pieces when it hit the floor. "And I know you sent those flowers." I picked up one of the old, musty tomes off his shelf, one I hadn't looked at before, and flipped it open. Just as I thought. Spell work. Herbs. Everything a growing magician needs to entertain his friends and screw with the local champion. "Doing a bit of herbalism on the side, are we?" His heavy, crystal AGENT OF THE YEAR AWARD actually bounced when I swept it off the shelf, gouging a chunk out of the hardwood.

His gaze followed me around the room as I created destruction and havoc, but he said nothing. He didn't have to.

"Axel came to see you, to tell you I was coming. But someone else got to you first, didn't they, Reggie? Made you an offer you couldn't refuse, no doubt. Gave you the giant shape-shifting Ken doll, to carry two hundred and seventy-six souls. Where were they going next? Who were they for?" Reggie glared daggers at me from his chair, jaw working as he bit off every curse word he knew before it could escape. I didn't expect him to answer. At least, not right away. I stopped in front of him again, Ivan turning the chair so I could crouch down at Reggie's eye level. "Who loves ya, baby?"

He turned away, directing his gaze out the window, until Ivan squeezed his shoulder again. "I would advise you to answer, Reggie. I'm a pretty decent guy, but him up there? He's old and cranky." Ivan gave me a dirty look over Reggie's head, but I ignored it.

It looked like the agent was going to keep mum, so I threw in one last bluff. At least, I hoped it was a bluff. "Ivan, break his knees." There was a split second where I was actually sure Ivan was going to do it, before Reggie caved.

"Wait! A name! They gave me a name I was supposed to use." I swear, Ivan growled when he reached down again, and Reggie squirmed frantically. "No! Seriously! They wanted her to name a master. Gave me a name to use."

"What was the name?"

"Do you think I'm insane? Saying it would draw them down on me in a heartbeat." Sweat dripped down his fake tan cheeks, and he wriggled in the chair, trying to shrink away from Ivan's iron grip on his shoulder.

"Fair enough." I hopped off the desk to pace again, mulling that over. "The souls were supposed to transfer directly to your . . . we'll say employer. So what was the golem for?" That was a damn good question, now that I heard myself say it. "You had him in place long before you ever knew I was coming out here, so it wasn't just to keep me occupied. What were you doing with the mud man, Reggie?"

Ivan must have squeezed him again, because Reggie made a choked whimper. "I . . . was going to get her to put the souls in it. A vessel to carry them."

"Why? You didn't need that if they were going to get funneled right into some demon's power bank." I turned from the windows again, eyeing the agent thoughtfully. Axel had sent me because I was an honest man. This man here? He wasn't. "You were gonna be a bad boy, weren't you, Reggie? You were going to keep those souls for yourself."

He went paler under the orange tan. "No rules against trying to make a profit. They didn't explicitly say that I had to turn the souls over to them, and there's this auction. A big auction with lots of buyers, and I was going to take the golem there, see what price I could get. I swear to God, it's the truth."

I looked up at the big man towering over us with a questioning quirk to my brow. Ivan shrugged. "There have always to been rumors of such things. A black market in the worst possible meaning."

It stood to reason. If souls could be passed around like worn-out dollar bills, they could be bartered and sold. I shook my head with a low whistle. "Damn, Reggie. You were gonna double-cross a demon, twice. Your life isn't gonna be worth spit after this." If he was pale before, he went ashen then. I'm not sure he'd realized the precariousness of his position until that moment. "Where is this auction?"

"I don't know." Ivan clamped down, and Reggie flailed in his seat. "No, I swear, I don't know! They text the location when it's time, a couple of hours beforehand. By now they know I failed, they won't text me again. You'll never find this one, and then they'll clear out of town." He was about thirty seconds away from dissolving into tears, clawing vainly at the bigger man's viselike grip.

"Let him go, Ivan." I shook my head. "That's all he knows." Reggie may not know where the auction was, but I was willing to bet I knew someone who did. "If you run across my path again, Reggie, it's not going to end well for you. You know that, right?"

"You can't just leave me like this! They'll kill me! Can't you protect me?"

"Yup. Could. Won't." I gave him a shrug. "See that there? That's the bed you made. Lie in it."

Reggie hunched over in his plush chair, huddled around the mass of pain that was his right shoulder, the pleading in his eyes shifting quickly to seething hate. "You're a dead man, Dawson. You know where those souls went, I know you do. And *they* won't stop until you give them back."

I punched him in the face, knocking the chair completely over to spill him out on the glass-littered floor. "Be seein' ya, Reggie."

I've come to the conclusion that I should probably just start punching agents when I see them. It's how it always turns out anyway, and it would just save time.

Ivan gave me an amused smirk in the elevator on the way down.

"What?"

"Nothing. To being nothing at all." I swear, he was chuckling all the way out to the car.

My brilliant idea to locate this auction came to nothing. Mystic Cindy's shop was not only empty, it was apparently nonexistent. I found the door where I recalled it being, but there was no little sign hanging on the side, no indication that the door had been opened anytime in the last century, and the chain on it looked like it had been there for fifty years or more. I thumped my fist against it with a soft curse, and when that wasn't satisfying enough, I kicked it, resulting in a shower of rusty dust raining down over our heads.

"Do not to be worrying, Dawson. I have encountered her many times. She enjoys to be meddling too much to stay away. We will to be finding her again." Yeah, that was what worried me.

Needless to say, Ivan followed me home. I felt like asking Mira if we could keep him, but then I was afraid he really would never leave.

My darling love met us at the airport, kids in tow. She flung her arms around my neck for a proper welcome home hug, then instantly sprang away from me with a horrified gasp. "What . . . ?" I guess I should have expected that she'd feel those extra souls, lurking there just under my skin.

"When we get home. Promise." I hugged Annabelle without any harmful repercussions, but she did wrinkle her pert little nose at me. "You smell funny, Daddy." Great.

The explanations took longer than I'd hoped, first because I had to retell the part with Gretchen kissing me about four times. More for Estéban than Mira, really, but still. I mean, it wasn't my fault, I hadn't done anything wrong, but I still squirmed under my wife's gaze every time I had to say it. Luckily, she didn't seem to be angry. I think she was more interested in the end of the tale, the part where I got stuffed full of two hundred and seventy-six extra souls.

The second reason the telling took way longer than I wanted was because we kept having to stop for Ivan to take calls on his phone. Some of them were in Ukrainian, some were in his butchered English, but the meaning of all of them was clear. I was being assigned my own set of champion bodyguards until we could figure out how to get these extra souls out of me. Reggie had been right. Once they—whoever "they" were—figured out that I had them, they'd come for me, just like they had Gretchen.

And speaking of coming for me . . .

Jet lag kept me awake far later than the rest of the household. At least, that was my excuse when I slipped out the back door in the dead of night, crunching my way through the half-melted snow. "Axel . . ." No sooner had the whisper left my lips than I caught the distinct whiff of sulfur behind me.

The bastard was still wearing my denim coat. "It's about time. I thought the old man was never going to leave your side."

"Well, keep your voice down or he'll be out here and put a boot up your ass before you can blink," I growled in return. "I suppose you know what all happened?"

"Of course I do. That's my job." He smirked in the darkness, his eyes flaring red for the space of a breath. "Let me tell you, people are scrambling now. No one else knows where those souls went, and oh, aren't they hopping mad."

"Yeah, well, you need to vet your employees better next time. Reggie turned on you, tried to sell out to the highest bidder."

"What?" The demon's eyes flared red and stayed that way, lighting the night in a crimson glow. "The little bastard. I'll kill him."

"Don't think you'll have to. He was planning on double-crossing the other side too, and if they think he knows where these souls are . . ."

"I'll never find all the pieces. Good point." Slowly, the glow in his eyes faded. "Just as well that fortune smiled on me then, hm?"

"Fortune, my ass." I knew him, better than I ever wanted to. "You planned this from the get-go. Got two hundred and seventy-six extra souls right where you want them, don't you?"

Axel chuckled, but didn't try to deny it. "I'll say I'm not displeased with the outcome. It could have ended several different ways, most of which were beneficial to me. Though, I have to say, I was actually partial to the ending where she seduced you and added your soul to her collection."

"I oughta kick you in the nuts. Do you even have nuts?"

"Aw, Jesse's all mad . . ." He reached out to pinch my cheek, but even as I moved to slap his hand away, he froze, all the humor draining out of his face. "How many did you say?"

"What?"

"How many souls did you say?"

"Two hundred and seventy-six. Why?" I wasn't ready when Axel grabbed me by the collar of my coat and yanked me close. "Gah! Get off!"

He took a deep breath, scenting my hair, my skin, like

a tracking hound. "No . . . no this isn't right . . ." Finally, he let me go, staring at me thoughtfully.

"What? What isn't right?" I brushed his touch off of my arms, making it very clear that I was displeased with him coming close to me at all.

"You only have two hundred and seventy-five souls."

"Okay, fine, two hundred and seventy-five. Whatever."

"No, not 'whatever.'" He walked a slow circle around me, shaking his head as he muttered under his breath. "What have you done, Jesse? Tell me *exactly* what happened out there."

So I started all over with the saga of Jesse Goes to Hollywood once again. When I got to the part where I blasted the golem into so many atoms, Axel stopped me. "Again. Tell me exactly what you did again." So I told him. I explained about the thin threads of magic wrapped around the clay figure, how I severed them with a mere gesture of my hand. I pictured it in my head, how the golem burst into a shower of dust, returning to that from whence he came. I told the story again. And then again, and then once more.

"And you didn't collapse. You had no fever, no seizures, no blackouts."

"Well . . . no. Not after. I think I blacked out at the beginning, when the souls hit me . . ." The demon looked concerned. Or at least as concerned as I'd ever seen him. "What is it? What do you know?"

"You've never had magic, Jesse. Never in your entire life. And yet you used it that night, used it to simply unravel a spell far more complicated than most could accomplish. It hasn't occurred to you to wonder why yet?"

"Well...no..." But you know, now that he mentioned it..."How did I do that?"

"You burned one up. Burned up a soul to power your magic, because for whatever reason, you can't access your own." Axel leaned close to sniff me again, and I gave him a warning look. "Two hundred and seventy-five souls. One short."

"But they're not actual souls. They're...markers. If they were real souls, all these people would be dead." Right? That's what Gretchen had said, so it had to be right? Right?

Axel shook his head. "It doesn't work that way. They're...it's all tied together. A direct link back to the source. What happens here happens to the person."

"So...somebody just dropped dead that night? Just...poof, gone, because I blasted that golem?" Suddenly, I felt sick. I sank down into a crouch, steadying myself with a hand in the cold, cold snow. It didn't really help.

"I think it would be in everyone's best interest if you didn't try to cast any more spells."

"Ya think?" Seriously, I thought I might throw up. Every single tattoo I could feel on my back suddenly felt like someone's eyes, watching me from afar. Lives. I was carrying people's lives around in my goddamn skin. "I gotta get these things outta me."

"I'm working on it." In a whiff of sulfur and the pop of recently vacated airspace, he was gone. I sat out in the cold for a long time after that.

That's way more responsibility than I ever wanted. I mean, I could barely look after myself. How was I supposed to look after two hundred and seventy-six—sorry, seventy-five—other souls? I did try to find out who that lost soul might have been. I pored over the obituaries in every Los Angeles newspaper that I could find, looking for unexplained or unexpected deaths. There were way too many. In the end, I had to resign myself to the fact that I'd probably never know. Sorry, whoever you were. I'm so damn sorry.

It was hard to get life back to normal after that. Ivan stayed of course, waiting for his reinforcements or replacements or whoever. Axel kept way closer tabs too. I caught him lurking often, usually in the guise of some furry rodent, but he seldom came down to talk. He didn't want to confront Ivan, for whatever reason. Couldn't fault him there. I never wanted to piss off the old man, either.

I kept tabs on Bobby until he was released from the hospital. After that, I kinda lost track. But really, I was just glad to know that he was all right. He was good people. He didn't deserve to get mixed up in this.

Tai, on the other hand . . . also released from the hospital, he was blowing up my phone the very next day. After some discussions with Ivan, we agreed that it was in the Maori's best interest to get some magical training, harness that explosive power he just had lying around. I know in the back of Ivan's mind, he was eyeing Tai as a potential champion recruit, but deep down, I was hoping that Tai would say no when the time came. Deeper down, I knew he wouldn't.

To add to the lunacy that had become my life, I got one text message much later from a number I didn't recognize. It was a Web site, and when I went to investigate it, I discovered that there was a movie in the works that looked suspiciously familiar. They were touting it as the "A-Team with demons," and while they were still in the casting stages, the lead was apparently going to be played by that guy. You know, that guy, from the show with the island and the polar bear? Yeah, him. And guess who the screenwriter is? C'mon, guess, you know you want to. I'm tempted to text Spencer back and tell him I want my fair cut. It's my story, after all.

So now I sit, waiting. Waiting for my new bodyguards to arrive. Waiting for Ivan or Axel to figure out how to get these souls out of me. Waiting for something bigger and badder than either of them to come and try to take them.

Waiting for the middle of August, when my wife will give birth to my second child. Is it all right if I hope for a boy?

A DEVIL IN THE DETAILS

A Jesse James Dawson Novel

Jesse James Dawson was an ordinary guy (well, an ordinary guy with a black belt in karate) until one day he learned his brother had made a bargain with a demon. Jesse discovered there was only one way to save his brother: put up his own soul as collateral, and fight the demon to the death.

Jesse lived to free his brother—and became part of a loose organization of Champions who put their own souls on the line to help those who get in over their heads with demons. But now experienced Champions are losing battles at a much higher rate than usual. Someone has changed the game. And if Jesse can't figure out the new rules, his next battle may be his last...

ALSO AVAILABLE
FROM
K. A. Stewart

A SHOT IN THE DARK
A Jesse James Dawson Novel

Jesse James Dawson's vacation is interrupted by a pack of
hell-spawned creatures. To save friends, family and
himself, Jesse will have to put his trust in his most
dangerous enemy-his personal demon.

**"If you want your life saved you call the cops. If you
want your soul saved, you call Jesse James Dawson."
—New York Times bestselling author
Rob Thurman**

Available wherever books are sold or at
penguin.com

facebook.com/AceRocBooks

AVAILABLE NOW FROM

SIMON R. GREEN

LIVE AND LET DROOD

**The brand-new book in the series
following *For Heaven's Eyes Only*.**

Eddie Drood's family has been keeping the forces of evil
contained in the shadows for as long as Droods have walked the
earth. But now Eddie's entire family has been banished to an
alternate dimension. And when he finds out who—or what—
attacked his clan, there will be hell to pay...

Praise for the Secret Histories novels:

"Another action-packed melding of spy story and fantasy,
featuring suave sleuthing, magical powers,
and a generous dash of dry wit."
—*Kirkus Reviews*

**Available wherever books are sold or at
penguin.com**

facebook.com/AceRocBooks

R0108

DOUBLETAKE

A CAL LEANDROS NOVEL
by
ROB THURMAN

Half-human/half-monster Cal Leandros knows that family is a pain. But now that pain belongs to his half-brother, Niko. Niko's shady father is in town, and he needs a big favor. Even worse is the reunion being held by the devious Puck race—including the Leandros' friend, Robin—featuring a lottery that no Puck wants to win.

As Cal tries to keep both Niko and Robin from paying the ultimate price for their kin, a horrific reminder from Cal's own past arrives to remind him that blood is thicker than water— and that's why it's so much more fun to spill.

"Thurman continues to deliver strong tales of dark urban fantasy."
—SF Revu

Available wherever books are sold or at penguin.com

facebook.com/AceRocBooks

R0117

JIM BUTCHER
The Dresden Files

The #1 *New York Times* bestselling series

"Think *Buffy the Vampire Slayer* starring Philip Marlowe." —*Entertainment Weekly*

STORM FRONT

FOOL MOON

GRAVE PERIL

SUMMER KNIGHT

DEATH MASKS

BLOOD RITES

DEAD BEAT

PROVEN GUILTY

WHITE NIGHT

SMALL FAVOR

TURN COAT

CHANGES

SIDE JOBS

GHOST STORY

Available wherever books are sold or at penguin.com

R0037